IN THE TROPIC OF THE POSSESSED

Carlos was shaking with the tenseness of his passion. For an instant he reminded Laura of the storm. Then she had been lashed by cold wind and rain; now she was being sucked into the whirlpool of Carlos' desires. She was not ready for it—and she was not going to have it happen when it pleased him.

He took her into his arms, crushing her ribs, squeezing the breath out of her. Laura did not plead pain. "All right," she said, "I'm not going to call it rape, Carlos, because I'm not going to fight you. You're much too strong."

"No," he said. "No, I don't want you that way."

"Come on. If you're going to dirty me up, you might as well get started."

"No, no!" he groaned in agony …

CAST OF CHARACTERS

LAURA RENDELL

Every man she met stopped, removed his hat and bowed to her as his eyes undressed her.

CARLOS

The force of his passion could conquer any man or woman, but not the ancient law of his people.

ANTONIO

What this *torrero* forgot was that an enraged man can be as dangerous as a maddened bull.

ALMA

She would fight for her jungle lover with the ways of a tigress.

ALMIRANTE

Though a clever actor, he could not impersonate manliness.

ROSARIO

This experienced guide stumbled into the greatest adventure of his life.

LASH OF DESIRE

LASH OF DESIRE

MARCOS SPINELLI

CUTTING EDGE

ISBN-13: 978-1-957868-75-2

Published by
Cutting Edge Books
PO Box 8212
Calabasas, CA 91372
www.cuttingedgebooks.com

To
Bruno

CHAPTER ONE

S HE WAS mistakenly called the Senhora Engleza at the hotel where she had been staying for the past eleven days, waiting for the guide the travel bureau was supposed to be getting for her.

As she was not used to sleeping in the afternoon, she spent the siesta hour in the cocktail lounge because it was the coolest spot in town. For it was now late January and the heat was fierce, especially here in Cuiaba, which was sweltering in a heat wave from the north.

So today too, after lunch, when almost all the green shutters on the upper floor began to be closed, and people undressed and stretched out on bedsheets that soon grew sticky, and the hotel itself became as quiet as a museum, she took herself into the cocktail lounge where she sat at a round table before a frosted glass of gin and lemonade. She sipped and smoked and tried not to think.

Although she was the only customer in the dim, cool lounge she did not look forlorn or forsaken. She was the type of woman whose personality created its own company. She stood out in a crowd as strikingly as she did now that she was alone.

She had leaf-shaped eyes, green and shiny as ivy, but not as serene. Between her eyes and the world there was a film of life lived intensely, and perhaps not too wisely. Her lips were sensuous; her bosom carnally cleft and pointed. She was clad in white linen, simply and tastefully. She wore no jewelry, not even a wrist watch. Her plainness was arresting, perhaps premeditated. She looked as if she had just arisen from a milk bath. The native sun had not yet claimed her exquisite complexion. Her auburn hair cascaded down to her shoulders in soft waves. She wore a delicate perfume. She appeared to be twenty-five or twenty-six years old.

The siesta hour ticked away. The hotel, the town, slept.

The bartender behind the bar and the waiter before the bar were napping standing up. The waiter's left arm bent at the elbow, was slipping down, the napkin over his wrist about to fall.

The woman, oblivious of them, oblivious even of the cigarette burning unsmoked in the crystal ashtray before her, was now wondering, not for the first time, what kind of welcome her brother would give her when they met. Whatever his welcome would be, she was not worried about it. She had not seen her brother in five years and he was not expecting her. He had absolutely forbidden her to visit him in the interior of Mato Grosso. She hated to be forbidden anything. Too dangerous, he had written her. Dangerous, she thought scornfully. There's more danger in falling in love with the wrong man than in a jungle full of wild beasts. At least you can shoot the beasts.

Obviously, the long separation had dulled her brother's clear understanding of her true character. She sipped from the glass. She crushed the cigarette in the ashtray, mechanically lighted a fresh one.

Then she thought of the travel bureau in the hotel and she felt provoked again, and again cursed them for their slowness.

Had she been in a different frame of mind, she would have realized that a guide such as the one she had asked for is like a star actor, booked months in advance. She knew she should have made arrangements the moment she landed in Rio, or even from back home. She knew she should have done a number of sensible things which, as usual, she had not. And here she had been waiting only eleven days.

But eleven days of inactivity—except for a few dull hours of sightseeing—meant eleven days of introspection. *Get thee behind me, Satan!* She hated to baby-sit for her inner self, a nasty little monster that gave her no peace. And that was not all.

Every bloody man in the hotel was in love with her, including that idiotic captain of the bellboys. She kept them at arm's length. But even so, every man she met stopped, removed his hat and bowed to her as his eyes undressed her.

She was used to being undressed by men's eyes. Her beauty drew such a compliment. But not like this. This at times was downright indecent and would have aroused another woman's righteous indignation.

But she was not another woman. She was not going to make an issue of the way these men undressed her with their eyes, because she very well knew that that was exactly what they were waiting for: the rich opportunity to start at once to protest their innocence in injured accents, and then to apologize for the unfortunate misunderstanding, and then to introduce themselves humbly, and then to offer their humble services, and thereafter to follow her about until she either told them off brutally or accommodated them. To hell with them.

The siesta hour kept ticking away.

The waiter's arm dropped to his side and the napkin fell on the floor by his left foot.

First one, and then two, and then another musician entered the cocktail lounge with unwilling steps. She watched them idly. They were not quite fully awake yet, she thought. The musicians walked to their platform in the corner and sat down behind their instruments. They smoked and talked in lazy tones.

As the church bell on the square tolled four stately strokes, the orchestra erupted into the opening number, a fast and furious maxixe. Literally intended as an eye opener, the music officially ended the long siesta hour, and people began to drift into the cocktail lounge for their pleasure.

At this point she usually got up and left the cocktail lounge. Standing, she was long legged and straight backed, with the firm, trim buttocks of a healthy adolescent. Her step was lithe as she walked into the hotel lobby and went over to the reception desk. Again she noticed the clerk's ears. He was a fine-looking man, except for his ears. His ears stuck out like bullfiddle frets. She asked the clerk if there had been any calls, if there was any mail, for Mrs. Laura Rendell—New York, N.Y., U.S.A., read the hotel register.

"You are being paged by the travel bureau, Mrs. Rendell," the clerk informed her. "Your guide has come."

"Thank heaven," said Laura Rendell. "I've been waiting for him for two weeks now."

"Not quite, Mrs. Rendell," the clerk said, bowing respectfully. "Only eleven days. If I may say so," the clerk bowed again, "we congratulate ourselves for having secured him in such a short time." Then he added, "Rosario, is a man much in demand."

"Where is he?"

"There. Standing by the palm tree." The clerk pointed to a potted palm tree in a corner of the lobby.

"Thank you," Laura Rendell said, and walked toward a tall, angular, mustachioed man who was obviously uncomfortable in his white cotton suit, wilted collar and readymade bow tie. He was wearing black riding boots under his trouser-legs, and the mark of the absent spurs was fresh around the heels. His broadbrimmed black hat, with the chinstrap stuffed into the crown, lay on the marble floor beneath the wicker chair he had been sitting in.

"Do you speak English?"

"No."

"I'm Senhora Rendell."

"At the service of God, and yourself, *senhora*," said Rosario the guide.

They looked at each other with unrestrained curiosity.

So this is the famous Rosario, Laura Rendell thought. Looks more like a farmer. How old is he? Fifty?

Rosario the guide was sixty-six years old. But he still had all his teeth—strong, square, yellow teeth. And all his hair, too—thick and straight and coarse, like a mule's mane. His bony face was sunblackened, his nose hooked, his long mustache drooping. His small round brown eyes had a disconcerting steadiness; they looked at you unblinkingly. You felt like waving your hand before his eyes. Laura Rendell looked into the guide's unblinking eyes with unruffled composure.

In a country of good guides Rosario was probably the best, even now that he was carrying his age on his shoulders like a *mar de lama*, as he put it. A sea of mud.

Rosario the guide had traveled far and wide and seen many strange things and known everybody worth knowing, from the Father Superior here in Cuiaba, to Thomaz, the notorious Amazonian *cangaçeiro*. He had had words with the famous bandit and they had exchanged shots, shooting each other's guns out of each other's hands. Then they had shaken hands.

Rosario the guide had also known and been befriended by the late Pedro Diaz, or the Tamer, as he was more commonly referred to, a ruthless, legendary character, the builder of Fazenda Boa Vista, a feudal estate in the heart of Mato Grosso.

Rosario the guide had a strange idea about words. He thought of them as whores ... "The cheap ones who lift their filthy skirts up at the jingling of a few coins." And he kept his mouth shut until he was fairly forced to open it. Then he spoke readily and with angry assurance, as if he wanted to be finished quickly, so that he might resume the rustic dignity which he thought he had lost by consorting with words.

Like a dog scenting game, Rosario the guide was now sniffing at his client's delicate perfume, as if it would lead him into her private life. I hope she will not cause me an exaggeration of troubles, was his conclusion.

Thank God, he isn't one of those *divine* movie guides who always sleep with their clients, Laura Rendell was thinking. "Shall we sit down, Senhor Rosario?" she said.

"At your service, *senhora.*"

The mist was rising heavily, but Laura Rendell could not see it because it was too dark. She could only feel it, settling on her face and on the back of her hands like cold sweat. Laura could not see anything about her except dank darkness. She could hardly distinguish Rosario the guide and Antonio, his nephew, riding a short distance ahead, and the pack mule, plodding between them and her.

The route was soggy. The darkness smelled of rotten mushrooms. At rare intervals the moon-bleached sky could be seen through the tall, swaying treetops. The sky looked like the part in a woman's wind-blown hair.

Although the jungle was still asleep—it is dangerous to disturb the jungle in its sleep; it has a thousand angry eyes and fangs and claws—Rosario had broken camp, gotten into the saddle and ridden off to meet the rising sun on the open road, refusing both to explain his sudden decision and to listen to Laura's angry remonstration.

For a senseless moment Laura had thought of firing him on the spot, and she might have done so if Rosario had not anticipated her by looking at her and asking with his unblinking eyes,

Do you want to fire me? Aloud Rosario had said, "You are my responsibility, *senhora*. We ride."

A hasty breakfast of black coffee and biscuits, and they were in the saddle.

And Laura was still angry, not really with Rosario, whom by now she had learned to trust and respect, nor yet for having been awakened in the middle of the night, or so it seemed to her, for still another day-long ride.

Laura knew that her anger now was a pretext to distract her from herself. She was weary of thinking about herself, her past—her inhibited scorn for marriage, her turbulent, inconstant romantic liaisons, her search and failure to find inner balance. She was tired of dominating herself destructively, of suffering in silence until she thought her heart would break. Now she had reached the point where she no longer cared to plan beyond the immediate present. She made a joke of life and, because she strongly suspected she had lost her sense of humor, she didn't give a damn whether the joke fell flat or not. In her sober moments Laura knew that the joke was on her. She thought of herself as a raft drifting nowhere.

Even in daylight such thoughts were bad enough. But alone at night—and especially on a night like this, when she could clearly visualize her thoughts—her memories, taking bodily shape, reeled off in the darkness before her as if on a screen.

Her marriage. She had fallen in love with her husband the moment—

"*Quidado, senhora!*" In the darkness Rosario's warning whipped Laura out of her recollection. "Be careful."

"What is it?" Laura called back.

"The path is growing steeper, slippery. Take care."

"I can't even see where I'm going."

"Do not try to lead your mount, *senhora*. Hold her steady on the bit and she will take you down safely, *comprende?*"

Laura gathered the reins tighter in her hands.

The path began to incline. Laura's mule started to skid downward on her hind legs. The bowels of the Earth breathed forth a stronger odor of rotten mushrooms as the path grew steeper and Laura's mule skidded faster. Now the mule was going downward on her own impulse, gathering momentum as she went. Laura's legs were stretched forward, her feet pushing hard against the stirrups, almost even with the mule's head. The mule's whole body was leaning in a dead weight against the bit in her mouth, and Laura was pulling at the reins with all her might. At any moment now Laura expected to sail clear over the mule's head and plunge headlong into the unseen hell below. But then, by abrupt degrees, her legs bent at the knee and hung limply along the mule's flanks; the mule straightened herself up on her hind legs and her head came level with her back, and then she plodded on fairly steadily again.

"*Senhora?*"

"Yes?"

"Was it too perilous then?"

Damned perilous, old boy. "Not at all."

"She is a brave woman," Rosario said to his nephew.

I wish she was much less brave and much more obliging, Antonio thought. Mother of God, her legs are driving me crazy. "Yes, uncle. She is a brave woman," Antonio said dutifully, and remembered Laura's legs as he had seen them as she washed them in a stream. Mother of God, he sighed, I need a woman, and his mind filled with the vision of a naked woman that looked exactly like Laura.

Antonio's skin was olive with a golden underglow. He had long-cut eyes slanting slightly toward the temples.

He was not quite six feet tall, but looked taller because of the way he carried himself. He was vain, bold and arrogant, allergic to true or fancied insult, and impulsively handy with the knife.

Antonio was the infant of nine children of Manoel, a good bullfighter who had lost his nerve and taken to drinking, and had ended by decorating a bull's horns with his intestines.

Manoel was a relative of Rosario's good wife's, Anna. Rosario had adopted Antonio to satisfy his wife's longing for a child, as she could not have one of her own. But neither Uncle Rosario's threats nor Aunt Anna's entreaties had been able to stop Antonio from finally running away from home and following in his father's footsteps.

Like his father, Antonio had served his apprenticeship in Venezuela, and now, at twenty-one, he was as good a bullfighter as his father had ever been. And much more popular, too. He was particularly successful with the women, who idolized him to a point where he thought of them indiscriminately as domestic animals with whom he could play whenever the mood struck him.

Like all tough men, Antonio, too, had his Achilles heel. He could never forget his early love and respect for his adopted parents, to whom he returned loaded with gifts after every season. And now he had canceled a whole season across the border because Aunt Anna had asked him to. She had explained to him that this was to be the old guide's last long ride, and, although no man alive knew the jungle better than he, she feared for his age and she wanted Antonio to go along with him and watch over him. "Please, son, do this for me."

Antonio had combed out his coleta.

But, although Antonio's respect for his uncle was strong, his much tested opinion of himself as a lover was stronger. Moreover,

Laura was a new type that he had never encountered before. Her green eyes and foreign beauty whetted his desire, and behind his uncle's back he had naturally tried to make love to her.

Like all bullfighters, Antonio was a profoundly religious man. He wore a silver crucifix and the medal of his patron saint around his neck. Yet he would have bartered his Christian soul for the chance to sleep with Laura only once.

Eight days after they had left Cuiaba, Antonio had sneaked into Laura's tent in the middle of the night and begged her to remove a thorn he himself had stuck in his left arm. And, while pretending to help her find the storm lamp in the dark, he had started to feel her. Laura had made no outcry, thinking of Uncle Rosario.

The lamp finally found and lighted, Laura had literally dug out the thorn from Antonio's arm with the awl Antonio himself had brought along, confident that she would not have the intestinal fortitude to use it. The operation over—it did feel like that to Antonio—Laura had presented the thorn to him with a sweet smile and told him with serious eyes to keep it as a souvenir, *comprende?*

Under different circumstances Laura would have handled Antonio in a fashion that would have left an everlasting mark on his ego. She had behaved thus only to prevent the small party from breaking out in fatal violence, as she was fully conscious that Uncle Rosario would not hesitate to kill his own nephew, were he ever to catch him taking liberties with her, much less making love to her, *his client.*

Moreover Antonio was not Laura's type, in spite of his good looks and virility. He was young and raw and overanxious. Laura damn well knew that Antonio would take a woman, any woman, to gratify his enormous ego and then his urge. To hell with him. Let him find himself a bitch.

CHAPTER TWO

THE PARTY rode on, toward the dawn. In the hollows beyond the eastern horizon, dawn and daylight were whispering hurriedly together.

And now it was a few miles after dawn, judging from the point on the horizon where the sun had appeared and risen into the sky without almost any discernible transition.

But in spite of the early hour it was already inexplicably hot, even for the jungle of Mato Grosso, where the torrid heat is dry and steady. And the air had a peculiar odor. It smelled of baking clay, a sweet-sour, throat-catching tang that made you swallow dryly.

On this oppressively hot morning many of the old natives were standing on the threshold of their thatch-roofed huts, looking at the sky, sniffing at the air, wondering.

Emerging from the clammy dark womb of the jungle and into the glaring sun of the open road, Laura's eyeballs sparked with pain. She loosened her chinstrap and pulled her broad-brimmed gray hat low over her eyes and rode on, staying a short distance behind the guides, as jungle etiquette demands.

This was the seventeenth day since Laura had left Cuiaba and the comforts of civilization. And by now her lovely face was so suntanned that it looked black in the dark, and her green eyes shone like pools of limpid water. The sun had by now not only claimed her complexion but also her hair, streaking it yellow. Her breast had two different hues: the upper part was bronzed, the lower milk-white. She wore riding breeches and a gray cotton shirt with pockets and long sleeves, which she kept rolled up to her elbows in spite of the mosquitoes. Her only weapon was a revolver. The hardships she had already endured were beginning to tell about her mouth. Unconsciously she kept her sensuous lips pressed together, as if she were constantly straining against a physical barrier. Her stamina was amazing. But then, back home, friends and foe alike had always thought she was an amazing woman, a woman who drank greedily from the cup of life and never staggered away. They had no way of knowing that she had promised herself never to let the world even suspect how truly drunk she was inside all the time.

The party rode on steadily, too steadily. At times Laura caught herself swinging in the saddle as if she were keeping time to the fast beat of a tomtom. She loved it with a masochistic ardor. For the faster they rode, the longer the distance she put between her and herself, she thought, without really believing it. With such a love she accepted whatever came her way, in the guise of hardship and discomfort and danger, uncomplainingly.

Now that they were riding on the open road, Uncle Rosario and Antonio carried their rifles hanging from their necks and lying horizontally across their chests. Each also carried a revolver and an elbow-long knife on his person, and a machete hanging from one side of the saddle and a drinking horn from the other. The wheels of Uncle Rosario's spurs were as large as small saucers; the mark of his profession, they jingle-jangled now in time to the fast lope of his mount.

Since they had ridden out of the jungle and onto the open road again, Uncle Rosario's eyes had kept returning to the sky as if to read, to discover something hidden therein. Something which not only seemed to escape his eyes but his sense of smell also, and which was obviously puzzling him.

Antonio kept spying on his uncle's mood, unable to suspect its origin.

A thick-tongued iguana, the size and shape of a baby crocodile, scurried clumsily across the road a few yards ahead of the guides. Uncle Rosario's mule shied. Uncle Rosario spat as his whip uncoiled hissing in the air, cracked like a shot upon the iguana, and slashed it in two.

The reptile's greenish, scaly tail was still wriggling when Laura came abreast of the halved body. Laura made a face and looked the other way.

Now Uncle Rosario turned in the saddle, caught Laura's eyes and tossed his arm forward. "Faster!" he cried.

The old buzzard's mad, Laura told herself. *Incredibly, absolutely and completely mad*, she thought, and set spurs to her already fast-moving mount.

A few more hours of sunlight passed.

The sun was now straight overhead.

The road bent toward the west. At every turn of the way Uncle Rosario studied the distance ahead, as if he were trying to discover a new feature in a familiar picture. Then his eyes returned to the sky.

Antonio kept spying on his uncle's mood.

May I be spiked in the groin, Antonio thought to himself. What is there in the sky that the old man can see and I cannot that is making him nervous? Whereupon Antonio again lifted his eyes to the sky and scanned it with spiteful concentration.

But Antonio saw nothing unusual in the sky. The sky today was exactly as it had been yesterday. Or a week before. A monotonously beautiful sky. A tropical sky. The sky of the dry season. The sun's vermilion surface seemed to be melting in its own heat and pouring down rivers of molten light whose shimmering whiteness blinded the eye. Not a breath of air stirred the torrid stillness. But insects, like buckshots, punctured the great patches of heat that hung motionless above men and beasts. As far as the eye could see everything was red, colored by the stale-smelling dust that lay thick over the whithering vegetation.

A bird flew high in the sky, crying shrilly. Another one followed. Then there was a whole flock of them, racing and pursuing each other as they flew south.

In the distant west the sky was growing lumpy with smoky blotches.

They rode on, increasingly faster.

The pack mule had fallen in step with the saddle mules, and the sound of their hoofs in the thick dust was like the even beat of a sodden drum. The mules' coats were running with sweat, and a greenish froth was bubbling at the corners of their mouths, speckling their bumpy chests.

The insides of the riders' boots were soaking wet. Their faces were covered with a thick make-up of dust and sweat. Uncle Rosario's long drooping mustache looked as if it had been dyed with henna.

The road, which miles behind had begun to narrow steadily, now drew into a cobra-head and snaked into the thicket. The sudden transition, from the glaring, scorching light of the sun to the clammy, dank darkness of the path, blinded the riders for a time, while their ears filled with a faint sound, like the hum in a seashell.

Eternally out of the sun's purifying and cleansing reach, the jungle at this point had reached a state of chronic putrescence. And the path, like a jagged cut made by a dented machete into a spongy surface, was deeply imbedded between two cankerous growths of entangled vegetation that met overhead like clasped fingers—leper's fingers, eaten to the bone, with open sores from which there ceaselessly dripped a viscid substance that struck the gumbo-like earth with a lifeless drumming.

Thus it dripped ahead, behind, and on all sides; on the hats and shoulders of the riders, and on their hands. And on the heads and necks and rumps of the mules which soon shone as if they were shellacked with some gummy substance smelling of rotten moss. The odor got into the riders' very clothes.

Laura felt as if she had been caught in a viscous net. She kept moving her hand in front of her face, as if to brush it away.

Uncle Rosario was leading and setting the pace. He was riding even faster on this route than he had on the open road. And under the sharp reminder of the spurs, the mules plodded on, skidding and swaying, regaining their footing with grunting effort.

A noise that was like pebbles and wet leaves being shaken fitfully in a tin container suddenly ran through the path, ebbed out into the jungle. Without turning in the saddle, Uncle Rosario raised his arm and threw it forward, bending his long torso low over his mule's neck. He seemed to be fleeing before an evil presentiment.

The noise, or the tremor—or was it a quaking?—recurred a second time. Then a third and a fourth. Whenever it recurred it seemed to loosen the trees and the bushes from their roots, and then the earth released a peculiar odor of mustiness, the mustiness of the sewer.

Unable to look at the sky through the dense tree-canopy overhead, Uncle Rosario sniffed this way and that like a famished hound. He was frantically trying to smell something through the dankness of the unsunned vegetation.

From the simmering, hot, dry outside—which now seemed as far away as is the bottom of the sea from its surface—there presently came a mighty, pit-of-the-stomach-hitting gust of air that pushed the riders back in their saddles, while the path grew unexpectedly darker.

Now the going was getting tougher and tougher. Laura's mule missed her footing, lurched across the path, fell on her foreknees. Laura's heart leaped into her throat, and she felt as though she were taking a high dive. Without knowing how she did it, Laura pulled her mule up, set spurs to her and rode on.

Now a tremor shook the earth, seeming again to loosen the jungle from its roots. The mules shied from the center of the path and, puzzled as the tremor recurred, shied back to the middle again, trembling, their ears as stiff as knives, opening and closing like a compass.

Then a fit of ague possessed the cankerous growth rising along the sides of the path. Every branch, fiber-limb and bush, shook frenziedly. The dripping, mucky-smelling substance was scattered about like a shower of rain in sudden wind. A thunderous sound reached into and ran through the path with a resonance that had the effect of a strong vibration.

Laura caught her breath. She felt her mule tremble violently beneath her legs. "Don't go scared on me," she cried to the mule. "One of us is enough."

Now the jungle seemed to turn over on its side. The whole western half rose and leaned towards the east, exactly like a ship giving away to broadside waves. Then, amid the groaning and cracking of the tree trunks, the convulsive shaking of the lower vegetation, the sudden, explosive clamor of the frightened underbush creatures, it swung back towards the west. It lasted an endless two minutes, this monstrous convulsion of the jungle, this writhing and snapping and snarling. Then it fell pantingly still, like a body after a severe fit.

Uncle Rosario pulled up, motioned Laura to stop.

"It has commenced, *senhora*," he said. "It has left the west and is riding fast this way. This storm has been playing hide-and-seek with me since last night. Now it has commenced."

"Is that why we broke camp at dawn, and have been riding like mad ever since?" Laura asked.

"Already this forest is full of scared life," Uncle Rosario said, ignoring her question. "And soon there will be a stampede of fear. We must ride fast, out of this path, onto the open road again where I know of a cave that will give us shelter."

"Is that why we broke camp at dawn, and have been riding like mad ever since?" she repeated.

"Yes."

"You might have told me," Laura snapped. "I'm no child."

"I did not even tell my nephew, *senhora*. I might have been mistaken and—"

"It would have hurt your pride, wouldn't it?"

"No no, *senhora*. It is not my duty to alarm you unnecessarily."

"Damned considerate of you!"

Uncle Rosario turned to Antonio. "Halter the pack mule to your saddle and ride behind us until we gain the main road again. Then pull abreast of us, *comprende?*"

Antonio promptly did as he was told.

Then Uncle Rosario said to all, "Ride with God."

"With God we ride," Antonio answered.

They had ridden about two miles with comparative ease, when the wind, a foreign wind that did not belong to the dry season, burst, flood-like, into the path. The wind was so heavy that it felt tangible. It covered the path, and the path seemed to grow narrower, and darker, an unfamiliar darkness that smelled of the bottom of a stagnant well.

The stampede of fear was beginning. Monkeys were popping up on every other tree branch, their round, stony eyes rolling in their flat heads, baring their teeth as they spat and screeched at the riders below. Present, but as yet unseen, there could be heard, even above the tumult of the wind, the strained growls of the jaguars and onças as they moved restlessly in the enmeshed thicket. The birds had long since taken flight. Already smaller creatures, the size of cats and piglets, were bounding across the path ahead.

As the wind still gained in force and fierceness, the cross-jungle exodus grew denser, more frantic.

Now a family of hysterical monkeys started to pursue the riders from tree to tree, pelting them with everything within their reach. Something hard hit Laura on the head. "You bastards," she cried.

Uncle Rosario turned in the saddle and, cupping his mouth with his hand, shouted, "Faster. Ride faster." Snatched out of his mouth by the wind, the sound of his voice reached Laura like a dying cry for help.

With spurs and voices they urged their mules on.

The earth quaked. The mules shied. Laura's mule swung on her hind legs and turned back. Promptly Antonio whipped her across the face and the mule turned around.

Fifty or sixty yards ahead, the mules swerved again as they came to a jagged gap across the path. It was a fresh gap, its intestine-like roots torn, bleeding a juicy matter. Feeling the riders' hands firm on the bits, and unable to turn back, the mules leaped over the gap and raced on.

Now the earth began to boil from within. Its surface quaked like jelly, and the air was filled with the prolonged, cracking reverberations of the tree roots snapping like steel cables. Even the darkness seemed to be cracking. And presently the jungle writhing along the borders of the path disappeared from sight. It stood on both sides before Laura's unbelieving eyes, like the incredible pictures she used to get by spilling a drop of ink in the fold of a white page and then pressing the two halves together.

And she was still gazing at this awe-inspiring sight when a flash of lightning exploded before her eyes, a clap of thunder pierced her eardrums. A blinding, deafening stillness followed, and then, like a landslide, the bottom of the sky fell, and the rain came.

The rain beat down the bullish fury of the wind. It set about flaying the treetops with a thousand hissing rods, bending and breaking the jungle's back.

The lightning flashed through the trees, uncovering mobs of crazed beasts dashing and bounding about. The thunder joined the chaos with rumbling voice.

The lightning scythed down primordial trees with one single stroke. The thunder applauded the feat. The surrounding trees stood firm by their struck kin, easing their fall. They fell then, through supporting branch-like arms, making a noise as if invisible hands were trundling enormous bundles of brambles.

Now the rain broke through the canopy-like roof over the path, hitting the earth and bouncing back in gurgling leaps.

The rain was so heavy that Laura thought she was riding under a waterfall. It was a weird feeling, as though she were being drowned from above. She hunched her shoulders, bent her head down against her chest, and wondered how much longer she could stand the merciless pounding. She was not actually praying with her mind, but her every breath was a prayer. And she breathed as if she were fleeing inevitable doom.

But she would not betray fear. Her shirt had become one with her skin. The shape of her bust showed with naked plainness. The rain flowed between her breasts, gathered in her crotch, flowed into her boots. Her nipples were painfully hard with cold, her crotch was cold, her feet were cold. The more hopeless Laura felt, the fiercer she fought for life. She fought for the sake of the fight, as she had once fought off the effect of an overdose of sleeping pills she had taken by mistake. Since then she had nicknamed herself Lazarus. "Top of the mornin' to you, Lazarus," she would greet herself on waking up in the morning.

In the storm-ravaged distance between earth and sky, visible now through the great gaps overhead, the treetops were hurled against each other with the swashing sound of clashing waves, became entangled in leaf-shedding wrath, were rain-slashed apart, rain-leashed back, to begin again.

The jungle smelled of nothing but cold, cutting wind and rain.

And through this miserable thing that was the jungle in the writhing, uprooting clutch of the storm, Uncle Rosario led his small party out of the path and onto the open road again. The road was already a river of flowing mud into which the mules— all except the pack mule, who had cut herself loose somewhere back on the path—sank kneedeep.

After a half-mile contest with the wind, Antonio managed to ride abreast of Laura, who now rode next to Uncle Rosario. There was but one thought in the old guide's mind: the safety of his client. Would that he were able to attract the fury of the storm upon himself alone.

"Up, up."

Their heads down, their backs arched like cats about to leap, their knees clasping their saddles, tugging at the reins to keep their mules' heads up, blinded by the slashing rain, resisting the snatching passes of the wind, they floundered on in a desperate effort to gain the cave.

"Two more miles. Only two more miles." Risking being snatched off by the wind, Uncle Rosario leaned over to impart the news to Laura. Uncle Rosario spat a mouthful of rain with every word he uttered. He looked as if he were viciously biting at the rain. And he looked pathetic, too, with the wind now twirling his long mustache crazily, now whipping it against his face.

Her broadbrimmed hat flapping madly behind her, the chinstrap fairly choking her, her hair now plastered against her head and face, now streaming behind her, seemingly yanking her head back, Laura hugged the saddle with frenzied strength.

"One more mile."

The recurrent, flare-like flashes of lightning revealed ugly, zigzagging gaps and gashes in the road, into which the liquescent mud was rushing as if into a sewer.

The mules floundered on, their bellies seemingly slit open lengthwise and bleeding mud, their tails frozen between their legs, their ears flattened against their heads, their necks stretched out, straining at the bit for support.

Laura's mule was falling back. Her hands were growing numb as she strove with all her vanishing strength to keep her mule's head up. Now her mule was a half-length behind. It seemed to Laura that the road was rocking and rolling in an earthly ground swell. Her stomach heaved. She opened her mouth and took in some rain. Now her mule was three-quarters of a length behind.

Laura had no idea what followed next. It happened quickly and silently, in a shorter time than it took her to gather the reins tighter in her numb hands. She thought she heard Uncle Rosario's warning shout. Then she saw Uncle Rosario leap out of the saddle, land before her mule and start whipping the animal back. For a moment Laura could not believe her eyes. She was seeing things. Too much rain. Until her mule reared and, neighing, boxed Uncle Rosario with her forelegs while he kept whipping her, barring her way ahead. Has Rosario gone mad? Is he rain-shocked? flashed through Laura's mind. At times the wind seemed to lift Uncle Rosario off the ground and toss him about like a puppet on a string. Then Laura's mule slipped, fell on her hind legs, turned over and pinned her down, deep into the mud.

And as her mule slipped and fell and turned over, Laura caught a fleeting glimpse of Uncle Rosario, stumbling about drunkenly, his head in his hands, and Antonio's mule, closely followed by Rosario's mule, leaping forward, disappearing into the earth, which parted before them like the jagged mouth of a shark.

Laura felt the bone-crushing weight of her mule pushing her deeper into the mud as the animal rocked and struggled to regain her footing. Laura felt as if she were drowning in mud. She gathered her strength to scream for help, and then she lost consciousness.

CHAPTER THREE

LAURA LOST consciousness within reach of the promised haven. The cave was now less than half a mile up the road, about two hundred yards west in the thicket, and it rose amid the storm-ravaged vegetation like a huge ant hill.

Inside, the cave was dark and clammy and pregnant with stinking odors. Bats squeaked as they moved in disorganized flight overhead, while smaller creatures crept about on the mildew-covered floor.

Two men were sitting on the ground against the wall facing the mouth of the cave. Their bodies were hardly distinguishable in the deep shadows.

There were two deeper shadows nearby, the men's mounts, stamping, saddles creaking, stirrups thumping dully against their flanks. A warm odor of fresh dung rose about the animals.

"Carlos?"

There was no answer.

"Sleep long and well," said the other and chuckled, as though it were possible to sleep in such a storm.

The man called Carlos was not sleeping. Among other things he had been counting how many streaks of lightning had flashed past the mouth of the cave. He had grown bored at eight. Now he was thinking how to get rid of the girl he was sleeping with. As a lover she had no equal, he readily admitted. But he was sick and tired of her aggressive jealousy. She had wanted to come along on this trip, so sure was she that he was going to see another woman. She had threatened to kill him. To hell with her.

A cold blast of wind rushed into the cave. It was really cold and the man called Carlos forgot about the woman he was planning to get rid of and caught himself remembering winter in another continent and the first time he had seen snow. His friends had pulled his leg about the snow. He tried to remember his friends' faces, but he could only manage to evoke a few blurred images. For awhile he wondered what had become of them; then he lost interest in their destinies.

The storm departed in the same way it had arrived, suddenly, leaving only an echo or a buzzing sound in the air. But perhaps the echo or the buzzing was in the ears of those who had lived through it. As if seen from the end of a tunnel, the outside now appeared bathed in cool, clear moonlight. For, although the storm was over and the sky had lifted, the darkness remained. Night had fallen with the rain.

"Carlos."

"What is it?"

"She has fought herself out. You want to ride on?"

"Get the mules ready."

"Son of a great whore," the man suddenly cried.

"What's the matter with you?" Carlos asked.

"He shit in my face," the other explained, meaning a bat.

"That should disprove the idea that bats are blind," Carlos said and grinned in the darkness.

"Speak short and straight," the other said.

"Let's go," said Carlos.

Laura regained consciousness. Still stunned, she could think of nothing except the great stillness about her. Then she realized how comfortable she was, lying in a coffin of mud.

Laura moved, and at once cried out in pain. Then her mind came fully alive again. In a panic of fear she found she could not move her left leg. The leg was bent at the knee, like a jackknife, and though she tried repeatedly, she failed to straighten it out. The effort clouded her eyes with fainting darkness and made her body break out in a cold sweat.

After a while Laura tried to move her leg again. Then another pain, even sharper than the first, awakened in the left side of her body. With every breath she took, she felt as if her ribs had caved in upon her heart and were stabbing her from within.

She lay still in her coffin of mud, nursing her pains, her fears.

She thought of Uncle Rosario, of Antonio. She mourned them as dead.

She was alone, hurt, helpless, hopeless. The end. But Laura was not so much afraid of that end as of the one that was lurking somewhere nearby in the guise of some wild beast.

But Laura fought back the surging crisis. She began to concentrate on ways and means of self-preservation. Ignoring her pains, and in a tremor of weakness, she started to lift herself upon one elbow, her mud-matted hair dangling from her head like a sodden mop. But strength failed her again, and she dropped back into the mud.

A hot breeze came tumbling down the road, stirring the pungent scent of the freshly washed wild vegetation. And even stronger was the odor of the newly exposed tree roots, shining now in the moonlight like polished bones—in heaps, in coils, scattered about.

The mud around Laura was getting cold, and she shivered with fever. She imagined the mud to be a cast. She thought of her injuries as permanently crippling ones. Her reason took issue with her fear, but her exhausted will sided with it. She turned to the sky for support. *Help me. Please help me.* And for a time she actually expected help from the indigo above. Then resignation set in. Then bitterness. She told herself she had never harmed anyone in her life. And Laura, who had always despised self-pity, now felt abjectly sorry for herself. She fed her mood richly with the worst of her memories.

Her marriage.

She had fallen in love with her husband the moment she saw him, that wonderful spring week end when he came to pick up his young sister, her roommate, at Smith. And then, on the spur of the moment, he had invited her to come along, too, and spend the week end with them.

How she had never been able to see through him during their engagement was something which had puzzled and humilated her for the longest time.

I was madly in love with him. I was blind. He was my dream come true.

But she ought to have had an idea of what type of man he really was when he showed surprise at her being a virgin.

I never gave a damn about my virginity as such. I just happened to be a virgin because I never loved a man well enough to lose my virginity to him. My future husband could have taken my virginity any time he wanted to.

Whether he was pretending or not?

No, he was not ...

He had mocked her virginity that very wedding night.

I was trembling with anticipation. I wanted to become a woman. I wanted to know him as my husband and my lover.

He had tried to hide his incompetence by getting drunk and rough with her.

He ripped my nightgown off. He threw me on the bed ... he fumbled and fumbled ... hurting me, not with the pain of love ...

A man possessed of a frantic desire he was unable to satisfy.

The weeks and the months that followed were a constant rehearsal of the same frustrated, messy tragedy. He had even suggested that she have a child by another man. He wanted an heir, to perpetuate his name. He was very proud of his name.

Yet she had been faithful to him to the very bitter end, when, fearing to lose her self-respect altogether, she had divorced him.

Divorce is not the end of a woman's life, she knew. Sometimes it is the beginning. But she had brought more to her marriage than her physical virginity; she had brought her moral virginity as well. And he had stepped hard on her moral virginity. Too hard. He had ground his heels on it. She had recovered, but the scars were still there for her to see whenever she lowered her eyes. That is why she chose to look straight ahead, and tried to find happiness again.

He was very handsome, kind and thoughtful.

God has answered my prayers.

He made love efficiently rather than ardently. A journey-man. But because she hardly knew what love was, she thought that that was it and was satisfied. It took so little to make her happy then.

But he did not tell her that he was already married and had two children. She had been loving him as his future wife for a whole year, when his wife, discovering the liaison, threatened to sue him for divorce on the ground of adultery. Then, and only then, did he find it necessary to tell her of his family, of the children he loved so dearly that he could not bear to be parted from them.

They were in her apartment—she was living uptown then—when he told her of his wife's ultimatum. He told her about it *after* they had spent the evening in bed together. He was feeling so sorry for himself that he even wept. He had been used to having his cake and his damned belly full too.

I couldn't believe he was the same strong man who a short while before had held me so tight in his arms, the same man who swore he couldn't live without me. I could have made a scene, ranted, threatened him. I wouldn't give him the satisfaction.

She had handed him his hat and showed him out, saying, "You might have told me. You're not too repulsive. I'd have loved you in a different way." She had seen in his suddenly sly eyes that he was glad to get off so easily. He inspired contempt.

Thereafter she had loved other men in that *different* way. She had trained herself to receive love without returning it. Thus shielded, she had lived life to the hilt. But that, she knew, was not the answer. Living life to the hilt was like staying drunk around the clock. In worldly experience she had grown much older than her age. No one, nothing, could surprise her any more. She thought she knew all the answers, and her acid tongue deflated men and women alike. The women slandered her in the powder room. The men crouched at her feet because of her beauty, and because they expected to take their silent revenge once they had gained her favor. She was drying up inside, fast. The faster the better. The sooner she forgot about having moral qualms, the freer she would be from herself. She coined a saying which for a time became the password of the crowd she was running with— "It's wonderful to be a moral eunuch ..." But all along she knew perfectly well that she was playing a part utterly incompatible with her nature. And that was her tragedy. Blessed be they who can lie to themselves, she told herself. They cease to know the difference.

Her few friends swore by her.

Her enemies rather avoided her.

Once she slapped a well-known actress in the face. *She had it coming. But no member of the feline family had the guts ...* screamed a tabloid. To hell with the tabloid.

She drank like a man but carried her liquor like a gentleman. No one ever caught her off guard. In time she reached the point where she could almost make herself believe that she was bored with love, through with life. Through with life! But she never suited the action to the thought, because she could not lie to herself.

And that was why she, so willful and self-assured, seemingly scornful of life and the living alike, felt a twitch of fear when she met those eyes—there were so few understanding eyes—that could look through her lovely bosom and see beneath it the tormented soul of a lonely woman, a woman who had been cruelly hurt, and was seeking a break from the life she was leading.

That perhaps was the reason that had driven her to Mato Grosso. And perhaps not. She had been studying Portuguese for the past year and a half, and so the idea must have been with her for sometime. A number of reasons, such as her growing discontent with herself, her genuine desire to see her brother, his forbidding her to come, might finally have persuaded her.

Her brother, William Burgess, was chief engineer of an American corporation developing the rubber region in Santa Caterina in northern Mato Grosso.

Of a well-to-do family and left orphans at an early age, brother and sister had drawn close to each other. Although William Burgess was four years older than his sister, he had always respected her quick mind, admired the force and attractiveness she naturally possessed. But at times he had also been a bit uneasy at the obstinate streak that ran through her. Even as a little girl, he remembered, if he wanted her to do something promptly, he had to tell her not to do it.

And he had absolutely forbidden her to come to Mato Grosso, not only because no one was better aware than he of the dangers and hardships such a journey entailed, but also because for the past six months he had been planning a pleasant surprise of his own for her.

Laura lay in her coffin of mud, staring at the sky, wishing the same wish all trapped mortals wish.

Whenever the breeze blew harder, showers of raindrops fell from the surrounding trees. Laura envied the raindrops. She imagined them to be free, beyond hurt and fear.

Her attention was caught by a broken tree branch arching over the mud in the distance up the road. The few scattered leaves on the branch shone like little mirrors in the moonlight. As her eyes glided along the branch and reached its end, dipping in the mud, her heart twisted in her bosom. It had come, the violent death she dreaded.

Something was moving at the end of the branch. A beast of prey, Laura was sure. Half-buried in the mud, the beast was drifting slowly towards her, like flotsam in mire. Now and again the moonbeams shone upon something metallic where the beast's neck should be.

Wide-eyed and breathless, Laura beheld the beast floating floating nearer and nearer, until it stopped, like the pause of doom, and crouched down, a thing born of the convulsion of the storm.

Laura started to tremble as she tried to drag herself away. She clawed the mud. She gained one, two, three, four yards. She dropped face down in the mud, exhausted. She felt she had received her fill of all agonies. She turned over on her back. She didn't care to wipe the mud off her face. She looked at the sky. How clean the stars were … how safe.

Then something strange happened to Laura. She grew calm. Too much fear had stunned her mind, even as a prolonged beating will make a body insensitive to pain. She started to weep. She wept softly, a little girl in the dark. She wept for the many things she had wanted to do but did not do, and would never do now. She wept for shame. She wept for love. She wept because she was conscious of all the life that was in her. She felt like rebelling against God, but didn't. She feared to anticipate the inevitable. She wept looking at the beast out of the corner of her eye.

Now the beast straightened itself up and, as soundlessly as before, advanced upon Laura. The distance between them grew shorter and shorter ... fifteen ... ten ... five yards. The beast stopped again, sniffed at the breeze, howled deep down in its throat, suddenly recoiled on its hindlegs and sprang forward. Laura crossed her face with her arms and her scream turned into a dying lament as the beast's mud-dripping belly leaped low over her.

CHAPTER FOUR

L AURA slowly took her arms away from her face. The beast was crouching at her side. She froze, and then relaxed as she saw that the beast was only a dog. The metal shining about his neck was a wide leather collar spiked with sharp steel. He didn't have much of a tail, just a wiggling, two-inch stump, and one of his ears, the right one, was split in two. From his muscle-humped back, over his sloping head and down to his flat, black-tipped nose, there ran three furrow-like, parallel scars where the hair no longer grew. He was a hunting dog, a veteran of many a deadly battle with the jaguar and its cousins.

Laura thought of the dog's master. A dog who wore a spiked collar must have a master. But who was he? What was he? Where was he?

A whistle rent the still night. The dog bounded off to meet the whistle.

Two riders appeared in the arch of the broken tree branch drooping over the road. From the distance one of the riders looked like a mountain strapped to a mule's back, while in comparison the other looked like a youngster.

The dog met them as they approached, leaped about them excitedly, darted back to Laura.

The riders pulled up at a prudent distance from Laura. The mountainous one climbed down the saddle and, rifle in hand, started toward her.

Now the man stood towering over Laura. Her expectant eyes met a black face framed in a long tasseled chinstrap, which rested on her breast as the Negro bent lower over her. He slung his rifle over his shoulder and, with unexpected gentleness, slipped his hand under her head, lifting it. Laura's mud-caked head rested in the palm of the Negro's hand as comfortably as on a pillow and she soon felt the heat of his hand warming the back of her head and neck.

"Santissima Madrel" said the Negro. He laid Laura's head back in the mud and stood up. "Carlos," he called. "Come afoot."

Carlos dismounted. His white neckerchief and gaucho pants flapped in the breeze, and his spurs squelched in the mud as he walked. Beside the Negro, now, Carlos appeared to be average in height and rather thin. Actually, he was over six feet tall and very well built. The breeze was buffeting the soft brim of his black hat against the crown, and his face was bare in the moonlight. He was a white man, burned dark by the sun.

Carlos tossed his rifle to the Negro, who caught it in the air, and knelt down beside Laura. At once Laura noticed Carlos' fine, smoldering black eyes, then his clear-cut features, then the keen expression of his face. There was an animal tenseness, or magnetism, about him that was almost palpable. Instinctively, Laura compared Carlos to a drawn bow. He looked to be twenty-five years old. He was thirty.

For a moment longer Laura and Carlos gazed at one another with inquisitive curiosity. Then Carlos turned to the Negro. "Bring me some *pinga*."

"Are you in pain?" he asked Laura.

Laura nodded.

"We'll try and make you comfortable."

The Negro returned with the *pinga* in a silver-ringed drinking horn. Carlos slipped his hand under Laura's head and lifted it, held the horn to her lips.

Laura drank thirstily, not quite aware that she was drinking sugar cane alcohol. The drink settled in her stomach, started a small fire.

Carlos tossed the remaining drink over his shoulder and the empty horn to the Negro.

"Where are you hurt?" Carlos asked Laura.

"My mule fell on me ... pinned me down. We were riding in the storm ... they ... I saw them ... there ..." The alcohol was working.

"Please, be calm. You're among friends now. Diaz is my name. This is Anteiro, my overseer."

"From Fazenda Boa Vista," Anteiro said. "At the service of God, and yourself."

"I'm Senhora Rendell," Laura said to Carlos.

"English?"

"American."

"How many in your party?"

"Three. Two guides and myself."

"Where are you hurt?"

"Won't you see if the guides—"

"Of course. As soon as we have made you comfortable. Where are you hurt?"

Laura told Carlos.

"Anteiro will take care of you now. He's a good doctor, Senhora Rendell. The second best on the ranch."

"The best, Carlos," Anteiro said good-naturedly. "I only make believe that I am the second best because I respect Porfirio's great age. My hand is steadier than the old man's. The old man cannot really operate any more."

"Is he a surgeon?" Laura wondered aloud.

"Yes," Carlos said. "His only degree is experience, but he has had a great deal of it. I recommend him highly. That," pointing at the dog's scarred head, "is Anteiro's needlework."

"Oh, he's a veterinarian."

"What is that?" Anteiro asked.

"A doctor who treats animals." Carlos explained.

"Are we not all animals, Carlos?"

Carlos grinned. Then he started to speak to Anteiro in the Bororo Indian tongue, and they exchanged places. Carlos sat down in the mud, rested Laura's head in his lap and took her face in his hands, while Anteiro knelt down at her side.

"Relax," Carlos said to Laura. "You're too tense. Please, do relax." He had a cultured voice and he was very polite—obviously he was a man of the world, in spite of his native attire—yet there always was that animal tenseness, or magnetism, about him that made him faintly sinister. The drawn bow. No telling when it might start off on its ominous journey.

Anteiro began to remove Laura's boot. But the boot was sodden and the leg bent at the knee, and Anteiro's effort caused Laura great pain. Carlos spoke to Anteiro in Bororo. Anteiro reached behind his back, unsheathed his elbow-length knife, and with a clean thrust slashed Laura's boot down to the instep. He tossed the boot over his shoulder, and with his hands he ripped the leg of Laura's breeches above her knee. Laura's leg was startling white. Anteiro fingered her kneecap.

"It is painful, is it not?"

"Rather."

Anteiro spoke to Carlos in Bororo and Laura felt Carlos' hands grow firmer about her chin. She was about to say something when Anteiro dealt a short, quick blow on her knee with the edge of his hand, pulling the leg straight at the same time.

For an agonizing moment Laura thought she was going to pass out again.

"You are small and delicate," the gigantic Negro said. "But you are very hard. Why did you not cry then?"

"I forgot, I guess."

"You are a valiant woman, is she not, Carlos?"

"You had a lock knee," Carlos said to Laura.

"Is it all right now?"

"Yes. But you won't be able to walk for a few days. Where else do you feel pain?"

"I'm sore all over. But here"—she fingered her left side—"it's pretty bad."

"If it had not been for the thick mud your mule would have crushed you to death," Anteiro said.

"I realize that."

"And now let me have a look at your bust."

"My bust?" Laura turned to Carlos.

Carlos explained that anything from the neck down to the waist of a woman was bust to Anteiro. Then he said, "Please, let Anteiro examine your side, Senhora Rendell. We must make sure how badly injured you are. Our means of travel, as well as our speed, will depend entirely on your condition."

"What about the others? The guides?"

"Their turn will come. Now it's *you* we're concerned about." Carlos nodded to Anteiro.

Anteiro unbuckled Laura's revolver belt and tossed it away. The holster was empty, the gun buried somewhere in the mud. Then he started to unbutton Laura's torn shirt—and paused.

"What is that, Carlos?" He pointed at Laura's brassière.

"It's something women wear," Carlos explained.

Good heavens, Laura thought, doesn't he know that?

"Why do not our women wear it, Carlos?"

"They don't like it."

"Why they do not like it?"

"Well," said Carlos, "it isn't part of their culture."

"What is culture, Carlos?"

"It's the way people dress."

This kind of conversation was carried on in orderly school-room fashion. Laura listened, amazed.

"That cinch is not good for a woman," Anteiro said, pointing at the bra. "It suffocates her breasts. And look how muddy it is. I must take it off."

"Don't you dare," Laura said incredulously.

"Be serious, woman," Anteiro said. "How can I clean you with that filthy harness around your breast?" And before Laura knew what was happening, Anteiro had slipped his forefinger under the center of the bra and yanked it off.

"You beast!"

And to Carlos, "Why didn't you stop him?"

"I'm sorry," Carlos said. "But, please, don't make it worse by making him believe he's done something ugly."

Laura gaped. "Hasn't he?" She fairly whispered in her amazement.

"No. Not so far as he's concerned. I assure you, he only meant to be helpful."

"How noble of him—and rotten of you."

Bewildered Anteiro said, "Did you call me a beast, woman?"

"No," Carlos said quickly. "She cursed her pain."

Like hell I did.

"Oh," Anteiro said to Laura. "I could not be insulted by you, woman. Because I have developed a live affection for you."

Whatever that is. "I'm delighted."

Laura's lovely breasts now lay bare in the moonlight, the nipples quiescent.

Carlos handed his neckerchief to Anteiro. Anteiro started to clean Laura's muddy bust. He went about it as gently and dispassionately as a midwife would clean a newborn baby.

What kind of people are these? Laura was wondering, still incredulously. The big gorilla has never seen a bra, calls it a cinch. But what about the other? He looks like a decent sort of savage. She shot an angry look at Carlos. Carlos was looking on as if he had spent his life watching Anteiro cleaning women's busts. As indifferently as all that. I can't figure him out, Laura thought.

Now Laura felt as though Anteiro's fingers were digging into her body. The pain was acute. She closed her eyes, gritted her teeth. And as she writhed under Anteiro's probing fingers, the touch of Carlos' hands on her face grew softer and softer.

"No rib is broken," Anteiro said. "But they are all much sadly bruised. You must be in great pain. I feel for you, woman, and—"

"Anteiro."

"Yes, Carlos?"

"She's Senhora Rendell."

"Is she, Carlos?"

"Yes."

"To you. To me she is a hurt and suffering woman. And she is my responsibility now."

Carlos grinned.

Laura was mystified at Carlos' behavior. First he thinks it's perfectly all right for him to rip my bra off, and now he goes formal on me. Then she wondered what kind of feeling, of a bond, between Carlos and Anteiro, was responsible for this kind of relationship between them—white master and colored man.

"And now I will bandage you as we do babies when they are first born," Anteiro told Laura. He seated her up in the mud. "Carlos," Anteiro said, "give me your sash. Mine is too rough for her. Feel her skin, Carlos. It is like the skin of a baby. Go on, Carlos. Feel it."

And Laura was convinced that Carlos would feel her skin to satisfy his man, even as a father would blow smoke rings to please his little son. She looked at Carlos, daring him.

Carlos grinned quietly.

Anteiro wore a woolen sash around his waist to keep the temperature of his body even, Carlos a light cotton one.

Carlos unwound his sash and handed it to Anteiro.

"Take that filthy rag off her," Anteiro said to Carlos. "I must clean her properly before I bandage her."

This is crazy, Laura thought. I might as well take off my breeches too. She caught herself resenting Carlos for refusing even to pretend to be embarrassed for her.

Gently Anteiro started to scoop the mud off Laura's back with his hand, which he shook clean at arm's length, to begin again. Then he dried Laura's back with the neckerchief and swaddled her torso with Carlos' sash with speedy efficiency.

Now only Laura's shoulders and arms were bare. "I feel like a mummy," she said to Carlos.

"You'll be all right," he said quietly.

Carlos and Anteiro started to talk in Bororo. They agreed that Laura was too weak to sit in the saddle, that they could not take her along with them as they went looking for the guides, and that they could not leave her here alone. Having reached this understanding, they looked about them for a drier, less muddy spot. Then Carlos sat down where he was and Anteiro picked Laura up and laid her down across Carlos' open legs so that her head rested in the crook of his left arm. She found it very comfortable.

Anteiro unslung his rifle. "Up, Leon," he called to the dog. "Up."

Leon trotted across the road. Anteiro followed him, and they soon disappeared in the lacquered darkness ahead.

Bandaged as she was, down to her waist, Laura looked as if she were wearing some kind of an exotic strapless evening garment. Nestling close to Carlos she felt his heart thumping steadily against the side of her head, and then the heat of his body warming hers.

"Do you think the guides—"

"Don't anticipate bad news, Senhora Rendell. You've gone through enough. Relax now. Please, do." But Carlos soon saw that his words had no effect on Laura and he started a conversation to distract her. "You speak Portuguese well. Where did you learn it?"

"Back home, in America."

"May I ask what brought you to Mato Grosso—*alone.*"

"Alone?"

"Your husband."

"My husband? Oh, he was much too busy." Then Laura told Carlos why she had come to Mato Grosso, omitting the fact that she had done so against her brother's wish.

"I know the region," Carlos said. "Their headquarters is not too far from our ranch. You'll have no difficulties in getting there, as soon as you're fit again."

"What's taking your man so long?"

"Call him Anteiro, and you'll please him. As he told you, he's developed a live affection for you."

"What kind of an affection is that?"

"Heartfelt. And, please, forgive him for the bra episode."

"He might have unhooked it," Laura said with a tired smile. "He's forgiven."

"In that case I must thank you, too. For if Anteiro had not thought of removing your bra, I'd have removed it myself."

"You wouldn't have dared."

"I'd have unhooked it."

It was so peaceful, so comfortable, so safe, in this strange man's arms and, in spite of her anxiety over Uncle Rosario and Antonio, an overwhelming drowsiness enfolded Laura. She fell asleep in Carlos' arms.

Two gunshots rang out in the distance. Laura started in her sleep. She grew restive. She mumbled incoherently, uttered choked cries of fear. Carlos felt her forehead. It was burning. He drew her closer to him. After a while Laura grew quiet again.

Laura traveled in Carlos' hammock, which was slung on two poles running lengthwise through the shortened stirrups of Carlos' and Anteiro's saddles.

Over her swathed torso Laura was now wearing Carlos' white poncho. Since it was too long and too large for her, she had taken it in at the waist with a leather thong. She had thrown away the other boot. The moon shone upon her bare head, her bare feet. She was dozing restfully.

Rifle in hand, Carlos walked beside Laura, holding on to the hammock with the other hand to control its swinging.

Antonio was riding Carlos' mule, in the rear, his feet dangling out of the stirrups. Antonio's right arm was hammocked in his wide belt he wore like a bandoleer. Antonio thought his right wrist was broken; Anterio did not. Antonio had jumped out of the saddle before striking bottom. A falling tree branch had knocked him out and pinned him down. The thick mud had relieved the pressure, saving his life.

Uncle Rosario was riding Anteiro's mule, which Anteiro was leading by the bit. The old guide was seriously hurt and in much pain. He rode slumped in the saddle and Anteiro kept a sharp eye on him. Anteiro had had a hard time reviving Uncle Rosario. His head was bandaged and the bandage blood-soaked about the left temple. Laura's mule had struck Uncle Rosario's left shoulder and arm, dislocating the shoulder, as he stood whipping her, barring her way ahead. Uncle Rosario now had his left arm cradled in a blue neckerchief, which was tied behind his neck. He had absolutely refused to travel in the hammock, as they all, including Laura, had wanted him to.

But perhaps even more painful for the old guide to bear than his own injuries was the loss of his faithful mule. Anteiro had shot both Uncle Rosario's mule and Antonio's mule, rather than leave the broken-legged animals at the mercy of the beasts of the forest. All their weapons lay buried somewhere in the mud. Anteiro and the dog had been unable to find Laura's mule.

Although it was held under tragic circumstances, the meeting of Anteiro and Uncle Rosario had had its happy side too. They knew each other and were old friends. For Uncle Rosario had know the Tamer, Carlos' grandfather, and been a welcome guest at the ranch. As a matter of fact, Uncle Rosario knew Carlos also.

They traveled in silence. The poles supporting the hammock carrying Laura squeaked and groaned as they bobbed or swung slowly.

The road looked like a wound that has ceased to bleed and is beginning to form a crust. The tree trunks, stripped of their barks and bent over by the force of the storm, shone like elephant tusks in the moon-bleached darkness. The mist was rising, the air damp and clammy.

Leon was scouting ahead. Now he barked, probably to tell Anteiro that he was not loafing on the job.

Laura woke up, and the first person she saw was Carlos. He was a comforting sight, tall and straight and strong as he walked beside her. She had never met a man like him before. With a woman's eyes Laura again studied Carlos' face, the keen expression on it. With a woman's curiosity Laura began to wonder what Carlos did, what kind of life he led, and lost herself in conjectures.

Now the road began to narrow slightly as it turned east.

There was a sudden burst of barking and a violent jolt and with a cry of pain Laura found herself sitting upright in the hammock. The lead mule had been brought to an abrupt stop. Laura heard Carlos cursing under his breath.

"What is it?" she asked.

Carlos shook his head. He kept his eyes on Anteiro, who now raised his arm and motioned Carlos to come to him.

Carlos found Anteiro and Uncle Rosario talking in hushed tones. The dog was growling at Anteiro's feet. Anteiro pointed ahead across the road and Carlos saw a heavier shadow crouching among the shadows of the bushes. They held a brief conference.

As Carlos walked back he reached behind his back, unsheathed his elbow-length, silver-handled knife and passed it under his belt, handle downward.

"What is it?" Laura asked.

"Don't be alarmed," Carlos told her, and to Antonio, a few steps later, "There may be trouble ahead." He handed his rifle to Antonio to hold for him.

"What kind of trouble?"

Carlos began to unstrap the poles from the stirrups and, waiting for Anteiro's signal, he shouldered the poles and together they carried Laura to the side of the road and laid her down on the ground.

Then Carlos went back to his mule, gathered the reins, handed them to Antonio and took his rifle back.

"Ride ahead," Carlos told Antonio. "Stand by your uncle. If danger should go past Anteiro and come your way, ride off. We'll cover you the best we can."

"What kind of danger?"

"I don't know. Ride."

Somehow Antonio took offense at Carlos' abrupt tone, and for a moment it looked as though he were going to argue with him. But Carlos ignored Antonio and walked back to Laura. He handed her his revolver. "But don't shoot," he warned her. "Please don't shoot until I tell you." Carlos took his stand five feet before Laura, his eyes on Anteiro, who was now standing in the middle of the road a few steps behind the dog.

Laura wondered why Carlos was carrying his knife like that, handle downward. Anteiro was carrying his in the same way, now that he had handed his revolver to Antonio.

Two or three minutes passed. Maybe less. But in the stillness of the moment, in the darkness of the hour, everything grew tense, assumed forbidding proportions. Laura felt her mouth growing dry. The recent past was too fresh in her memory. She wondered if she would ever live to see her brother again. You asked for it, she reminded herself.

Now Anteiro whistled, a sibilant, almost inaudible sound. Then Laura saw Leon drop on his belly and, snake-like, move toward the shadow crouching in ambush farther ahead on the other side of the road. Now there came a sharp grunt that sent a shiver through the still night. Leon stopped in his tracks, became one with the earth, it seemed, but for his spiked collar. Anteiro cautiously approached the dog, knelt beside him, stroked his head, his back, his head again. It was a language the dog knew well, and, wiggling his stumpy tail, he started on his dutiful journey again.

Anteiro stood in the middle of the road, his legs spread wide, the barrel of his rifle in the hollow of his left arm. The distance between the dog and the shadow grew shorter, until finally it was enough to tempt the shadow to come out of hiding and offer itself as a target. Anteiro whistled his soundless whistle. The dog stopped, straightened himself up and started to bark. The shadow shot up from the ground and rushed out onto the road, stopped and stood grunting at the dog. The dog answered in the same challenging tones.

The moonbeams fell upon the shadow like a searchlight. It was a wild hog, as tall as a young bull, with shorter legs, heavier body. Its lower tusks, looking like white-enameled steel hooks, were clamped about its pointed snout.

Anteiro was taking aim when the hog rushed the dog. The dog leaped upon the hog's back, sinking his wolfish teeth into the hog's neck. For a moment hog and dog looked like a monkey riding a bucking bronco, as the hog tried to shake off the dog. Anteiro was about to squeeze the trigger, when the hog threw itself down on one side and started to rock from side to side in an attempt to crush the dog. Anteiro's sighting eye could not separate them, and, rather than take the chance of hitting the dog, Anteiro rushed the hog, holding his rifle high by the muzzle. Just as Anteiro was bringing the rifle butt down upon the hog, the hog rolled away, got up and, leaving the dog half-crushed and stunned on the ground, charged Carlos and Laura.

Carlos was squeezing the trigger when a shot rang out behind him, then another. Carlos flinched, and by the time he had sighted on the target again, the target was upon him. Carlos dropped the rifle and crouched down on his right knee; then, as the warmth of the hog's panting breath touched him, he snapped to his feet and, left arm across his face, right hand gripping the handle of his knife, he leaped to meet the hog, bringing the knife up and plunging it handle-deep under the hog's left shoulder. The impact as they collided with one another sent Carlos stumbling backwards; then he staggered forward again, like a man breasting a great wind. The hog stood trembling, blood spurting from under its left shoulder until, dropping its head, it charged again. As Carlos was steadying himself for the next encounter, Anteiro fired, the bullet whanging and hitting the side of the hog's neck with a dull thud. The dog, now recovered, raced and pounced upon the hog, which went down under the violent impact, crumbling at Carlos' feet.

The entire action, taking place as it did within a matter of seconds, affected Laura like a wild film reeling before her eyes at a dizzying speed. It stunned her.

Anteiro came running over to Carlos. Carlos told him he was all right and pointed to the dog, who was tearing away at the hog's throat. Anteiro dragged the growling dog away.

By degrees the hog shrank into a shapeless mass, folding its legs with their incredibly small and elegant hoofs against its belly, as if it were hugging itself. Its large, stinking body writhed once or twice more and then was still, its tongue slipping out of its mouth and lolling on one side, its bloodshot, porcine eyes staring glassily into the night.

Carlos ran his bloody knife into the ground a few times, then sheathed it, handle up, and slipped it behind his back again.

CHAPTER FIVE

I N SILENCE Carlos and Anteiro strapped the hammock back to the stirrups. Then Carlos went back to Laura. Mechanically she handed him his revolver. Carlos took it, avoiding Laura's eyes, thus failing to see their stunned, glazed look. He picked Laura up and laid her back in the hammock, still avoiding her eyes.

They set off again, in the same order and, to the naked eye, in the same mood.

First the storm, and then the dog she had mistaken for a wild beast about to devour her, and now the wild hog rushing straight at her—one ordeal following so closely upon the other had finally drained whatever energy Laura had left, and thrown her in a state of shock. Teeth clenched, she stared at the moon, until finally she let out the long, quivering sigh of relief that had been jailed in her bosom for the past half a mile. Then she felt as though she had surfaced from an endless dive. Again she breathed the air of the living.

Carlos heard Laura's sigh, and for a moment he turned and looked at her. Carlos' eyes were still heavy with a sort of bestial dullness that to Laura betrayed the other side of Carlos' nature. She felt as if she had now had a clear look inside Carlos and discovered that underneath his cultured exterior there existed two opposite natures, making him appear romantic and faintly sinister by turns, and that attracted and repelled her at the same time.

Laura saw Carlos now as clearly as she saw Anteiro, an essentially primitive man. But Anteiro was genuine in his primitiveness, whereas Carlos' primitiveness was glossed over with a veneer of civilization.

Laura could feel the tension growing between Carlos and herself as they traveled on. His seething anger, his animal tenseness, needled her into a suspicion of uneasiness. Carlos was the first man who had ever made Laura feel physically uneasy, as though he were threatening her bodily.

Now Carlos tripped and stumbled. He grabbed at the hammock as he regained his footing, and the hammock swung roughly.

"You must be tired," Laura said. "I'm sorry I'm such a burden to you." She wanted to break the tension. She wanted to tell Carlos her side of the story, and perhaps apologize as well.

"I'm not tired," Carlos said. "And you *are* a burden."

If Carlos had slapped her across the face with a wet rag, Laura would not have been more humiliated. Laura was quiet for a moment, knowing that her voice would tremble if she spoke immediately. Then she said, "Senhor Diaz, I was fascinated by your courage. I think you're the bravest man I've ever met ... and also the most *villainous* one! You may choose to be as brutal as you please, because you *damn* well know that I can't get up and walk away."

"Think as you wish, Senhora Rendell. But I like my life well enough to scorn any hysterical woman who endangers it."

"I was frightened. It's no crime to be frightened. The gun went off by itself."

"Twice?"

"I was frightened, I tell you."

"And so was I. And so was Anteiro. And so was the dog. We were all damned scared, including the mules."

"You're despicable."

"No thanks to you. Thanks to you I might be mangled to death by now."

"For God's sake, don't be so damn dramatic."

"You don't seem to understand that all I'm trying to say is that I hate an hysterical woman, that in this part of the country a woman does as she's told, frightened or not frightened."

"I'm not one of your women."

"True. You're the kind of a woman that nearly had me killed—and yourself, too." Then he added, "Is there anything you wish now? A drink? Something to eat? Or would you rather we stopped a while?"

"No, thanks. The thing I most wish for now can't be fulfilled."

"What's that?"

"To be rid of you. To be able to get up and walk away. To relieve you of my hysterical presence."

Slowly Carlos turned to Laura. His eyes were burning. No, Laura thought. Not even he would dare. She feared Carlos was about to strike her.

"But that's not the point," Carlos said in an anxious voice, suddenly a different man, in a mood that escaped Laura's understanding altogether. "That's not the point at all."

"Then what *is* the point?"

"*You* might have been killed."

Now the moon was blending with the sky and the remaining stars were blinking feebly, vanishing like dying sparks. Then the east was covered with a pinkish hue, like a slow-spreading flame seen through a dark celluloid, and the jungle, as if relieved of the weight of darkness, began to straighten itself up, like a giant stirring from a torpid slumber.

Carlos' party traveled on through the shifting dawn, in and out of pockets of air that were dank and dark in the hollows, warmer and lighter in the open spaces.

At a turn in the road the sun shone in their eyes.

Laura's first movement to shield her eyes from the sun tore a sound of pain from her lips.

Carlos turned to Laura and their eyes met. For a moment they took stock of one another in the new light of day.

Aside from his fight with the hog, Carlos had walked at Laura's side throughout the night: he looked as fresh as if he had just got out of bed. Laura wondered how she looked. *To hell with my looks.*

"Are you in pain?" Carlos asked.

"No," Laura told him. "I'm hysterical. And you?"

"How's the knee?"

"Also hysterical."

"You're my guest. You owe me the courtesy of an answer."

"I'll not be your guest for long, I hope. The knee's all right."

"And the ribs?"

"Fine."

"You're truly an Amazon."

"And you a superman. What a rotten combination."

Slowly Carlos turned to Laura. "Are you still angry with me?"

"Oh, of *course* not!"

Carlos bent down and kissed Laura on the lips.

Recovering she said, "Why did you do that?"

"An impulse of my heart."

"Praiseworthy, no doubt, to your way of thinking. But was it necessary?"

"Yes," Carlos said seriously. "Or I'd have started ranting at you again."

Carlos stopped and waited for Antonio to come abreast of him.

Just as he had the night before, Antonio resented Carlos' voice and offhanded manners, a resentment of which Carlos was completely unaware. Moreover, Antonio was dying to know what Carlos had done when he had bent down over Laura. Carlos' hat had screened off the kiss.

"My wrist has turned blue," Antonio said. "It's numb with pain."

"Well," Carlos said encouragingly, "you don't have to worry about doing the cooking now."

"What cooking?"

"Aren't you the cook?" All along, Carlos had taken Antonio for the cook in Laura's party.

As a bullfighter, Antonio had appreciated better than anyone Carlos' coolness before the hog. For a moment Antonio's mind had substituted a bull in place of the hog, and he had felt as he usually did in the ring when another matador received a warmer ovation than he. And now, on top of this feeling of jealousy, he had been taken for a cook! Antonio's ego revolted.

"I'm not the cook. I've never cooked in my life. Women are glad to cook for me." Contemptuously Antonio told Carlos who he really was.

"Never heard of you."

"You would have heard of me if you lived among people."

Carlos eyed Antonio. "Where do you do your bullfighting—in Portugal?"

Antonio fairly jumped out of the saddle.

In Portugal the bull has his horns truncated and padded, and the bullfighter, mounted, sticks him with a blunt-tipped pole. Neither bull nor fighter is ever allowed to be killed.

Antonio was so insulted, so mad, that he bit his tongue as he tried to answer Carlos. He cursed in pain.

"Anteiro doesn't think your wrist's broken," Carlos said.

"What does that enormous ape know?"

"That enormous ape, as you call him, knows more than you suspect, man. He also can and will tear you limb from limb if he hears you call him that."

"I do not frighten so easily."

"Provoke him."

"At my convenience."

"We have room in our cemetery. You're welcome."

Carlos walked away, past Laura, at whom he smiled, up to Anteiro.

Uncle Rosario looked bad. His eyes were like the eyes of a dead chicken. But being the man he was, he pulled himself together at seeing Carlos.

"Good morning, Carlos Diaz, grandson of my friend, the Tamer," Uncle Rosario said.

"You knew my grandfather?"

"Yes, Carlos," Anteiro said. "Rosario the guide has been a friend of the house since before you were born."

"And I know you, too, Carlos Diaz," Uncle Rosario said. "Do you not remember me?"

Carlos wished he did.

Then Uncle Rosario started to explain how many times he had seen Carlos on the ranch when he was a boy. "And then I heard of the Tamer's death and I was much grieved. And soon after that I heard that your father had come back to the ranch and taken you away from the land and your friends."

"Yes," Carlos said, and to spare Uncle Rosario from carrying on a conversation that was visibly exhausting him, he turned to Anteiro and told him to stop at the first convenient spot so that they could eat and rest.

Carlos stopped and waited for Laura to come abreast of him.

"We'll have something to eat as soon as Anteiro finds a spot for us," he told Laura.

"How's Rosario?"

"Not so good, I'm afraid."

"Poor man. I have a feeling that he holds himself responsible for what happened to us, for allowing himself to be caught in the storm."

"I wouldn't be surprised," Carlos said. "He's that kind of a guide."

"In Cuiaba they said he's one of your best guides."

"I don't doubt it, but I really wouldn't know," Carlos said. "I was away a long time."

"From Mato Grosso?"

"Yes. I went abroad."

"Where abroad?"

"Europe."

So that's where he learned his erratic good manners, Laura thought. "Where in Europe?" she asked.

"Italy. France."

"Were you studying there?"

"Pretending to."

"How long were you abroad?"

"An eternity, it seemed to me."

"Did you like it?"

"What?"

"Italy."

"No."

"France?"

"Worse. I don't like anything that's forced on me."

"Didn't you want to go?"

"Of course not. But after my grandfather died, my father came back to the ranch for the first time since I was born. I was fourteen then. And he deceived me into following him to São Paulo, where he put me in a private school from which I promptly escaped. I was on my way back to the ranch when he caught up with me and, to make sure that I wouldn't escape again, he shanghaied me to Europe. He had decided to make a gentleman of me, and he succeeded. I've learned to be prudent and to disguise my thoughts."

That's news to me, Laura thought. "Is that your definition of a gentleman?"

"That's what we think of a gentleman in this part of the country. That's what they think of me now, I'm afraid."

"What do they think of a reckless, outspoken man?"

"We have neither reckless nor outspoken men in this part of the country, Senhora Rendell."

"As I'm forced to be your guest," Laura said with a smile, "hadn't we better drop the formality, Carlos?"

"I don't know your first name."

Laura told him.

"It's a beautiful name," Carlos said. "A Latin name. Are you part Latin somewhere in the past?"

"Not a bit. One hundred percent cold-blooded Anglo-Saxon."

"What a pity."

"Isn't it, though. But getting back to what you said before, what kind of men *do* you have in this part of the country?"

"Men, and women, too, who think and act simply. People who can't help behaving as they do because they don't know the meaning of pretense or lie or deceit. Anteiro's an average example. You've had a taste of him, haven't you, Laura?"

I've had a taste of you, too, my friend, Laura thought.

"Among other things Anteiro insists on calling you woman," Carlos was saying. "I've tried to stop him. That shows how stupid I've grown, how—"

"You needn't apologize, Carlos."

"I'm not apologizing. I'm explaining, Laura. Anteiro calls you a woman as he would call a general a soldier. And what greater compliment could one pay a general than to call him a soldier?"

"So I'm a general now," Laura said. "In America, in the South, the standard promotion is colonel. Isn't that ridiculous?"

Carlos grinned. "Let's drop the military," he said.

"If we do, what else's left for us to talk about while we wait for breakfast?"

"You."

"Me? All right, let's talk about me. What do you want to know? When and where I was born? My mother's maiden name? The schools I went to? Shoot."

"Are you in love with your husband?"

"Whoa!"

"What does that mean?"

"Stop that line of questioning right here and now."

"I asked you a civil question."

"God save us from your uncivil ones."

"Well, are you in love with your husband?"

If you only knew, my friend. "Yes."

"Very much?"

"Deliriously."

"Does he reciprocate your love?"

"This is no longer a conversation, Carlos. It's a cross-examination. I hate to be cross-examined."

"Does he reciprocate your love?"

He won't let go. Shall I tell him to mind his own damn business? No. Don't spoil it. "I refuse to answer," she said.

"On what grounds?"

"Your impudence."

"I don't think he does."

"Think what you please."

"I don't believe you."

"Are you calling me a liar?"

"Aren't you?"

Here we go again, Laura thought. Well, say it. "I was never so insulted in my life."

"That's because you're so beautiful. If you were just another fairly good-looking woman you'd have been 'so insulted' at the age of fourteen, or even sooner. There must be a beginning sometime."

"You made an early one, a good one, during the night."

"That's very unkind of you."

"Please, forgive me. I'm still hysterical."

"That's damn unkind of you."

Laura grinned to herself.

They traveled on in silence for a quarter of a mile.

"No," Carlos said, betraying the direction in which his thoughts were wandering. "Your husband can't love you as much as you say."

Laura held her peace.

"If he loved you as much as you say, he wouldn't have allowed you to take this trip."

"Why not?"

"If you were my wife I would never let you out of my sight."

"How thrilling! Thank God, I'm not your wife."

"But if you were—"

"Time's up. Now let's talk about you. What were you doing in Europe? Never mind that. You told me. Shall I have the pleasure of meeting your mother at the ranch?"

"Who?"

"Your mother."

"My mother's dead."

"I'm sorry."

"I never knew my mother."

"Was she a local girl?"

"No. She was from São Paulo. My father met and married her there. But when my grandfather heard that she was with child, he ordered my father to bring her to the ranch, the only place where his grandson ought to be born. My grandfather never doubted that I was going to be a boy. My mother died the same day I was born. Probably the long ride was too much for her. My father held my grandfather responsible for his wife's death and left the ranch, vowing never to come back."

"Why didn't your father take you with him?"

"Gun in hand, my grandfather dared my father to take me away from him."

"It was your grandfather, then, who brought you up."

"Yes."

"Gun in hand, too?"

"You seem to have formed a wrong opinion of my grandfather, Laura. Most people have. My grandfather was truly a good man, as good as the circumstances permitted at the time. They've made a legend of his ruthlessness. He was an early *bandeirante*—"

"Pioneer?"

"Yes. He had to machete and shoot his way through the jungle, through men and beasts alike. True, he drove the fear of hell into the Indians, but also into those whites who massacred the Indians, for the sake of bloodshed only. It was thanks to my grandfather's so-called ruthlessness that the Catholic missionaries were finally able to enter the jungle safely."

"And he must have been kind to you, Carlos, to have earned such admiration." Laura's voice was thoughtful.

"Well, he never treated me with kid gloves, to be sure. Sometimes he was even cruel, but it was the cruelty of a man who loved too possessively. I sensed that even as a child, and

I never feared him. I always loved him, even when he used to grab me by the scruff of the neck and toss me onto a bareback bronco, and then he wouldn't speak to me for days because I was thrown."

"How old were you then, Carlos?"

"Five or six."

"Weren't you a bit too young for that kind of treatment?"

"I never knew the difference. My grandfather never treated me like a child. He always thought of me as his future heir, and he started training me for the job as soon as I could walk."

"Doesn't the ranch belong to your father?"

"No. It never did. It belongs to us."

"Who's 'us'?"

Carlos smiled. "Betta, Anteiro and me."

"You mean legally?"

"What's legality got to do with it."

"So your father lives on the ranch now as a guest, as it were."

"My father doesn't live on the ranch. In fact, he's hardly ever lived here. He was still in his teens when he decided he could never become the rancher my grandfather had in mind, and he packed himself off to São Paulo. He's lived there ever since, first as a student, then as a businessman."

"What business is your father in, Carlos?"

"Coffee exporter. Probably you've drunk his coffee in America."

"Probably. Have you seen your father since you came back from abroad?"

"Yes. Once. Six or seven years ago. It was evening, I remember. I happened to be passing by his house, and he was standing in the open doorway, pulling on his gloves."

"Did you have a pleasant visit?"

"I didn't even speak to him."

"Why?"

"I'll never forgive him for having sent me off to Europe. Europe taught me nothing."

"Maybe you refused to learn, Carlos."

"Absolutely!"

"Your father may want to see you again."

"Here?"

"Yes."

"I hope not. For his own sake I hope he never sets foot on the ranch again. I fear Betta and Anteiro might kill him."

"Kill him!"

"Since my father took me away from the ranch, they've nursed a rage against him, like a chronic toothache. Especially Betta. When you meet her, you'll see what I mean."

"Is their any reason for them to have developed such animosity toward your father.

"My grandfather left me to them in his will. They believe I'm theirs, like an heirloom."

"What?"

"So when my father took me away, Betta and Anteiro thought, and still think, that he stole the most treasured item in their personal belongings."

"*Stole?* Your father was merely taking back what was legally his."

"Not so far as Betta and Anteiro are concerned. To them, to this day, my father's a thief. And on our ranch theft's the most unpardonable crime of them all. That's the law, and so far no one has ever dared break it. But should someone break it, I'd hang him myself. So you can well imagine what would happen to my father were he to let his sentimentality get the better of him and come back to the ranch to see me."

"Aren't you ever going to see your father again, Carlos?"

"I don't know. Not in the near future, anyway. I can't rid myself of the resentment I have against him for having uprooted me."

"It was only for a few years."

"It was for long enough to make me feel, sometimes, that I'm neither fish nor fowl any more."

Laura eyed Carlos. "Don't worry about that," she said with a smile. "You're very much a native."

Carlos looked at her and grinned.

About two hundred paces later Carlos suddenly took off his hat and put it on Laura's head.

"No, thanks," she said. "My hair's thick." She handed the hat back to him.

"Not against this sun," he said. "I insist."

"In that case I'll make my own headgear," Laura said. "Help me, please." Laura, holding onto Carlos' arm, leaned forward in the hammock, pulled the back of her poncho from under her and draped it loosely over her head and shoulders.

"You're an artist," Carlos said. "You look like a nun, now. No, like a madonna. I've seen you before, in some gallery in Florence. A green-eyed, suntanned madonna. A very beautiful madonna." Then he said, as if they were alone in the dark, "I shall worship at your feet. Will you answer my prayer?"

Laura felt his animal tenseness reach her, suddenly awakening in her a thrill that developed like the growth of pain. She nursed the feeling for an instant. Then she smiled and said, "You remind me of my darling husband."

Carlo stiffened, then relaxed, like a taut rubber band snapped loose.

CHAPTER SIX

Anteiro led the front mule to the left side of the road and stopped before a large gap in the compact growth along the roadside.

"There is water nearby," Anteiro said to Uncle Rosario.

"A stream, running from the north," said the old guide.

Laura saw Uncle Rosario start to climb down from the saddle, unaided … and tumble into Anteiro's expectant arms. Anteiro carried Uncle Rosario into the gap.

Carlos put his hands out to pick Laura up.

"Let's test the knee," she said. Slowly she swung her legs over the edge of the hammock, sat still for a moment. Then she stood up and took a few steps, grimacing, limping heavily on her left foot. Carlos walked Laura into the gap and seated her down on the ground opposite Uncle Rosario.

The old man's in bad shape, Laura realized. "How do you feel, Rosario?"

"Very well, *senhora*. And you?"

"Fine."

Anteiro beamed down upon Laura. "I dreamed of you last night," he said.

"When?"

"While I was walking."

"In your sleep?"

"Do not confuse me, woman," Anteiro said, frowning. "Accept my dream."

"Accepted," Laura said, feeling rather confused herself.

What Anteiro meant was, I was thinking of you. To dream and to think were the same thing to him, as he visualized his thoughts as if they were dreams, and thought of his dreams as work of his mind.

Antonio came into the gap. He looked displeased. Throughout the night and since sunrise he had been traveling alone, feeling unwanted. On top of that, he was sure Carlos had displaced him from Laura's favor. And on top of that, he had been mistaken for a cook. Antonio hated Carlos. Antonio was going to get even with Carlos the first chance he got. In this mood Antonio even scowled at Laura when she smiled at him in greeting. Antonio sat down cross-legged beside his uncle.

Carlos and Anteiro unsaddled the mules, gathered their gear and brought it into the gap.

The dog supervised all these operations, then disappeared.

It was not easy to build a fire so soon after the storm. Yet, Laura noticed, Anteiro never lost his patience. He coaxed the fire as if it were a moody child.

Anteiro's small round head was perched on his massive shoulders like that of a thoughtful boy. When he smiled his whole boy-like countenance lit up, as if the sun were shining on his face. Now that he was bareheaded—he was fanning the fire with his hat— Laura noticed gray in Anteiro's hair, like scorched wool.

Anteiro was a guileless but formidable human machine, Laura clearly saw, which no one could control once it got out of hand—no one, that is, except Carlos, to whom he was enslaved by a primitive worship, and by whom he was treated like a friend and an equal.

Laura knew that Anteiro was the overseer of Carlos' ranch. She took it for granted that Anteiro was born on the ranch and had worked his way up to that responsible position.

Actually, the Tamer, Carlos' grandfather, had found the future overseer when he was still a boy in age, but already in possession of a strong man's body. He had found him alone in a hole in the jungle, half-starved and badly wounded, fighting off a jaguar with a Bororo arrow which he had extracted from his own thigh. The Tamer had shot the jaguar, tossed his machete to the boy and ridden off—only to ride back a while later and toss him his revolver, and ride on again. The third time back, he'd ridden off with the boy, and kept him at his side throughout his turbulent life.

From one of his saddlebags—Anteiro's saddlebags were really small packsaddles—Anteiro now took an iron pot. As he carried it down the path to the stream, Laura, who was seated on the ground, could not miss noticing his feet. She wondered what size shoe Anteiro wore. When Anteiro lifted his feet he uncovered yards of ground, it seemed.

While Anteiro was gone Carlos emptied Anteiro's saddlebags and placed the food and the tableware on the ground next to the fire. The tableware was of tin and there were two of everything: two cups, two dishes, two forks.

Now Anteiro came back, hung the pot on the rod over the fire, squatted on his heels beside it. They all waited in silence, each nursing his own pains and tiredness.

The water began to simmer. Anteiro took up a pouch-shaped, udder-bottomed cloth bag and half-filled it with finely ground coffee.

Finally the water began to boil, and Anteiro reached for the pot. He held the bag over a cup while he poured the boiling water into it. At once the bag swelled out and then collapsed as steaming black liquid flowed from its udder-like end into the cup. Never before had coffee smelled so good to Laura.

Carlos offered that first cup to Laura, and the second one, a moment later, to Uncle Rosario. The coffee was scalding but its aroma so tempting that Laura drank it greedily. She and Uncle Rosario refused a second cup not to keep the others waiting.

Uncle Rosario started to fidget in his place. He spoke to his nephew in secret tones and Antonio got up, helped his uncle to his feet. Slowly they made their way down the path and disappeared into the thicket.

Carlos glanced at Laura. "Your hair's still caked with mud," he said. "Your face could stand a good scrubbing, too. Shall I ring for your nurse?"

"Please, do."

"Anteiro, have you forgotten your responsibility?"

Anteiro stood up. He was indignant. Shaking his fore-finger at Carlos he said, "There is life in our forest, man. There is love in our affection. There is a drop of blood in each sorrowful tear we shed for our friends, man, and—"

"Bravo!" Laura said.

"I have not finished yet, woman. And there is a *pampeiro* blowing in your head, Carlos, my son."

"What does he mean?" Laura asked.

Carlos smiled. "He's just finished calling me a fool."

"Why?"

"For reminding him of his responsibility. In short, he was hurt."

Anteiro slung Carlos' saddlebags over his shoulder, picked Laura up in his arms and carried her down the path. Anteiro's chest was burning, Laura felt, and he smelled of hot molasses.

Carlos sat down on his heels before the fire and started cooking: beans and rice which would be served with mandioca flour instead of bread.

The beans were boiling when uncle and nephew came back. Uncle Rosario looked exhausted, cadaverous. Carlos gave Uncle Rosario a stiff drink of alcohol and told Antonio to help himself.

A startled expression came over Carlos' face when Anteiro came back with Laura and deposited her on the ground.

Laura's sun-bleached auburn hair, still damp, was combed back and parted softly in the center. Her suntanned face, washed clean, was feverishly radiant and her green eyes were shining. Carlos thought there was something different about her now. Then he realized what it was. Laura had discarded her riding breeches, and the poncho, taken in at the waist with the leather thong, was spread around her like a flaring skirt, sagging softly between her thighs. Carlos wondered what she was wearing underneath.

"Well eat presently," he said. "Would you like a drink?"

"Scotch?"

"Of course."

"With a little soda, please."

"Coming up."

Carlos poured some alcohol into a cup and handed it to Laura. "May you never grow old."

"What's that?"

"A native toast."

Laura lifted her cup and drank. "Best damn Scotch I ever had," she said, and in her present mood she meant it.

Having only two dishes and two forks, they ate in the same order in which they had drunk the coffee: Laura and Uncle Rosario first, then Carlos and Antonio, while Anteiro ate from the pot with his knife. He said he was too hungry to wait.

As they were drinking second cups of coffee, Carlos offered Laura a rice-paper cigarette, lighted it for her.

Carlos and Anteiro decided that, since the rest of the journey would have to be made on the open road, they would do better from now on to rest during the day and travel through the night. In this way, Laura and Uncle Rosario would be more comfortable. Of course Carlos asked Uncle Rosario if that would be agreeable to him. Uncle Rosario said he did not mind relinquishing the leadership to Carlos Diaz, grandson of his friend, the Tamer. Carlos thanked Uncle Rosario but said that Anteiro was the leader now. Anteiro said of course Uncle Rosario was still riding the lead mule.

Anteiro kept an eye on Laura. He waited for her to finish her cigarette; then he got up and strung out Carlos' hammock between two trees. Without a word he picked Laura up and laid her down in the hammock.

"Best damned service I ever had," Laura said. Laura marveled at the way she allowed herself to be treated by these two men, Carlos and Anteiro. What's more, she rather liked it. In their warm, spontaneous actions she recognized a quality which she had once possessed but now kept buried deep inside herself. Laura laughed to herself as she remembered Carlos saying, *I've learned to be prudent and to disguise my thoughts.* Ye gods! And the other one, Anteiro. *Woman, I have developed a live affection for you.* It was so novel, refreshing, friendly.

Now Laura heard Carlos and Uncle Rosario starting an argument as to who should have Anteiro's hammock. Uncle Rosario insisted on sleeping on the ground with the others. Carlos finally won, but it was a strenuous contest. Uncle Rosario was no mean debater on matters of personal pride, and he conceded defeat only after Anteiro had lifted him into the hammock. There the exhausted old guide fell asleep at once ... and soon was moaning in pain.

Carlos got up. He stood by Uncle Rosario's hammock, looking down at him, wondering if the old guide would have enough strength left to finish the homeward ride in the saddle. Maybe he'd have to travel in Laura's hammock, whether he liked it or not.

Thinking of Laura, Carlos looked at her. She was staring at him, and for a moment their eyes met. Then Carlos whispered, "Why aren't you asleep? Go to sleep." How sweetly the savage could give orders.

Carlos walked over to Laura, stood looking down at her. His eyes journeyed the length of her body. He reached down for her ankle, lifted it slightly. His hand felt dry, hot, and Laura began to feel his animal tenseness reaching her. Then he laid her foot back in the hammock, walked away without looking at her. She saw him stretching out on the ground next to Anteiro. For a moment longer Laura felt Carlos' hand around her ankle. She closed her eyes and remembered his kiss. Then she heard Carlos' voice in her mind. *I shall worship at your feet. Will you answer my prayer?* Was that being friendly, too? Go to sleep, Laura told herself.

Leon trotted into the gap, a turtle hanging by its short tail from his slobbering mouth. The dog dropped the turtle on Anteiro's chest. Without opening his eyes Anteiro felt the turtle, thought what a good soup it would make for his friend Rosario. He patted the dog, then pushed him away. The dog laid himself down at Anteiro's feet. The turtle stuck its head out and slowly started to climb down Anteiro's chest. Anteiro put the turtle down on the ground. The turtle went past the dog. The dog reached out with his front paw and raked the turtle back. They were going to play that game for a long while.

Carlos spoke to Laura.

"Of course," she said. "I'm feeling fine, really."

Then Carlos spoke to Uncle Rosario and Uncle Rosario was sorely offended. He spoke in angry tones. "*Hiyayaya*, Carlos Diaz. Your grandfather would not suggest that I travel in my client's hammock, even if she was a man."

Stubborn old man. Carlos gave the order to start off. The evening was warm. The sun and the moon were staring at one another in the clear sky. Then the sun dropped out of sight. Carlos' party disappeared into the night.

The rising sun found them in Las Almas Lauca, a deserted village. Carlos' party rested in a wild tamarind grove outside the village. The river was infested with piranhas. No one except Anteiro went near the river that day.

The incoming moon found them on the go again. A humid wind came blowing from the north and throughout the night the jungle sounded like an ocean, wave upon wave rolling and breaking on an unseen shore.

At dawn the next day they reached O Morro Verde, The Green Hill, and paused to rest. The hilltop was bathed in moonlight and steeped with the odor of dew-drenched alfalfa, as this was pasture land. On the eastern side of the hilltop, overlooking a slope, there was a wooden shrine with a statue of Jesus Cristo, also in wood. The Savior was primitively carved with machete and hatchet. He looked like a native, with kinky hair and beard.

Carlos led Laura to the western side of the hilltop and pointed out to her the jungle-fringed plain below.

Laura saw a river, the Xingù, black and swollen, sneaking cobra-like in the distance. And then she saw a shadow, a sober, somber shadow.

"What's that?" she asked Carlos and pointed.

"That's Fazenda Boa Vista—our ranch. The shadow you see is the *casa grande*."

And there it stood, or rather, squatted, the massive ranch house under the moon. For generations it had stood thus: a self-sustaining pastoral oasis in the heart of Mato Grosso, isolated and proud, resisting the Indians' attacks, scornful of elements and beasts alike.

With the rising moon that night they came to the outer gates of the ranch.

Three men, rifles slung over their shoulders, were sitting on their heels before a small fire. They leaped to their feet and ran to open the gates.

"*Boas tardes, patrão,*" they said and raised their hands.

Carlos returned the greeting.

Anteiro led the front mule down the wide, well-kept road that ended at the main entrance to the *casa grande.* As they approached it, Betta, followed by a crowd of servants, rushed out to meet them.

"Welcome home, son," she cried to Carlos as her eyes darted from Uncle Rosario to Antonio, came back and stayed on Laura.

Carlos helped Laura out of the hammock and walked her over to meet Betta.

"This is Betta," Carlos said to Laura. "The mistress of the house."

Betta was lighter of skin than Anteiro, and her hair, although she was probably younger than he, had more gray in it than his. But they were of a breed of people who had no notion of time and never really aged. Betta was compact, heavy, like a bag of sand. She had round small eyes that squinted merrily in a full face the color of polished brass. But her eyes would grow as hard as pinheads and her face turn a rusty green when she flew into a rage. She was strong and she had a sharp tongue, and even Anteiro, her lifelong companion, disliked arguing with her.

"This is Senhora Rendell, Betta. She's going to be our guest."

"Was she caught in the storm then?"

"Yes."

"Is she injured?"

"Not too seriously."

"Welcome to the *casa grande*, daughter," Betta said to Laura. Then she added, as if she could not keep it to herself, "*Santa Madre*, I have never seen green eyes before. They are beautiful, are they not, Carlos? And you, too, daughter, are very beautiful. Welcome."

"Thank you, Betta."

Betta turned to Anteiro. "*Xêcô*, man, take the men into the house and make them comfortable."

"One thing at the time, woman," Anteiro said calmly.

"A lazy time, if I know you."

Chuckling, Anteiro helped Uncle Rosario to climb down the saddle. Uncle Rosario's knees buckled under him and Anteiro fairly carried him to Betta.

"My Jesus, my Mother and my cross," Betta cried. "Is that you, Compadre Rosario?"

"The storm, Nhâ Betta. The storm."

"Are you badly hurt, Compadre Rosario?"

"Insignificantly so, *nhâ*."

"Welcome to the *casa grande* again. Maybe we had to have a storm to have you visit us again."

Uncle Rosario introduced Antonio to Betta. "My nephew. Antonio by name; a bullfighter by call."

Betta eyed Antonio. "A very distinguished-looking lad."

"A man of some aspect," Uncle Rosario said.

Betta turned to Anteiro. "*Xêcô, xârâ*, man! What is this of doing nothing? Take the men into the house and make them comfortable."

"Do not hurry time, woman," Anteiro said calmly.

Betta placed her short, powerful arm about Laura's waist and half-carried, half-led Laura into the house.

As Laura walked with Betta, looking and smiling at the people about her, she suddenly noticed a pair of strange glowing eyes fixed intently upon her. When she searched the crowd again, they were gone. It must have been my imagination, Laura decided. But it left an unpleasant impression.

Laura was startled by Betta's booming voice, calling, "Maria! Santa! Linda!"

From several parts of the house there immediately sounded the noise of approaching feet, and Laura had the first opportunity to see how efficient Betta was as mistress of the house.

Away back when Betta was a slim and quick-legged girl of no more than twelve, shy and very religious, the Tamer had one day ridden into the Catholic Mission on the left bank of Rio Barreira and kidnaped her—tired of having the boy Anteiro cook for him, he had decided he wanted a woman cook.

Betta had been in the house ever since, and together with Anteiro had seen it grow from the original cowhide shelter to its present size and state.

As loyal to those whom he trusted as he was implacable with his enemies, the Tamer had placed and kept Betta in full charge of the house even after he was married. And Betta had run the ever-growing house with a firm hand and an understanding heart. She was a benign despot, respected and loved even by those whose misfortune it was to incur her wrath.

CHAPTER SEVEN

BAREFOOTED, the girl slipped into the sleeping house and ran from room to room until she came to the sewing room. There she stopped, looked up and down the corridor, and then quickly sneaked into the room and hid herself behind a laundry basket.

The room was stuffy with the odor of women. In addition to Betta there were five other women in the sewing room making a dress for Laura.

Now only Felicia and Inocencia were working under Prudencia's supervision. Prudencia, the official dressmaker of the house, was an unmarried, virgin woman of forty-seven who prayed thrice a day and ran her "shop" like a convent. The other two girls were sleeping sitting up on a bench beneath the window with the blue curtains.

Her stubby broad hands clasped upon her hard belly Betta was rocking herself in a chair beside Felicia and Inocencia, plump, fun-loving, copper-hued girls not yet eighteen.

Now the girls whispered to each other without looking up from their work. Then their shoulders shook with convulsive giggling. Betta grinned.

"Laugh less and work more," Prudencia told the girls. "Laugh less and work more or I shall send both of you back to the tannery, where the work is heavy and the stink insufferable, as you well know."

Felicia and Inocencia, still apprentices and on probation, shut up at once.

The girl hiding behind the basket started to sneak away. Out of the corner of her eye, Betta saw the shadow sliding along the wall. She leaned forward in her chair and called, "Who is there? Alma! What are you doing here at this time of day? Come here."

Alma came into the light. She was a nineteen-year-old mamaluca, the offspring of Indian and white. Her body was tall and supple, and she moved with feline grace. Her blue-black hair, now carelessly combed back from her forehead, reached down to her waist. Her face was a slightly elongated oval with high cheekbones and heavy, well-shaped eyebrows that almost met over her straight nose. Her eyes were almond shaped, the pupils like black enamel, the whites like porcelain. The quivering of her nostrils, a bit broad, together with the velvety down shadowing her upper lip, filled her face with a feverish sensuality. Now she was pale and there were black rings under her eyes.

"Why are you not in your house?" Betta asked.

"I cannot sleep."

Betta did not ask why. Betta knew.

"Where is he, Nhâ Betta?"

"Sleeping."

"Why has he not come to me after the ride?"

"You cannot force a man's mood, Alma."

"True. But it is also true that I have a dagger which needs sharpening. I will need a sharp dagger to protect what is mine!"

Betta knew Alma's sickness and recognized the symptoms in the threat. Betta stood up.

"Be careful, girl," she said. "A guest is a guest. Under this roof an Indian guest or a white woman share our respect alike. It is the law. Do not break that law, Alma, or, upon the Tamer's soul, I swear I will drown you in the river."

"Like a jealous cat," Felicia said and giggled.

Alma leaped at Felicia with clawed fingers that sank and tore into the girl's face.

"Let go of her, viper," Betta cried and was about to grab Alma when a gleam of metal caught her eye. Quickly Betta wheeled and hit the other girl, Inocencia, in the mouth, and then she twisted the long shears out of the girl's raised hand.

Dropping the shears into a pocket of her skirt, Betta turned and grabbed Alma by the hair, pulled her head down and struck her on the neck with the edge of her hand. Stunned, Alma stood reeling. Betta took Alma by the arm and led her out of the sewing room.

Sometime later Betta came back and seated herself in a chair directly in front of Inocencia and Felicia. The girls' heads were bent over their work and they took care to avoid meeting Betta's eyes.

"Inocencia."

The girl looked up.

"Were you going to hit Alma?"

"*Sí*, Nhâ Betta. Felicia and me are friends. I saw she was help-less and—"

"You lost your reason."

"Truly so, Nhâ Betta."

"Let us finish the dress," said Betta.

A puff of fresh air ballooned the curtains at the window. The weathercock spun rustily atop the house. Blanched fight was lap-ping the sky.

"The dress is finished," Felicia said.

"Inocencia," Betta called. "Go have your breakfast now. Then pack up your things and leave the house. Go back to the tannery and stay there until you think God has forgiven you for what you were about to do."

"I am going back to the tannery with Inocencia," Felicia said.

"Brave words," said Betta, "but your wish shall not be respected."

Betta turned to Prudencia. "Have the dress pressed and send it to me," she said and got up and left the sewing room.

A little black girl in pigtails leading an old black man by the hand entered the western side of the house.

The little girl led the old man to a sturdy timber frame work that was really a belfry built on the ground. She reached for the rope and placed it in the old man's hands.

"All right, Grandpa," she said. "Now."

And the old man started to pull the rope and the bell to toll the Angelus.

The little girl knelt down on the ground, joined the whitish palms of her black hands before her closed eyes and uplifted chin, and recited her prayer. The old man chanted his in time to the tolling of the bell.

Although most of the house had been up for sometime now, the tolling bell opened the day officially.

Laura awoke and cast a wondering look about the room before she remembered where she was.

The orange curtains at the windows were fluttering gayly in the warm breeze.

Laura stretched under the sheet. She could not recall ever having slept so well, feeling so refreshed. She was wearing one of Betta's lace-trimmed nightshirts, and it was absurdly large and much too short for her. Laura sat up in bed. She ran her fingers through her hair, then she shook her head and her hair parted in the center.

There was a knock at the door.

"Come in."

Carlos stepped in, carrying an armful of orchids.

"Good morning," Carlos said. He walked over and spread the orchids across the foot of the bed. "With the compliments of the management." He offered Laura an orchid.

"Thank you, Carlos. They're gorgeous." The orchids were so richly hued that they looked as if they had just been painted. "What kind of orchids are they?"

"Laelias. The queen of the orchid family. Did you sleep well?"

"Like a top."

The room was filling with the scent of the flowers.

Carlos had bathed and shaved and was wearing white linen pants and shirt and thick-soled sandals.

"How are the ribs?"

"Fine. No pain so far this morning. Betta removed the sash last night. She gave me a sponge bath and a drink. Then she told me not to let Anteiro touch me anymore."

"The old rivalry between them," Carlos said.

"It seems that I'm now Betta's exclusive responsibility."

"Why is it that everybody falls in love with you, Laura?"

"How's Rosario?"

"He had a bad night. He's burning with fever. Anteiro's sent for the Negress Mullô."

"Is she another of your unlicensed doctors?"

"Yes. The Negress Mullô's a midwife. They say, those who ought to know, that she delivers babies as pleasantly as they were conceived—or shouldn't I have said that?"

"Why not, if that's the way she works?"

"The Negress Mullô's as big as a whale and as gentle as a lamb. Her vitality is such that her nearness comforts the downhearted, gives strength to the sick. She'll nurse Rosario back to health."

"And Antonio, how is he?"

Carlos shrugged his shoulders. "Nothing much is the matter with him." Then he said, pointing, "That French creation you're wearing is most becoming to you."

Laura gathered the big shirt about her neck.

And Carlos said, his eyes meeting in Laura's, "Not even Betta's ridiculous shirt can alter your beauty."

"It's too damn early in the morning for that kind of flattery, Carlos."

"Flattery?" Carlos looked surprised. "Laura," he said, "you may slap my face if you ever think it necessary, but don't ever call me a flatterer. I'm not a flatterer. Take it back." Carlos leaned toward Laura, as tense as a drawn bow.

Laura's languid body stirred with a sensual emotion. "No," she said to feed the emotion. "I won't take it back. You're a flatterer."

Carlos reached out for Laura's arm and his fingers bit hard into her flesh. Carlos' grip on her arm affected Laura like an angry embrace. She felt as though she were being crushed into his arms.

Then Carlos dropped his hand. He said, as if he had just entered the room, "Do you prefer a shower or tub, Laura?"

Laura was still feeling the weight of Carlos' grip on her arm. She looked at her arm. The imprint of Carlos' fingers was still on her flesh. She looked up at him, felt his growing tenseness. A deafening instant of stillness followed. One false move, one false look on her part and she would bring him upon her. The bed was there, and the privacy, and the swelling urge. Laura forced her body to relax. And Carlos relaxed too. They felt drained, as after quick, violent love-making.

"What did you say, Carlos?"

"Do you prefer shower or tub?"

"Either."

"We have neither. We bathe in the river, the sexes strictly separated. But we can easily rig up a shower for you. Or make a tub."

"Oh, no," Laura said. "Please don't go to any trouble on my account. I'll love bathing in the river."

"Betta has some clothes for you."

"Betta's clothes?" Laura pulled at her shirt. "I'll be lost in them."

"Betta had some clothes made for you."

"Made? When?"

"During the night. She's going to surprise you. I suggest you show the proper amount of surprise."

"That was awfully nice of her."

"She'll be here shortly."

"Carlos, did I put you out of your room?"

"No. I sleep in my grandfather's room. This was my grandmother's. It seems that shortly after their honeymoon it became rather dangerous for my grandmother to share the same bed with my grandfather. He went back to drinking and having nightmares and beating up anything or anybody within his reach. I was born in that bed. My mother died in it. My grandmother found safety in it." Carlos paused. And you, Carlos' eyes asked Laura, what will you find in that bed—love or loneliness?

"It's quite a bed," Laura said with a sweet smile.

"I hope it's comfortable," said Carlos.

"Very."

"I hope that its history won't interfere with your dreams."

"Hardly. Besides, I don't dream."

"Ever?"

"Never."

They smiled at each other.

Then Carlos walked over to an iron-clamped wardrobe trunk which was standing in a far corner of the room. He opened the trunk, took out a large mahogany box and walked back to the bed. He handed the box to Laura.

Laura laid the box on her lap and opened it. It was a toilet case containing comb, hairbrush and mirror, small scissors, nail files and perfume bottles, all finished in gold. Printed on the damask lining in the lid were the words, *Coty, Paris.*

She looked up at Carlos.

"It was my mother's," he explained. "She brought it along when she came here from São Paulo."

"Thank you," Laura said. "Thank you very much."

Carlos left the room walking backwards, looking at Laura. He closed the door after him softly.

Laura listened to Carlos' footsteps receding deeper into the house and felt as though she had just escaped from some kind of danger. Men had never made her feel like that before. It was a new experience. Laura pigeonholed it in her mind.

Laura was brushing her hair when Betta came into the room followed by Miranda, carrying a tray. Miranda was the baker. Laura noticed a small, red heart embroidered under the left breast of the baker's white dress.

Laura laid the brush back in the toilet case, closed it and pushed it aside.

Solemnly Betta took the tray from Miranda and laid it across Laura's knees. And Laura let out a little cry of surprise as she looked at the familiar but long-missed breakfast. Ham and eggs with corn muffins and milk and coffee. The breakfast was served on a large plate of dark-red wood. The fork, the knife, the spoon, the milk pitcher, the coffee pot and the butter dish, all a trifle too large, too heavy, were of solid silver.

"Who told you I like ham and eggs, Betta?"

"Carlos. He said it is your national breakfast. But eat now, daughter, before it gets cold."

As Laura was eating, the room began to fill with visitors. By now the news of her arrival had spread far and wide, and both the household members and the neighboring ranch hands wanted to look at her, make friends with her.

There were about twenty people gathered in the room now. They were of both sexes and of all ages, with eyes of all shapes, from owl-round to slanting. And they were of all hues, from black to white. Some were white Negroes, and some were Negro-looking whites with all shades of sunburn, from black to lobster-red. But in all the faces staring and gaping at her now, Laura noticed the same expression of simple contentment. In vain did Betta try to make them leave the room after a brief stay. Not one of them had seen green eyes before.

From somewhere in the crowd a daring voice said, "By what name do you answer?"

"Laura."

They all chanted the name after her.

Now Betta saw a child peering out from behind a woman wearing a fringed leather apron.

The child was naked except for a red cotton kerchief worn diaper fashion. She was all eyes, luscious, soft, sloe eyes, with a small nose and rosebud mouth. She seemed to be sculptured out of butter.

Betta looked at the child, trying to place her in her memory.

"What is your name, little one?"

"Mira."

And the name told Betta that the child was the offspring of Franca, wife of Roul, a cowboy. While visiting her husband in the southern pasture six months before, Franca had been caught in a cattle stampede and kneaded into a pulp.

"Her father is riding down to take her to live with him. His friends are looking after her now."

"The devil he will," Betta said. "I will not allow this child to live on the range in a cowboy's lean-to. She stays here until her father finds himself another wife. Or I will find one for him. Now she becomes your responsibility."

The baker touched the small red heart embroidered under her left breast, thus showing her condition before time would reveal it.

Betta nodded. "Linda should make a good mother to this child," Betta thought aloud. "Yes. Linda's blood is hot and her skin is burning for a man. Linda it is." Betta turned to the visitors and shouted them all out of the room. "Not you, child. You stay here."

The crowd, like scolded, sulking children, filed out of the room. Then Betta picked the child up in her arms. "Let us go to find Linda," she said.

"Nhâ Betta," the child said, pointing, "I want to smell her."

"That is good. Smell her." Betta put the child down again.

Mira climbed upon the bed, crushing some of the orchids, and threw her slim arms about Laura's neck, squashed her nose against Laura's cheek and sniffed hard.

"You smell of milk," the child said to Laura. "My mother smelled of nutmeg. That smell I remember well. But you, you smell of milk. Milk with sugar. I like it. I like you, too."

"Thank you," Laura said.

"Come now, child," Betta said. "We must find Linda."

Mire scrambled down the bed. Betta took her by the hand.

"I will be back soon to dress you," Betta said over her shoulder to Laura as she and the child crossed the threshold.

And now, after having shown complete surprise, as Carlos had suggested, Laura was wearing a lime-colored, one-piece cotton dress with a long waist and tight-fitting bodice; flared at the hips, it fell to her ankles in a number of wide soft folds. It had a low round neck and elbow-length sleeves, and it fitted Laura perfectly. Betta, who could tell the size and weight of a fowl or a woman at a glance, had found a girl of Laura's build and pinned the material on her. Prudencia had cut it, the girls had sewn it. Laura was wearing cream-colored, peccary-skin sandals with tasseled thongs. The sandals were a size or two too large for her.

"Come now, daughter. Lean on my arm and I will take you to the river where we will wash together," Betta said, allowing Laura one last look at herself in the mirror.

Laura had gotten some idea of the vastness of the house from the quick look she had had at it on her arrival, before Betta had taken charge of her and whisked her off to her room. But how big the house actually was, Laura first began to discover now as she walked with Betta past or through countless huge rooms, in some of which, to her amusement, she saw orange and avocado trees with flowering branches, and plants that smelled of peppermint or basil. And all the rooms, no matter what they were used for—even rooms with nothing in them but hammocks strung out at the corners and small or large sandals on the floor beneath each hammock—all the rooms were as clean and orderly and quiet as convent cells. Huge cells.

Leaning on Betta's arm, mostly to please her, Laura walked past a padlocked door, the gunroom. Later they came to a large, square-cut door with a cross carved in it. It was the chapel (the belfry was outside) which had been built for Carlos' grandmother, Dona Conçeicão.

Some of the floors were plain clay; others, the majority, were inlaid with yellow or black or pinkish wood. The furniture was made of the same woods and all the pieces—tables, chairs, chests and closets—were heavy, large and comfortable, polished and smoothed by time.

"How old is this furniture, Betta? Did it come from Cuiaba?"

"No, daughter. It was all made here in the course of time. When I first came here from the Mission we had not even a chair. We sat on the floor, in hammocks, on saddles or on drums. Then the Tamer married Dona Conçeicão. She was a gentle and quiet creature. But many a time I caught her crying by the riverbank. She missed the comforts of her home, she told me, and I told the Tamer and he at once got Alcantara, the hunchback, and put him to work. Alcantara was a rare carpenter. He could do with the wood what the baker does with the dough."

They came to Uncle Rosario's room. The door was ajar.

"He is a guide without equal," Betta whispered to Laura. "Also a man of unequaled pride. He told me this morning, and he was shivering with fever, that he is responsible for what happened to you in the storm."

"We must tell him not to worry about me any more," Laura said.

They stepped into Uncle Rosario's room. The Negress Mullô had not come yet. Uncle Rosario was snoring open-mouthed.

As Laura and Betta were approaching the dining room, a little girl with a birthmark on her cheek came running up to them.

"Nhâ Betta," she said. "Almirante told me to tell you that he is tired of waiting for you."

Betta grunted.

There were twelve or thirteen children in the dining room and they were sitting on low, wide benches along the wall.

"Where is Almirante?" Betta said.

"He just left, Nhâ Betta," the little girl with the birthmark said.

"Run after him. Tell him to come back at once, or I will pluck his mustache off for him."

The little girl took another little girl by the hand and they both skipped out of the dining room.

Betta led Laura to the table and seated her almost at the center. Then she left to give some orders.

The children watched Laura with curious eyes. Many heads, both wooly and straight-haired ones, poked in and out of the doors opening on the dining room.

Laura's eyes swept slowly over the table. Then her lips started to move silently as she counted forty-eight chairs comfortably spaced around the table. Laura wondered if they were all filled at once. And by whom.

There was a double paneled door with iron clasps and bolts in the center of the wall facing Laura. The door led outside. Green fiber mats were drawn over the windows. The walls were decorated with hunting trophies, ancient bows and arrows, two blunderbusses, a collection of pistols, and blow-guns, ornaments and weapons of the Chevantes Indians, the cruelest of them all.

Lamps, of many shapes and sizes, hung from iron arms brackets or horns on the walls.

A "straight hammock," really a long, wide canvas swing, was strung out in each of the four corners. After the evening meal, children fell asleep in these hammocks; mothers suckled their babies; old men and old women reminisced; women in trouble confided in Betta; men in trouble talked to Anteiro; boys and girls sat stiffly side by side, staring stonily ahead in a pathetic effort not to betray their thoughts.

But all alike, the young and the old, the men and the women, were the most proud when they sat with Carlos in one of these hammocks. The children thought of Carlos as their uncle; the older generation as their master; the old-timers as their son or grandson. These hammocks were the heart of the *casa grande*, the soul of the ranch.

There was a massive credenza against the wall behind Laura. The wall over the credenza was draped with a faded, worn-out, leather-hemmed grayish poncho, in the center of which, where the hole was, there hung a battered black hat with a long thin chinstrap, a coiled bull whip with a tufted end, and a pair of enormous iron spurs. They had belonged to Carlos' grandfather, when, hardly twenty years old, he had first entered the jungle from the southern side and emerged, God knows how long after, at the northern end. There was still something ominous in the shape of the battered hat, in the powerful bull whip, the brine-cured, tufted end of which could, and did, razor-slash man or beast twenty times simultaneously, and in the spike-like wheels of the iron spurs. Together they clearly told the history of their owner. Old-timers touched their hats in a gesture of respect whenever they stepped into the dining room and looked at those relics.

Laura started as out of the corner of her eye she saw someone standing beside her. He must have tiptoed up to her, Laura thought, and, a bit annoyed, she stood up and faced him questioningly.

The man removed his hat, revealing a shock of coarse black hair, parted in the center and plastered down over his ears like folded wings. He was a squint-eyed, cunning-looking little man in his late thirties, with a boy's shoulders and a fat woman's hips. He was sporting the most foppish mustache Laura had ever seen, together with a red silk shirt and dainty boots of fine light-colored leather.

Laura's annoyance at his having crept up on her turned to amusement at the sight of him, and she had to control herself lest she burst out laughing in his face.

This was Almirante, the bootmaker, son of the late Zuca, from whom he had inherited his remarkable skill and nothing more.

Almirante was a rascal. An exceptionally lucky rascal, he somehow managed to remain alive while indulging in the deadly pastime of courting married women. He owed his life more than once to Anteiro's timely intervention. Almirante enjoyed the reputation of being a man of the world because every so often he saddled his mule and went off to Cuiaba—or so he said—whence he returned with the most fantastic stories of his exploits with the city women. He would have his listeners believe that he never failed to cuckold the whole town. Almirante was the only conscious liar on the whole ranch.

It was obvious that Almirante had taken even greater pains than usual with his appearance today. His hair and boots shone like mirrors and his clean-shaven face was blotched with rice powder. He smelled strongly of musk.

He introduced himself.

"I believe Betta is looking for you," Laura told him, and coughed in her hand to hide her broadening smile.

Almirante shrugged his frail shoulders contemptuously. "Nhâ Betta holds no curiosity for me. I am at your service." He bowed from his broad hips. He eyed Laura. "Be kind enough to acquaint me with your name." And on learning it he chewed on it thoughtfully. "Rôndôl. Rôndôl. Rôndôl. It is a name full of signficance."

"What?" Laura said.

"I shall explain. Your name is—"

"Hush!"

Almirante shrank in his place and looked up at Laura like a frightened child. He knew the voice well.

"Shameless, where were you?" The voice drew nearer. But as no blow hit him Almirante at once regained his impudent behavior. He faced Betta and sized her up. Betta had a secret fondness for Almirante, who was truly a harmless man, and he, being cunning enough to realize it, took liberties with her. But he also knew when to stop, as he did now.

"Sit down, daughter," Betta said to Laura, and to Almirante, "Take our guest's foot measurements."

Obediently Almirante fell down on his knees before Laura. From his back pockets he took out a roll of leather and a sharp awl. He unrolled the leather and smoothed it out on the floor. He asked Laura's permission to remove her sandals. Then he asked her to stand on the leather and he traced her feet on it with the awl.

"What kind of boots do you wish?" he asked Laura.

Betta spoke for Laura. "Pigskin. Flat heels. Broad toes. Accordion-like, not leg-fitting. Comprehend?"

"I comprehend," Almirante said with sarcastic patience. From one of his back pockets he took out a waxed string and circled Laura's right calf.

"That is too tight," Betta told him.

"I am the bootmaker," Almirante cried angrily.

"And a good one, too, except for your temper."

Almirante could think of no suitable retort, and Betta, smiling now, turned to Laura. "Do you want shoes, too, daughter?"

"No, thanks, Betta. I prefer to wear sandals in the house."

"Put the sandals back on her, Almirante."

This done, Almirante stood up. Laura thanked him. "Do not mention it," Almirante said. "It is always a privilege to serve a lady of distinction—a *rare* privilege around here." He shot a glance at Betta. "See you subsequently, Dona Rôndôl." He made a deep bow, strutted away, his fat buttocks quaking, the strong smell of musk trailing after him.

"He is a rare animal," Betta said and chuckled.

CHAPTER EIGHT

LAURA AND BETTA walked through the other half of the house. They came to the "leather quarters," the original house, where everything was either covered with or made of leather. Not one iron nail or bolt or clasp or hinge had been used here.

Again Laura was surprised at the vastness, cleanliness and orderliness she saw as they made their way from room to room and into the kitchen, a huge, clay-floored expanse with three rather narrow, slit-like windows curtained with bamboo-cane blinds, and a heavy Dutch door with iron bolts and clasps.

There was a long clay stove with eight openings of all sizes, the center one large enough to roast a calf. A confusing array of pot and pans of all shapes and sizes, including primitive cooking gadgets of brass and iron, of pewter and clay and wood, hung from pegs on the walls.

The furniture was mostly Alcantara's work, heavy and massive, polished smooth by time and the grease of cooking. Some of the pieces were smoke stained, as were the walls, especially the wall over the stove. There the smoke had licked its way up to the ceiling and farther out, and the wall looked as if black waves had been painted on it.

Among the wooden chairs and stools Laura saw six very low, wide rocking chairs. She asked if they were for the children.

"No," Betta said. "They are for the siesta hour."

Followed by a crowd of children and young girls, whispering and giggling among themselves, Betta and Laura went outside.

The first thing that caught Laura's eyes was the river flowing in the near distance. Then she noticed a small forest of eucalyptus trees growing on the left side of the house, spreading out toward the western corrals. A soft odor of resin, melting in the sun, hovered over the small forest. Laura inhaled deeply.

Looking eastward, Laura saw a mountain rising in the distance, like a hump on the back of the jungle. Cowboys and ranch hands believed with superstitious reverence that whip-scarred ghosts were seen wandering in the mountain at night. And it might have been true, for it was there that all matters of honor were settled. It was called Serra da Tristeza. The Mountain of Sadness.

Directly behind the kitchen there was a lawn of escallonia flowers. The shrubs were planted in star-shaped groupings, their tubular white and red and pink flowers drooping somnolently in the sun. Squatting in a semicircle beyond the shrubs were the dwellings of the ranch hands and the artisans.

There were chicken coops on the right and pigpens on the left. Further out, on the right, there arose, like decorated Christmas trees, fruit and vegetable orchards. On the left, stretching toward the river, there began a plantation of sugar cane, with the thatch-roofed sugar mill and the clay-roofed distilling house, each with a large wooden wheel at its side.

Men and women were scattered over the land, engaged in their tasks. Children were playing in the sun and in the shade. Some of them were riding the pigs, their happy cries mingling with the squealing of their mounts. Others were sleeping in hammocks hanging basket-like from tree branches.

From the jungle, rising on the opposite bank of the river, there came the echoing yelling and calling and cooing of birds.

This is another world, Laura thought as she surveyed the scenery before her. It looked like an oil painting with the paint still wet and each color shining brilliantly.

Laura and Betta walked slowly toward the bathing grotto. The entrance to the grotto was screened off by trees whose trunks and limbs were decorated with purple-hued orchids, clusters of them hanging in mid-air like Chinese lanterns.

Now they heard the noise of running feet and they turned their heads in time to see Alma sprinting from tree to tree. Betta's call stopped Alma between trees. Alma stood there panting, her breasts rising and falling, her head high, and Laura was almost sure she recognized the glowing eyes she had caught staring at her on her arrival.

"Where are you running to, Alma?"

"To wash, Nhâ Betta."

"To wash? But you have already washed this morning," Betta said. "You washed with Miranda. Miranda mentioned it because she noticed the way you were washing yourself. She told me that you scrubbed and scrubbed your skin as if you wanted to make it lighter."

"She is a liar," Alma cried and sprinted away, her long hair waving after her.

"That woman is peeling her heart," Betta thought aloud.

"She's beautiful, isn't she?" Laura said.

"Yes," said Betta. "Alma is beautiful. She also suffers with the hereditary sickness of Eve."

"What's that?"

"She is passionate. Very jealous. And, at times, hard to handle."

"Who is she?"

"Alma is the woman of Carlos."

After a moment's silence, Laura said, "Does she live in the house?"

"No. Alma has her own house, where Carlos sleeps with her."

❧ ❧ ❧

Feeling rested and strong after a good night's sleep and a breakfast of beefsteak and rice, Antonio was at this time wandering down a graveled lane that ran west of the *casa grande*.

Now Antonio exchanged greetings with two light-brown women riding sideway on bast-matted, long-eared donkeys. Each woman had seven or eight straw hats balanced one on top of the other on her head. They were Constancia, the hatter, and her widowed mother riding to work.

The lane turned right and Antonio saw a low, flat-roofed timber building whence there came a whirring sound. It was the spinning house.

Pig-tailed, copper-hued girls clad in white were bent over their work. They heard Antonio's crunching steps and raised their heads to look at him.

Antonio smiled at them, winked, bit his lower lip. The girls whispered among themselves excitedly, burst out giggling.

Seeing so many girls reminded Antonio that he had not had a woman since he had left Cuiada. Antonio made a mental note of the place.

The lane curved to the right again. Here the gravel gave away to a powdery dust that was warm and soft to the touch. The treetops arched and met overhead, completely shading the lane. Birds sang in the trees, small animals scurried along the edges of the walk. It was cool and peaceful.

Antonio came upon the small house even before he saw it. The house, set well back from the lane, was almost completely hidden by the surrounding vegetation, and it was not until he was standing directly in front of the narrow entrance path that Antonio first noticed it. Now he studied the yellow curtains fluttering at the square-cut windows, the wrought-iron lantern hanging on a peg by the small Dutch door.

Antonio's curiosity was diverted now as he saw a woman walking up the lane toward him. He was at once struck by the voluptuous grace of her body. She was barefooted, and as she walked she angrily kicked small puffs of dust before her. She was walking against the lukewarm breeze, and her light skirt clung to her long, shapely legs.

"Good morning," Antonio said as he came abreast of Alma.

Alma ignored Antonio.

Indifference inspired Antonio. "Do me a favor," he called.

Alma stopped. Antonio walked up to her. "Which way to the *casa grande?*"

Alma pointed the way to Antonio.

"Much obliged," Antonio said. "Much obliged." And he merely shifted his weight from foot to foot. This woman is truly beautiful, he thought. I must find out if she is unattached. He introduced himself.

"I know who you are," Alma told him.

"I saw a child running into the forest," Antonio said. "Is she yours?"

"I have no children."

"Then you are not married?"

"I am the woman of a man."

"What a pity that your beauty should be wasted on a cow-hand, or on a toiler of the land."

"I am the woman of the *patrão.* Carlos Diaz."

Antonio's eyes glowed. Then he grinned and said, "You speak in joke."

"I speak with knowledge."

And by now Antonio was thinking of Alma's man as the one who had called him a cook, a Portuguese bullfighter, and who had robbed him of the foreign woman's friendship. Antonio felt his hatred for Carlos mount in him, and as he looked into Alma's eyes he vowed to wound Carlos' pride infinitely more than Carlos had wounded his.

Antonio laughed.

Alma frowned.

"You speak in jest," Antonio repeated. And on receiving Alma's contemptuous silence, he said, "And maybe not. Maybe you speak only half of the truth."

"What is the other half? Speak clearly, man."

And Antonio did. He told Alma that through the nights of their homeward journey he had caught Carlos and Laura making love in the bush.

"You are a liar," Alma hissed.

Antonio shrugged his shoulders.

"You are a liar."

"You bore me, woman," Antonio said. "I told you the truth as I saw it."

It was Antonio's indifference which finally convinced Alma that what she had suspected was true. And now as she watched him it suddenly came to her that she had found the tool she needed to carry out the revenge she had sought throughout her sleepless night. If she had been cast aside for the green-eyed woman, Alma told herself, then she would force Carlos to fight—fight and die, or fight a fight whose scars he would bear to the end of his life. Carlos would have to fight or she would strip him of his honor before the whole ranch, destroy his name throughout the forest. She sized Antonio up. Yes, he would do all right.

Antonio saw the fire die out in Alma's eyes. Her lips parted in what she intended to be a smile.

"I am sorry I called you a liar," Alma said.

"That's all right," Antonio said. "Maybe I shouldn't have told you the truth."

"I do not mind the truth," Alma said. "I do not mind it because I do not suffer with the sickness of jealousy."

"That's good," Antonio said. "Then you will not be tormented by jealousy when night comes and you lie alone in bed, while your man is lying with the woman who has stolen—is stealing—kisses that should be yours."

Alma winced. "You are right," she said. "I will not be tormented."

"And I," said Antonio, "I am an unattached man." And, thinking of the man who had insulted him, he took that man's woman into his good arm.

Impulsively Alma's fingers went for Antonio's eyes, but then they met and clasped behind Antonio's neck and she kissed him, thinking all the while of the man who had betrayed her.

"You kiss well," Antonio said.

"You please me."

Antonio slipped his good hand inside Alma's dress, took her breast in his hand. Alma gave Antonio the love-bite. Antonio panted in her ear, "Let's go into the bush."

But Alma coyly slipped out of Antonio's arm and ran up the lane, to her house, biting hard into the back of her hand to stop herself from sobbing aloud.

The siesta hour was approaching.

Carlos was standing at a window in the dining room having his first drink of the day. He heard the sound of rolling wheels; then a buckboard pulled by a mare stopped before the door. Betta was driving the vehicle. She got out and helped Laura down and together they came into the dining room.

Betta left to order the noon meal.

"Would you like a drink?" Carlos asked Laura.

"No *pinga*, please," Laura said.

"No," said Carlos. "I drink *pinga* only when I travel. You can now have brandy, rum or gin."

"Gin."

"I'm sorry," Carlos said, "but I'm all out of vermouth. The children found an open bottle, drank it, liked it, invited all their friends in and finished my stock."

"It doesn't matter," Laura said.

Carlos seated Laura at the table which was set for two. He went over to the credenza and returned with a drink of gin for Laura and a fresh one for himself. He sat down next to her.

"Cigarette?"

"No, thanks."

"Did you enjoy your bathing?"

"Very much."

"What did you do with yourself the whole morning?"

"We were coming back from the river when the buckboard came along. Betta requisitioned it and showed me around the— industrial, shall I say?—part of the ranch. It's quite remarkable. Except for one thing it has everything, from a silversmith's shop to a blacksmith's. This place is as self-sustaining as a ship at sea."

Yes, Carlos said. "We have everything we need, except for electricity, gas and telephone, which we don't want. By the way, Laura, what's the exception?"

"You have no beauty parlor."

"That also is unnecessary."

"Is it?"

"Yes. As unnecessary as—as the 'cinch' Anteiro removed from you."

"And you," Laura said, changing the subject, "what did you do with yourself?"

"I rode over to the western corral to pick myself a pony. I've got to start training him for the races."

But Laura showed no curiosity about the races and the conversation ran down for lack of interest.

The short morning's separation seemed to have aged their relationship to a point where they were now sensing each other's mood as clearly as if they were confessing them aloud.

In Laura, Carlos sensed a new reticence, almost an antagonistic feeling, which had not been there when he had left her a few hours before. Carlos hoped he had not inadvertently said or done something to offend her when he had visited her in her bedroom. Quickly he reviewed the situation in his mind, but he could find no fault with his behavior, not even with his gripping of her arm. She knew that that was his way of telling her he loved her and that, loving her, he wanted her. Perfectly natural. Then what was wrong? Should he ask her what was the matter? You never ask a woman what's the matter, he reminded himself, unless you want to listen to her lies. She'll tell you when she's ready, and not a minute sooner. And Carlos, although puzzled, kept his peace.

Carlos, Laura felt, had spent the morning nourishing his growing desire for her. Of course it was not something which she had just sensed; she had known that he wanted her since shortly after their first meeting, and she had been intrigued by it all along. But now Laura rejected Carlos' desire for her with contempt, for she couldn't help feeling that he had been deceiving her, or, at the very least, playing with her. He had ranted at her for shooting at the hog, telling her he was thinking only of her safety and not of his. And the kiss on the road: *An impulse of my heart.* Still on the road: *I shall pray at your feet.* And this very morning: *I'm not a flatterer.* And all along he had a woman of his own, and a very beautiful woman at that.

For an instant Laura was reminded of her affair with the married man. Although there was no true comparison between her past situation and the one which confronted her now—Carlos was not married to Alma—Laura nevertheless flared up inside at the old memory, and in this mood she believed she had been on the verge of making the same mistake.

Laura looked at Carlos with cold fury. She was about to ask him to give her another gin when their lunch was brought in. Laura started to eat immediately, warning herself all the while to calm down and not make a damn fool of herself. Carlos busied himself with the ritual of pouring the wine, being careful to pour the first few drops into his own glass, taste it, and then fill Laura's glass.

Laura looked up at him. "Carlos, who told you that ham and eggs is the typical American breakfast?"

"I had an American friend in Florence."

"Woman?"

"An art student."

"Who served the American breakfast to whom?"

"The one who had less of a hangover."

"You're like the proverbial sailor, aren't you, Carlos?" *Stop it.* "A woman in every port." *Smile.* She did.

"I am a man."

"Is that what it is?" Still smiling.

"I hope I haven't offended your sense of decency."

"Don't talk rot." Impatiently.

"I may have a woman in every port, as you put it, Laura. But I have never deceived a woman in my life."

"How boring for the woman."

"I have never told a woman that I loved her when I didn't," Carlos went on. "When I like a woman, when I need a woman, I ask her to live, to sleep, with me. Whether it's to be for money or for fun is up to her."

"Damn cold-blooded, aren't you?"

"When my love is not involved—yes. Why should it be otherwise? Why romanticize a dish of ham and eggs, or a portion of veal scallopini?"

"And when your love's involved, what happens then?"

"What *will* happen then."

"All right. What *will* happen then?"

"I love my people," Carlos said with growing feeling. "I love them in all humility. The old generation fought and died for this ranch. They made my grandfather very rich. The old generation's children are my responsibility now. And yet I'd forsake them all … sacrifice them all—"

"I like this wine," Laura cut him short as she lifted her glass and pretended to study the claret.

"It's Portuguese wine," Carlos said quietly. "I get it from Cuiaba. Of course I've got to send my own packmule train to pick it up. As you know, it's a long, rough trip, and by the time the wine gets here half of the shipment's broken and the other half so shaken it takes days to settle again. I'm going to experiment growing my own grapes here."

"Why not? You just about make everything else here—including *flattery*."

"I like wine," Carlos said quietly. "I learned to drink wine in Itally."

"I thought you said Europe taught you nothing … I learned to drink wine at Nino's in the Village."

"What 'Village'?"

"The Village in New York."

"Should I be interested?"

"Not really."

Coffee was brought in. Also rice-paper cigarettes in a straw basket with a flat lid.

Laura asked if she might serve the coffee. Carlos said he would be delighted. He served the brandy, offered the cigarettes. He lighted Laura's cigarette. Laura took a long drag, drew her head back, exhaled quiveringly. It was all so very polite, so very international. They might have been having lunch in New York or Paris or Rome, instead of in a hidden citadel in the wilderness of the Mato Grosso jungle.

Outdoors as well as within, the place was growing quieter and quieter, like waves rolling out to sea. So much so that Laura noticed it and said to Carlos, "What's happening? Where's everybody?"

"Sleeping. This is the siesta hour."

Just then a curly-headed boy of ten, wearing a beautiful silver-studded belt, came rushing into the dining room.

"I have a word for your ear, *patrão*," the boy shouted, meaning a confidential message.

At the sight of the boy Carlos tossed his cigarette into his coffee cup and, without excusing himself, got up and went to meet the boy, stopping him at the other end of the table.

The boy began to talk excitedly.

Carlos told him to lower his voice.

The boy began to whisper. Carlos listened to the boy, shaking his head all the while. Once he said, "No. I'm busy." The boy forgot himself and raised his voice again, and Carlos laid his hands on the boy's shoulders and shook him roughly, told him again not to talk so loudly.

The boy's feelings were hurt and he shouted, "*Bom, patrão,* then Alma said she will come here herself and scratch your eyes out."

"Get my horse ready," Carlos told the boy.

Carlos returned to Laura and apologized. Then, excusing himself, he strode out of the room.

Laura's eyes followed Carlos past the threshold. By now the whole house was asleep. Only the broiling sun outside was alive. Laura took herself to her room.

CHAPTER NINE

THE SUN was setting.

Laura had slept three hours, undisturbed by dream or noise. Now she was sitting in a wicker chair outside the main entrance, sipping a glass of gin which the child Mira had brought her with Betta's compliments.

In the west the first campfires blinked in the distant fields. The fires blinked like lights at sea, a sea rippling toward the edge of the jungle in a rhythmical succession of dark-green, oily waves that was the grass bowing under the touch of the evening breeze.

The blind bell-ringer, led by the little girl in pigtails, came up the road. They turned at the western end of the house. Then the chapel bell started to toll the Angelus.

Laura stood up and began to stroll about the grounds, tucking away in her memory the scenery and the atmosphere of an environment which, but one day previous, had been unimaginable to her.

Ranch hands were returning from work. They came from the sugar-cane plantation, from the mandioca flour fields, from the rice paddies. They came from the mills and from the river, where the irrigation system was controlled. They walked in single file, the men ahead, the women following, peaceful of mien, lax of body, chanting the evening prayers.

Artisans were closing up their shops, stepping into the next room or rooms which were their homes.

Cowboys cantered in. *"Boas tardes, senhora,"* they said gravely and raised their right hands.

"Boas tardes," Laura answered.

The household women were walking towards the river for their nightly bath. Among them Laura saw a tall black woman carrying a naked white child on her head. The child was prattling and clapping her hands and drumming her feet on the woman's face, while the woman walked on like an African queen.

As Laura walked farther down the eastern side of the house, she was met by the beat of active life. Mealtime was approaching and the food was on the fire.

Orderly tumult reigned in the kitchen. The brown-skinned priestesses of the stove wielded great authority over their under-lings, who, in their anxiety to please and learn, were in a constant state of storm and strife among themselves.

The hot odor of richly seasoned food, the richest of which tonight was that of roasting pig, was floating into the dining room.

The dining room was a beehive of activity. Nine girls, freshly washed and clad in white, their kinky hair tightly pulled and braided over their heads, were running back and forth setting the table, chattering like so many macacos, until Betta, wearing a fresh dress and a scowl, appeared. Then the thunder clapped and the girls huddled together in fright.

Betta examined the table with critical eyes, while the girls waited anxiously.

"Well done, children," Betta finally said and stepped outside where she was met by the guests for the evening, standing about in small groups. Some of them had brought their children along, scrubbed clean. A girl with her hair parted in the middle was standing by herself, near the door, with her baby in her arms.

Betta greeted Laura and told her they were waiting for Carlos.

Now a murmur traveled through the assembled guests an they looked in the same direction. It was Carlos, riding toward them on a stallion whose coat was as glossy and black as an eel's. Carlos pulled up and dismounted. As he walked towards them Betta noticed, as did Laura, that his right hand was bandaged with a handkerchief.

Carlos walked quickly past his people, hardly stopping to answer their greetings. He nodded to Laura. "Is dinner ready?" he asked Betta.

"What is this with your hand?" she asked Carlos.

"Nothing. My horse tripped and I fell."

Betta looked at Carlos' clothes. Not a speck of dust. "Where is Alma?" she asked. "Is she not sitting at the table?"

"No," Carlos said to Betta, and to Laura, "Shall we go in?" He tossed his hat on a bench outside the door and led the way into the dining room. The guests followed.

It was the proudest accomplishment of the day, to follow the master into the dining room, although the guests were not chosen for any special reason. They simply washed, put on clean clothes and gathered outside the dining room. First come, first served. And every evening quite a few were left standing outside, waiting patiently.

Carlos seated Laura at his right at the head of the table. Betta sat at the opposite end of the table between Prudencia, the dressmaker, and an empty chair that Anteiro presently occupied. But not before he had walked over to Laura and, patting her gently on the shoulder, asked her how she was feeling.

Antonio came in. Carlos motioned Antonio to him. Antonio sauntered over, sporting a cunning, knowing little smile.

"I'm sorry I had no time to visit your uncle this afternoon," Carlos said. "How is he?"

"A colossal nigger woman is taking care of him. He is all right."

Carlos stood up. "Say Negress," he told Antonio in a low voice that only Laura heard.

Carlos and Antonio glared at each other.

"Say Negress, I said."

Antonio dropped his eyes, again smiled his cunning, knowing little smile. "All right," he said. "Have it your own way."

"Say it."

Slurring over the word, Antonio complied.

Carlos sat down. Laura glanced at Carlos. Carlos' eyes had the dull, bestial expression she had noticed after the fight with the hog. Laura shuddered inwardly.

Antonio found a place a few seats down the center of the table.

Dressed in white and wearing a red ribbon in her hair, the child Mira came running into the dining room. She ran almost all the way around the table before she discovered an empty seat, and she was just climbing into it when Almirante, the bootmaker, sneaked up behind her and neatly lifted her out of the chair and set her down on the floor again.

"Good evening," Almirante cried to all. He looked like an owl with freshly lacquered wings. He caught Laura's eyes. Bowed to her. "My respects, Dona Rôndôl," he said as if he were the host.

Laura grinned.

"I want my chair," little Mira cried, pulling Almirante by the seat of his pants.

"Mind your manners, child," Almirante said sternly and wiggled the seat of his pants free from the child's stubborn grip.

Mira stood pouting behind Almirante. Then she ran up to Laura and climbed onto her knees.

"Betta," Carlos called.

"Please, don't," Laura said. "She's no bother."

"Come here, angel," Betta called. Then she sat the child on her lap, facing the table, and said, for everyone to hear, "Give no importance to that shameless one." This remark apparently did not bother Almirante, who, to his pleasant surprise, found himself sitting opposite Antonio, to whom he introduced himself as "a fellow city man." Antonio ignored Almirante.

As Laura's curious eyes swept slowly past the guests, she realized she was sharing the table with three generations of natives. Among them she recognized Jose the silversmith and Pedro the blacksmith, whom she had met that morning while with Betta. She also recognized some of the men she had seen working in the fields, some of the women she had bathed with.

On a smaller table crouched the roasted pig, fenced in by rice balls. Behind the table, ready to carve, stood Filomena, the chief cook, a handsomely built creole with fine arms and bosom.

On the dining table there were shoulders and legs of mutton with scallions and capers. Also sirloins of beef and breasts of veal. Hog's haslets, chitterlings and sausages. Mound of vegetables. Jugs of alcohol. Two kinds of bread, white and *rosca*.

Including little Mira, forty-nine healthy people were now eating in comparative quiet as they relieved the first pangs of hunger.

Filomena carved and carved until nothing was left of the pig but its leering snout and dainty hoofs. The guests paused to wipe their greasy mouths and chins. Then they attacked the food on the table.

There was a bottle of claret before Carlos and he kept Laura's glass filled. It was fortunate for Carlos that his people did not like wine. They would have bankrupted him.

City-mannered and nimble-tongued, Antonio was the center of attraction at his end of the table. He had the girls giggling and blushing, the men laughing.

To force his attention on Antonio and thus share in his popularity, Almirante had pushed aside all the food that lay across the table between Antonio and himself. He kept leaning forward, vainly trying to engage Antonio in conversation.

Now Antonio acknowledged Almirante's presence.

"You there," he called. "Would you mind giving me a haircut tomorrow?"

Almirante was dumbfounded.

"Aren't you the barber?" Antonio asked.

"No," Antonio the carpenter told Antonio the bullfighter. "He crows like a cock, struts like a peahen, makes love like a capon—but what is he?"

"An obscene frog," said Alfonso the miller.

"Do not insult the noble frog," said O Velho, the Old One, the beekeeper.

The dining room was rocking with laughter.

"Would you like to live on a ranch?" Carlos asked Laura.

"I wouldn't mind it."

"I mean on a ranch here, in the wilderness."

"Why not?" Laura said politely.

"You would grow tired of it. Ranch life in the interior after awhile becomes monotonous."

"I rather enjoy it."

"Wait until the novelty wears off."

"I won't be here long enough to grow bored."

"Nhâ Betta," Prudencia said. "Look at Felicia."

Betta's eyes found Felicia among the guests. To hide the marks of Alma's fury, and avoid gossip about the sewing room,

Felicia had bandaged her face with a white kerchief knotted on top of her head. She said she had an earache.

"Felicia has been moody all day," Prudencia was telling Betta. "She wants to go back to the tannery to be with her friend Inocencia. What shall I do?"

"Do not respect Felicia's wish," Betta told the dressmaker. "Inocencia has got to be punished. If God had not alerted me in time, Inocencia would have killed Alma."

A sturdy boy murmured to a full-breasted girl sitting next to him, "Meet me at the Three Forks with the incoming moon."

"Why?"

"I want you."

"In love or hunger?"

"Love."

"And then?"

"And then if I please you, and you please me, we will be married."

The full-breasted girl breathed deeply. Then she nodded, her eyes on her plate.

A woman wearing her wedding ring like an earring, said to Porfirio, the venerable veterinarian, "*Vovo*, my man has an incorrigible ingrown toenail that causes him great pain with every step he takes. What can I do for him?"

"Woman," Porfirio said, "send your man to me tomorrow. I will operate on him."

The woman looked at Porfirio's palsied hands, bent her head low over her plate and hurriedly crossed herself.

"I will tell Anteiro what to do," Porfirio said.

"Much obliged, *vovo*," the woman said aloud. I thank Thee, God.

And at the head of the table, the conversation continued in muted tones.

"Do you stay on the ranch all the time, Carlos?"

"Yes."

"Don't you ever go to Cuiaba? Don't you miss the city?"

"I never liked the city."

"But you've lived in Europe …"

"I was glad to get away from Europe. Until now, that is."

"Why 'until now'?"

"Now I have an urge to travel again."

"Where to?"

"I'm thinking of following you to America."

"I'll be delighted to introduce you to my husband."

Carlos asked one of the serving girls to bring him another bottle of wine.

Now the serving girls were running out of the dining room with the empty platters and promptly returning with fresh platters piled high with smoked meats, cured hams, cheeses and many kinds of fruit.

Little Mira said to Betta, "I want to go to sleep for awhile."

"Good. Go and lie down on the straight hammock." Betta stood the child on the floor. The child ran to the hammock in the nearest corner and curled up in it.

"This was a good meal, woman," Anteiro said to Betta.

"Had enough?"

"Could eat more, I think. And will," Anteiro said, helping himself.

What Carlos had been trying to do for sometime now had been accomplished in the afternoon. It had been a wild scene, but well worth having, he thought.

Carlos had answered Alma's summons, resolved to put an end to their affair. On entering Alma's house, even before he could open his mouth, Alma had leaped at him, reviled and scratched him and finally told him she was through with him. Amen!

And now, while making polite conversation with Laura, Carlos was thinking how to let the ranch know that Alma was no longer his woman. For the ranch must know it, or no man would dare go near Alma. The law was indeed strict on that matter on the ranch. As long as a man and woman lived together, she was to be respected as his wife, or else the whole ranch would become a great whorehouse and, therefore, a slaughterhouse.

The law also disapproved strongly of a married woman—or a woman living with a man, which was the same thing—dancing with any man other than her own.

At a dance, even a drunken man managed to respect a virgin. He was not so much afraid of the virgin's father's vengeance as of her mother's. Once an angry mother, helped by other mothers, castrated such a man.

Now four men stepped quietly into the dining room. They wore bandoleers and carried rifles. They seated themselves on a bench along the wall. They stood their rifles against their knees and looked on with grave eyes.

They caught Carlos' eyes and nodded to him.

"Valente," Carlos called.

The man stood up.

"Have you eaten?"

"Si, patrão."

"How's your thirst?"

"Thirsty."

Carlos motioned to one of the serving girls who ran out of the dining room and was soon back with a straw-skirted bottle of alcohol and four glasses.

The men filled their glasses and raised them to Carlos, who acknowledged the toast with a nod. The men drank.

"Who are they?" Laura asked. "The one in the middle looks ferocious."

"He does, doesn't he?" Carlos said. "Valente was truly a bad man. He ran away from the ranch and became a bandit. He once raided the diamond field of Esperance single-handed. Now he enjoys being good as much as he once enjoyed being bad."

"What are they?"

"Sheriffs."

"Sheriffs? You have your own police force, Carlos?"

"We don't regard them as such. We think of them as peacemakers."

"Do you have your own jail, also?"

"No. Though, now that you mention it, I think they'd rather be shot than jailed. They'd die in jail, for lack of freedom."

Prudencia said to Betta, "Excuse me, *nhâ*. I am going to chapel."

A woman standing outside came into the dining room and sat down in Prudencia's place. "Eat," Betta told her.

Now a few polite belches opened a new period at the table. With studious unconcern men were loosening their belts, unbuttoning their shirt collars. Women were leaning back in their chairs, hands slack in their laps. The girls' cheeks were flushed. The children were becoming restless. All eyes were glowing. Smiles were growing lazier, broader; voices thicker. Fresh jugs of alcohol replaced the empty ones on the table. Maize-leaf cigarettes, cigars and clay pipes were burning. The dining room looked like a bivouac after a victory, everyone consciously happy of his fight against hunger and boredom.

"What time is it?" Laura asked Carlos.

He shook his head. "I know I have a wrist watch somewhere, but I haven't wound it in three or four years. And that's the only timepiece in the house."

"In my country, time is money."

"Here time is something to be enjoyed, like a mistress, or a lover."

"And when there's neither mistress nor lover, what then?"

"Hope, Laura. A consuming hope that will thaw the cruelest heart."

"Are you sure?"

"I'm only a beggar, Laura. And you are rich. So very rich."

Laura looked the other way impatiently. She was sorely puzzled. She couldn't figure Carlos out. She was perfectly sure that he was not the "two-timing" type, and yet here he was giving her this kind of talk, asking her to sleep with him. It was not even, a matter of politeness that stopped Laura now from being rude to Carlos, from telling him, why don't you make your pretty speech to your woman? It was something else, something sincere about him that belied his present behavior.

The baby in the young mother's arms started to cry. She left the table, went to sit in one of the corner hammocks. She unbuttoned her white blouse, took out her swollen brown breast and the baby's crying turned into a sucking, gurgling sound. The mother grimaced contentedly as the baby gummed her nipple.

A man came into the dining room and sat down in the vacated seat. Betta motioned him to go ahead and eat.

The sturdy boy left the table, looking stonily ahead, as if fearing to betray the purpose of his journey.

A man took the boy's seat next to the full-breasted girl. She kept her eyes down. She was sure people knew what she was thinking, waiting for.

The children sitting near Tomaso had quieted down. If they were good he was going to tell them a story by-and-by.

Tomaso was the gunsmith, Felicia's bethrothed, a jovial man with a mole on his cheek.

Carlos asked one of the serving girls to bring him the bottle of brandy. Also black coffee for two, and the rice-paper cigarettes.

The full-breasted girl left the table, staring at the floor.

A man replaced her. It was difficult to keep an accurate count of the people who enjoyed the hospitality of the *casa grande* during the evening meal.

"No, thanks. No sugar, Carlos."

"Brandy?"

"Please."

Then Carlos lighted a cigarette for Laura.

There was the sound of dishes crashing on the floor. The girl stood rooted to the floor, looking at Betta.

"Good luck," Betta said. Then she added, "Amaya, I told you before, do not take too many dishes out all at once."

A tepid breeze was blowing in through the door and the windows, its fresh scent attacking the hot odors entrenched in the dining room.

The sun had long departed. Now its afterglow was fading fast. The moon, already in the sky, was waiting for more darkness to have a clearer look at the premises she was to occupy through the night.

The sturdy boy waiting at the Three Forks saw the full-breasted girl walking up the path and he went down to meet her. They met, stood looking at each other shyly. Then they joined hands and walked into the thicket, the girl lagging half a step behind. Night was falling.

But the guests' spirits were high and no one perceived the slow change which was invading the dining room, until faces and contours began to grow blurred.

"Lights, children," Betta called.

And the serving girls went from lamp to lamp, lighting first this corner, and then the other, until the four corners emerged like niches touched by a solitary light, a vigil light, casting its tremulous glow upon a sleeping Mira, a baby suckling at its mother's breast, two elderly women fingering their wooden rosaries, an old man talking to himself. And then the wall lamps were lit also, and a surging brightness filled the dining room, crowding the ceiling, the walls, patches of the floor, with shadows dancing in time to the swelling lights. A puppet show. Having routed darkness, the lights settled down, burned evenly, and the shadows grew still in their places, like pinned butterflies.

The battered black hat with the long, thin chinstrap, and the bull whip with the tufted end, and the enormous iron spurs, spied on the company from the wall over the credenza.

With the lights, spirits rose again.

The full-breasted girl was crying in the thicket, her face buried in her hands. The sturdy boy was terribly confused. The girl spoke through her fingers. "It was wonderful. Wonderful."

The boy felt like a man.

The venerable Porfirio started to snore in his place. With his long, snow-white hair and his parchment-like face framed in long, snow-white sideburns, he looked the patriarch that he was. He slept, but his palsied hands remained awake in his lap.

"How old is he?" Laura asked.

"I really don't know," Carlos said. "Nor does he, exactly. Maybe a hundred. Maybe more. He's been like that since I was a boy, except that his hands were steady and skillful then."

"I love these people," Laura said with sudden feeling. "They're so close to nature."

"Yes," Carlos said. "They're as simple as children and, at times, as unreasonable." Then he said, in that tense way of his, as if they were alone in the dark, "And you, Laura, will you be reasonable too?"

Laura looked the other way.

"The minstrels," the girls cried and clapped their hands excitedly.

Four men, one fingering an accordion, one picking at a guitar, one lipping a flute, and one tapping a cylindrical drum, trouped through the door.

"A concert?" Laura asked.

"A nightly affair. There will soon be dancing. Tonight they're going to play in your honor."

Betta was napping in her seat. She looked like a Buddha.

Anteiro left the table and went to sit with the sheriffs. "Where are you riding from?" he asked Valente.

"From Serra Ventosa."

At the name of the place Anteiro frowned. "Was it a duty ride?" he asked.

"Yes."

"Serious?"

"The Pinheiros and the Souzas."

"Bloodshed?"

"No. Not this time. We got there in time to prevent it."

"Good, Valente."

"Yes, this time. But maybe we will not be so lucky next time. Maybe next time we will have to stop their fighting each other with violence of our own. Those two clans should be separated, north and south, kept as far apart as possible, or there will be many orphans and widows."

"I will speak to Carlos," Anteiro said.

"That is why we came here tonight," said Valente. "But now you can speak to the *patrão*. Do it promptly and clearly, friend, before it is too late." Then Valente added, looking into the muzzle of his rifle, "It would grieve me much to have to break my vow never to kill again."

"Do not break the vow, friend," Anteiro told Valente. "Let those who have not taken the vow do the shooting. You use blank bullets in your rifle."

"Much obliged, friend."

As every adult knew, the fued between the Pinheiros and the Souzas was an old and bloody one. At a fiesta in Serra Ventosa a drunken Pinheiro had danced with a Souza married woman ....

Twirling his mustache and displaying a superior grin, Almirante was listening to Tomaso telling the children the story of the jaguar and the mouse. Almirante could not understand how grownups respected that kind of tripe. He moved in his chair as if he had ants in his pants. He caught Laura's eyes.

"How are you. Dona Rôndôl?" he called out, as if he were the host.

Laura motioned Almirante to be quiet. Almirante was taken aback.

"Fellow city man, I—"

"Shut up," Antonio told him. Almirante was insulted.

Anteiro snapped his fingers. Almirante turned to him. Anteiro took the ends of his neckerchief and wrung them. Almirante paled.

There was quiet in the dining room now, and a touching aura of simplicity, as Tomaso told his story, the children craning their necks, the grownups as anxious-faced as the children, or smiling indulgently. The dining room was a vast kindergarten, with some scar-faced, bearded and ferocious-looking children.

"Viva Tomaso! Viva the mouse!" The children applauded and laughed with the abandon of innocence as the story ended.

But Almirante was already on his feet, shouting in all directions at once. "Your attention, ladies and gentlemen. Listen. I have an enormous one to tell. There was once a padre, A Capuchin monk, and he was a man without much looks but

of extraordinary manhood. Ladies, he was a man, *zzzzut!*"
Almirante burst out into body-rocking cackle and his villainous
mustache began to bristle with excitement. The men prodded
each other and winked, the elderly women's faces grew stern,
the girls cast their eyes down modestly, the children beamed
at Almirante innocently. Betta was no longer napping. She was
watching Almirante through narrowed lids. Almirante's cackle
ended in a whine and he continued. "And so one evening, ladies,
this padre without much looks, but of *extraordinary* manhood,
visited a widow who lived with a monkey, a capuchin monkey,
he, he, he, he. And the monkey wore pants. Red pants, *hiyayaya*.
And the padre who was Capuchin monk, but not a capuchin
monkey, he lifted his skirt and the widow—"

"Not one word more, you shameless one!" Betta thundered
standing up.

"Obscene frog!"

"Capon!"

"Peahen!"

Boos and catcalls rained upon Almirante from the cardi-
nal points of the dining room. Then men rocked with laughter, the elderly women, crossed themselves, horrified, the girls
giggled convulsively, the children screamed happily. It was
pandemonium.

Almirante flopped down in his chair, took his head in his
hands, and noises that sounded like stifled sobs issued from his
frail frame.

"Is he crying or pretending?" Laura asked.

"He's pretending," Carlos said. "Almirante's so double-faced
that if you kick him in the buttocks he blushes."

Laura roared. Her laughter rose over that of the others like a
burst of silvery bells. She laughed and laughed. Carlos was rather
surprised that his puny joke had caused such a response. Too

much wine or brandy, maybe? he wondered. He looked at Laura, fascinated. She was laughing with her head thrown back and her eyes were sparkling, her teeth shining, her lips moist, her throat throbbing, her pointed breasts quivering ….

Lost in the rich enjoyment of their own laughter, no one noticed Alma when she first appeared on the threshold of the door leading in from the courtyard. She was dressed in white. Her face was frozen with suffering. She was forbiddingly beautiful. Her eyes were glittering as she stood staring at Laura and Carlos. Then, moving with her panther-like gait, she came into the dining room, and first one and then another saw her and turned toward her. An expectant hush fell over the room.

Carlos stood up. Laura, looking at Alma, took in her beauty again. Betta sat straight in her place. Antonio looked puzzled. Then a flicker of understanding shone in her eyes and the cunning, knowing little smile visited his lips again.

"What is it, Alma?" Carlos sounded casual.

"I have come to eat," Alma told him.

"Sit down somewhere and eat."

"This is my place." Alma pointed at Laura's chair.

"She is our guest, Alma. She must sit next to her host."

"And I must sit where I sleep. Next to you."

"No longer."

"I want my seat."

"By all means let her have her seat," Laura said and got up.

But Carlos reached for Laura's arm and made her sit down again. "Please," he said.

Laura flared up. "You don't expect me to quarrel over a seat, do you?"

"Please," Carlos said again.

"I will fight for my seat," Alma said.

"Not on my account," Laura told her.

"Then get up and let me sit next to him."

"Or else you'll scratch me, won't you?"

"*Si!*"

Laura tossed her head back defiantly. But contempt overcame her indignation and she ignored the challenge. Also, she knew that she could humiliate Carlos much more by acquiescing to his woman's demand than by resisting it.

"This is ridiculous," she said to Carlos, and to Alma, "Sit down where you belong, dearie."

"Alma!" Betta was hurrying toward them. Betta seemed to have left her personality draped on the back of her chair; now she looked like a bulky brown cat stalking a bird. She stopped beside Alma and rested her hand on the nape of Alma's neck. "Let us go away together."

"I have come to eat, Nhâ Betta. I have not eaten yet."

Betta's hand, closed about Alma's hair and jerked it warningly.

"I know," Alma hissed. "I do not please you. You are jealous of me."

"Careful, woman," Betta said. "I am old enough to be your grandmother. And you please me very much, when you do not lose your reason."

"You are talking with your tongue, Nhâ Betta."

"With my heart, Alma."

"You always abuse me."

"I have never abused you, until this morning, remember?"

"I remember this morning. And there is still gall in my heart," Alma said, beating her breast fiercely.

"And I will abuse you again, now, and for the same reason, comprehend?"

"You are no more woman than I am."

"Naturally not."

"You do not frighten me."

"That is as it should be. I do not favor cowards."

"I have come to eat, Nhâ Betta. I will eat in my place."

"Do as you have decided."

Alma moved forward and Betta yanked her back by the hair. Betta yanked so hard that one of Alma's legs flew up in the air. But Alma did not scream. She was past pain now. She was steeped in the poisonous passion of her jealousy, and she fought as she made love—with all the violent ardor of her heart.

Alma swarmed over Betta. Betta took Alma's blows without yielding an inch, like a sandbag against a wall. But Betta's complexion had by now turned a rusty green, her eyes were narrow slits, and there was saliva bubbling at the corners of her mouth. Betta's calm heart had reached the murderous stage. With a roar she grabbed Alma's right breast and twisted it this way and that, pushed and pulled it back and forth, keeping Alma off balance as she hit her face, the side of her head, her neck with the other hand, now a fist, now open, now a horny edge. Betta's hand was as busy as a sugar-cane machete at harvest time. Alma fought back blindly, desperately trying to sink her sharp teeth into Betta's flailing hand. They fought close to Laura's chair, pushing and rocking it.

"Damn it all," Laura cried and fled the room. She was crossing the threshold when she heard the scream of defeat. Then all was quiet.

And in the stillness of the echoing scream, the strains of a lively tune reached into the dining room from the front of the house where the minstrels now were playing and several couples already dancing.

CHAPTER TEN

CARLOS looked for Laura.

Laura's "Damn it all" and appalled countenance haunted Carlos. He felt that her flight had shattered his hopes. He must find Laura and explain before it was too late—although for what it would be too late he did not know. His was the anxiety of a blind man who has lost his way. He looked for Laura in her room. He looked for her in the crowd listening to the minstrels. He looked for her in the eucalyptus grove. He ran up to shadows that he mistook for Laura.

And now that he was about to abandon his quest, Carlos heard the plodding of a horse from off in the darkness. Then a cowboy, with his wife sitting sideway on the mount's rump, came riding out of the darkness and, in answer to Carlos' query, said that he had seen a woman walking towards the river. No, he could not tell who she was. It was too dark where he had seen her.

Carlos hurried along, shouldering his way through the darkness. He found Laura halfway down the loam path that led to the river. He fell in step with her. She ignored him, feeling the tension between them grow. Laura felt she had lived this moment once before. Whenever their hands, his right one and her left, touched inadvertently, she drew away from him.

"I must talk with you, Laura. Please, listen."

"Go away. Leave me alone. I've had enough for one evening."

They walked on, through alleys of darkness, across squares of moonlight. In the northern distance the jungle stood out in the night like a stormy sea caught in slow-motion, the crest of its horizon a foamy radiation in the moonshafts.

"Please, let me explain."

"I'm not interested. I'll never set foot in the dining room again. I'm not going to be the bone of contention between *you* and your *woman.*"

"She is not my woman."

The mist was rising in the open fields. In it the livestock moved about like phantoms. On the left the night was studded with lamplights burning in the ranch hands' quarters. The lights squinted like caged fireflies.

Laura turned about. But Carlos took hold of her arm, held her back.

"Take your hands off me. Don't touch me! *Don't touch me!*"

"Let's walk, please."

They continued along the path, the castanets-like voice of the bullfrogs growing louder as they drew nearer to the river. And then they were standing side by side, looking down at the flowing water. The cool air smelled of freshly crushed grass, and in the loneliness of the hour, the hum of the river, emphasized by the stuttering of the bullfrogs, was almost a song.

"She *was* my woman."

Laura faced Carlos, her lips trembling, her arms stiff at her sides. "Why tell *me*? What makes you think I'm interested in your bloody love affairs? I'm going back now."

Carlos barred her way. "Not before you've heard me out."

"Don't be silly. You're making a perfect ass of yourself, forcing your lurid confession on me. I'm only your guest, who'll soon bid you good-bye and forget your delightful hospitality. Now let me go."

"You're more than my guest."

"Don't talk rot. Let me go."

Carlos did not move.

"You're quite a man, aren't you? Perfectly masterful. But you don't impress me a bit, Carlos. Let me go. I'm tired. I want to go to my room."

"She is not my woman."

"For heaven's sake, not again. Throw the damn record away."

"She was my woman. But I never loved her. I made that clear to her from the beginning. She agreed to accept the situation without the love angle. Only I didn't know then the kind of jealous woman she is."

"Your pathetic confession bores me to death."

"You're right, Laura. It *is* a pathetic confession. I never thought the time would come when I'd care enough to explain myself to a woman."

"You don't have to. I don't want to hear it."

"My relation with her was physical. *Only* physical. A combination of laziness and indifference made me postpone breaking off with her. This afternoon she sent for me and told me she was though with me."

"Not judging by the way she acted tonight."

"That was for spite. The ranch will soon know that she's finished with me."

"*She* is finished with *you*. Aren't you the perfect gentleman!"

"I love you, Laura."

"I'm thrilled."

"I want you."

"My heart's breaking with excitement. May I ring up my husband and ask his kind permission to oblige you?"

"Look me straight in the eye, Laura."

"What the devil do you think I've been doing all along?"

"Tell me that you love your husband and I'll leave you alone."

"Otherwise?"

"I won't let go of you, Laura. I need your body to tell you how much I love you."

"Then I'll never know the extent of your devotion—isn't that a pity! Now take me back to the house."

Carlos shook his head.

"Don't make me despise you, Carlos."

"You can't think any less of me than you already do."

Laura turned to go, but Carlos grabbed her arm.

"Let go of me!" Laura cried. "Let me *go!*"

"You must listen."

"I'm not interested. Go back to your woman."

"You can't humiliate me."

"You're rotten."

"I'm past being insulted."

"I'm married."

"That is hardly a valid excuse any more, Laura. I love you. I fell in love with you when you were ugly with pain, disfigured with fear. When you were sexless. Now I need your body to tell you the rest of my love."

Carlos was shaking with the tenseness of his passion. For an instant he reminded Laura of the storm. Then she had been lashed by cold wind and rain; now she was being sucked into the whirlpool of Carlos' passion. She had not expected it to happen so soon after the scene in the dining room. She was not ready for it. And she was not going to have it happen when it pleased him.

Laura sought escape. Everything around her stood out in bold detail—the loneliness of the surroundings, the misty night, the humming river, the croaking bullfrogs. She smelled the odor of freshly crushed grass. She was certain that the birds in the trees had awakened, heard everything, were now waiting for the conclusion. She was conscious of everything, except why she herself was there.

Carlos made her aware of it. He took her into his arms, crushing her ribs, squeezing the breath out of her.

Laura did not plead pain. "All right," she said. "When shall we do it? Where shall we go?"

"No," Carlos said. "Not that way."

"That's the only way you're ever going to have me."

"No," he said. "No." His arms grew slack about her body.

"I'm not going to call it rape, Carlos, because I'm not going to fight you. You're much too strong."

"I don't want you that way." He dropped his arms.

"Got a coat or something to spread out on the ground? It's terribly damp and I catch cold easily."

"Please, don't talk like that."

"Come on. If you're going to dirty me up, you might as well get started."

Dawn was breaking when Laura finally fell asleep. She was not very proud of herself. She knew she could have handled the situation in a subtler manner. But she had been angry and conscious of Carlos' unyielding mood, and she had done the best she could on the spur of the moment.

Laura got up late. She wanted no breakfast. She bathed alone and by the time she came back it was lunch time.

There was a note propped against the wine bottle. *Please don't wait for me.* Laura gave the note to Betta and Betta had lunch served. Laura picked listlessly at the food, drank three glasses of wine, smoked a cigarette and then retired to her room for the siesta hour.

The sun was leaning hard against the orange curtains. Outside, fistfuls of mosquitoes were butting against the window-nettings, a buzzing crowd seeking admittance. The room was hot and Laura's body, running with perspiration, stuck to the sheet.

The bed smelled of damp linen. Unable to rest, Laura tossed about, wallowing deeper into a feeling of guilt.

Laura jumped out of bed in a passion of unrest. She slipped into her dress and sandals, grabbed up her now broadbrimmed white straw hat and left the room. A few seconds later she was standing in the courtyard.

The sun blinded Laura for a moment, the heat enveloped her like a steamy towel. The stillness was oppressive, the surroundings deserted. Laura felt as if she were alone in the world. She found herself walking down toward the river; it was a familiar route now and she had taken it automatically. She passed several windows behind which people were snoring or mumbling in their sleep.

Laura stopped, looked about her. Compared with this, Cuiaba was like Paris, she thought, smelling the pungent odor of scorched grass, listening to the desert-like silence, squinting at the blazing sun, at the sky-reaching, fence-like jungle. Good heavens, she thought, thinking of the monotonous days ahead of her, this is a tropical Siberia.

Laura walked on, with a pallbearer's step and countenance.

The river came into view. A sluggish breath of air staggered to meet her. Even that felt cool on her flushed skin.

Laura saw Carlos before he saw her. Carlos was watering his horse. He seemed to be dozing in the saddle, chin on chest, reins slack in his hands, his left foot dangling out of the stirrup. Laura had just decided to turn around and head back to the house when Carlos raised his head and saw her. She stood still where his eyes had found her, and so searchingly did they look at each other that their eyes bridged the distance separating them and they felt as though they were standing face to face, reliving an épisode that did credit to neither of them.

Carlos rode up to Laura and dismounted. He left the reins on the horse's neck and the horse wandered away.

Not a leaf nor a blade of grass stirred about them. Only the river was moving, as flatly as a shadow follows its living substance. They could not go on staring at the river, as they were doing. One of them would have to say something, would have the break the silence that was, in itself, all too meaningful.

"Where are you going?" Carlos finally asked.

"Nowhere in particular. Just escaping the heat. Or trying to."

"Does it bother you that much?"

"Today it does."

"It isn't any warmer than it was yesterday."

"It was pretty hot yesterday, too."

"No more than usual."

"Don't you think so?"

They fell silent, not anxious to continue in this vein.

Two parrots burst into rapid squawking somewhere in the hidden distance nearby. They sounded as if they were disrupting a perch. Then a gaily feathered parrot, with blazing eyes and ruffled crest, winged its way low across the river, hurling imprecations at the victor.

Carlos and Laura followed the bird's fluttering flight with eyes that voiced no comment.

Stillness returned after the bird had gone.

"It's hot," Laura said just to say something.

The river grew excited in its bed. For a few moody moments it purled into little circles; then, exhausted, it stretched itself out again, and flowed on, as flatly as before.

"Come with me," Carlos said.

"Where?"

"I know a place where you'll find some relief from the heat."

"Is there such a place?"

Carlos started to walk upriver. After a moment's hesitation Laura followed him. Tall and straight and strong he walked before her. She noticed that his hair grew long in the back, fell over his shirt collar. She noticed the line of his hard, lean buttocks, his long stride. She wished he would not walk so fast. The path was narrow and sandy, and the sand got into her sandals and felt gritty and hot. Carlos' spurs added a crunching sound to his footsteps.

Now the path curved to the right and grew steep, and they went down it by propping themselves against their heels. At the end of the path there was a boat held fast by a knotted rope tied to a tree stump cut in the shape of a capstan. The boat was an eighteen-foot pirogue with a tiller and a fringed white canvas roof in the center. The boat was painted green. A deep green.

Carlos motioned Laura to get into the boat. She eyed him. He met her gaze. With an expression of defiance Laura skipped lightly aboard and seated herself beneath the canvas roof. Carlos unfastened the rope, tossed it into the boat, gave it a shove and jumped in. He sat at the tiller.

The boat started on its calm journey downriver.

Now Carlos bent down to remove his spurs just at the same moment as Laura removed her hat. Startled, they searched each other's eyes, as if their simultaneous action was an occurrence of dire portent. Laura sat with her hands folded in her lap, the breeze playing with her hair. Carlos hardly troubled to steer the boat. Occasionally they would exchange banal remarks to interrupt their eloquent silence. Their silence needed no translation. Each was infecting the other with the tension he was feeling at the moment.

The boat rounded a bend in the river. A small family of jaguars, the mates and two cubs, came out of the jungle and paused to sniff and look at the boat.

"They look rather tame," Laura said.

"They aren't hungry," said Carlos. Then he added, "Everybody's tame when he isn't hungry."

Laura avoided Carlos' eyes.

"What are those birds?" she said, pointing to a path opening in the jungle.

"Garças. Recognize their feathers?"

"Should I?"

"Egrets."

And now the river grew festive with the calling and trilling and whistling of all sorts of birds as they flew back and forth in the arching treetops.

A score of flat heads with small ears and rodent teeth were peeping out of some burrows on the right bank.

Carlos pointed them out to Laura.

"What are they?"

"Coypus."

"Coypus?"

"Women wear them on their backs."

"Furs?"

"Nutria."

The river began to widen and the treetops meeting overhead drew apart, revealing a sky ablaze with yellow sunlight.

The boat got stuck and stopped.

"Algae," Carlos said. "I was steering too close to the bank."

Laura said nothing. Carlos did nothing. They remained, each in his own place, as if waiting for the boat to free itself from the weeds.

"Please, hand me the gaff," Carlos said and pointed.

Laura reached for the gaff behind her but she could not unhook it. Carlos got up and walked down the center of the boat, bending down very low to fit under the canvas roof. He found himself kneeling before Laura. He might have gone on kneeling before her forever. He was on his knees, the savage was, worshipping her as if she were the sun, or the moon, or any other elemental force that awed him. The savage prayed to his deity: he rested his hands, palms down, on her lap.

But soon the heat of his hands seeped through Laura's cotton dress and touched her skin. His hands tightened about her thighs. She did not dare move. She did not want to move. With still countenance and grave eyes they gazed at each other, building up a tremendous tension between them. The animal magnetism in him attracted her. She leaned forward and kissed him gently on the corner of his mouth. Then he took her face in his hands and kissed her lips as if he wanted to draw blood from them. They invaded each other's mouth with famished anxiety. In the secret darkness of their mouths they contested for each other's tongue. Still holding her face in his hands, his fingers gradually crept into her hair, baring and slightly tickling her ears. She trembled, and then their lips met again, softly, and then as before, she felt herself growing weak. He pulled her down towards him and they lay on the floor of the boat ....

She was in the ecstasy of enjoyment before she had time to seek for it. It was an emulsive explosion that rocked, tore within. Behind her closed eyelids everything appeared a reddish gleam and consciousness was obliterated for the moment. It left her body throbbing tensely. Later she compared the present episode with similar past experiences and she could not believe it. Now she wanted to rest. But he began to undress her. She thought it was happening in a dream as he bared her body to the sun's lambent glare. The sun consorted with her while he undressed himself.

Now in each other's arms, his hard, dark-haired chest against her smooth turgid breasts, they smelled a new odor in each other's body—a peculiar odor, almost incense-like, like the odor of heated heartwood, stronger in him, more profuse in her, that the body gathers during, and then releases, like a sigh of exhaustion, at the culmination of love making. The odor of life.

Later they slipped over the side of the boat and swam and played in the water. He swam like a fish. She was a good swimmer too.

Back in the boat he wrung her hair fairly dry, and then they lay side by side on the floor of the boat. Their bodies were cool, smelled of fresh seaweed. He propped himself on an elbow and adored her, as he studied her body—long and supple, the bosom small and firm, the nipples of a rose-bluish hue.

Laura had never suspected how passionate she truly was. She was proud of it, of being a woman, and she loved the one man who had revealed her to herself.

Resting in his arms, Laura told Carlos that she was not married, really. He grinned and said he knew it. How? Laura wanted to know. Carlos whispered a sweet obscenity in her ear—compared her to a virgin. Then she whispered an obscenity in his ear. He grinned quietly.

They parted where they had met several hours before.

What had then been a place of suspended conflict was now a spot dedicated to their love. Carlos said he was going to fence it in and grow red carnations in it.

He was sweet, her savage was, as sweet as pure alcohol flavored with honey.

Twice, as she hurried back to the house, Laura had a feeling she was being watched. She stopped on both occasions and looked about her, but she saw no one.

Laura went to her room to freshen up before dinner. She loved the face she saw reflected in the mirror. It was a strangely new face, bare of all worldliness. A face tranquil and happy. Her lower lip was a bit swollen. She soothed it with her tongue. And lip and tongue gossiped about the recent past. With the active memory of perception, Laura still retained the sensations she had absorbed in Carlos' arms. She smiled as she remembered what Carlos had compared her to. She wished she had a bra, to blindfold the impudent expression of her nipples. She felt like patting her body for having performed so gloriously.

What a few hours before had been a "tropical Siberia" had magically turned into a Garden of Eden.

CHAPTER ELEVEN

Now Laura heard the chapel bell tolling the Angelus. The previous evening's performance was reenacted. Like tributaries flowing into the Xingù, the ranch hands turned toward the *casa grande* and the guests for the evening found their places at the dining table. The food was different in selection, but not in abundance. Although quite a few familiar faces were missing, all the seats were filled. Little Mira had her own seat. Antonio's cunning, knowing little smile had aged and there was a new crease on each side of his mouth. Antonio had been seen slinking about Alma's house during the siesta hour. The same exuberance of spirits prevailed in the dining room. But Laura's mood was absent from it. Laura was holding a party of her own within herself.

Betta's all-seeing eyes kept returning to Laura, noticing how well she was eating and drinking.

"*Xârâ,*" Betta said to Anteiro. "The girl is starved."

"She is still growing," Anteiro said sententiously.

Laura was eating as greedily as she had made love. Laura was now a woman who had dropped all pretenses, all true or fancied rancors, all frustrations, all attempts at cleverness. During that afternoon she had shucked the bad from her life. She felt as though she were reborn and beginning to live again, thanks to the man sitting next to her.

Carlos watched Laura out of the corner of his eye. It was a wonderful feeling to watch a woman appease a hunger for which he was partly responsible. And it was a wonderful thought to know that this richly fed body was his. He felt a sensual pleasure at the idea that she was hoarding fuel for their love.

But to the casual observer, Carlos and Laura were now behaving as if they had not yet been introduced.

"The minstrels."

Warming up their instruments the four musicians went past the door.

"They are late tonight." How the speaker could tell was a mystery, unless he was judging time by his digestion.

Shouting happily, "Let us go to the dance," the children fled the dining room. The girls followed the children. The men followed the girls. Except for four elderly people napping in their seats, Carlos and Laura were left alone at their end of the table.

"You've got some explaining to do," Carlos said to Laura.

"What about, darling?"

"Last night. They were going to play in your honor and you didn't show up. They think you're a bit of a snob."

"Me, a snob! Oh, no. I'm a peasant at heart, darling. I love the earth. I love you."

Carlos warmed himself at the glow of Laura's emotion a moment longer. Then, "You should wear a black veil over your eyes. They are indecently beautiful."

"You made them indecent, Carlos. And I love you for it."

"How old are you, Passion Fruit?"

"Passion flower?"

"Passion Fruit, capital letters."

"Am I?"

"To the tenderest, sweetest, deepest core."

"Shut up, or I'll blush."

"How old are you, Passion Fruit?"

"I'm an old woman, darling. Twenty-seven."

"Liar. You're sixteen."

"No, no," said Laura. "I don't ever want to be sixteen again. That's a raw age. A lost age. I want to be an old woman of twenty-seven."

"Don't ever change."

"I won't, darling. Now take me to the dance. I want to dance with you. I want you to hold me tight. I—"

"Hush. Here comes Betta."

"What is this "hôllô," daughter?"

"Greetings. Salutations. *Felicidade.*"

Betta stared at Laura. Under the scrutiny Laura grew a bit uncomfortable. "What's the matter?" she asked.

"Your eyes. I have never seen your eyes so beautiful as they are tonight. Your husband should be here to see them. Do you miss your husband, daughter?"

"Good heavens," Laura said. "Shall we go, Carlos?"

Betta followed them, like a duenna.

The mist was rising. Flaring torches were holding night at bay in the courtyard before the main entrance. The wafting glare of the torches swabbed the mist an oxblood hue, stained the face sof the onlookers standing or sitting or squatting in a circle on the ground.

There was no dancing now. The minstrels were playing a folk song, and the people clapped their hands and rocked their bodies in time to it, and the oxblood wall of mist swayed with them.

Now a subdued humming joined the clapping and the rocking. Then the humming swelled into a chant, which ranged in pitch from a love lament to an angry howling: a counterpoint of human voices and animal sounds. It was a music, a rhythm, Laura had never heard before. It told of the moods of the jungle and its creatures, men and beasts alike. The accordion wailed sonorously, the flute cried shrilly, the drum thundered and rolled, the guitar punctuated the score with the twang of whining steel, while the chanting, the clapping and the rocking, steady and unchanging, was as alive as a tremendous heartbeat.

Laura had a weird feeling that she was no longer among people she knew, but among natives holding a tribal ritual in the depth of the jungle.

Laura looked at Carlos, sitting in a wicker chair next to her. Carlos was listening to the music with the primitive reverence of his humblest *peón,* seemingly ready to answer the summons of the drum, to leap into the air and shout and dance in savage rapture.

Laura looked at Betta, sitting on the other side of her. Betta's face was convulsed with the achingly ecstatic expression of one who is coaxing a sneeze.

Laura looked at Anteiro, who was standing now beside Betta. Anteiro's mouth was parted as if in an arrested scream of exaltation, and he clapped his huge hands and swayed his massive body as if in a trance.

Laura felt herself being infected with the animal-like sensuality that seemed to be flowing from the core of everybody about her. It was like a spiritual orgasm that never matured. The suspense was oppressive. She wished that the music would stop. She wished that Carlos would pay attention to her.

She spoke to Carlos. He did not hear her. She rested her hand on Carlos' knee. He turned to her slowly, his eyes seemingly focused on some distant atavistic image. Then he took her hand and placed it back on her lap, his eyes now warning her not to do that again.

It was fortunate that neither Betta nor Anteiro nor anyone else saw Laura rest her hand on Carlos' knee. In their society a man's legs was as private, in public, as a woman's pelvis.

The music ended. It was as though padded doors had been shut tight upon a tumultuous multitude.

Getullio, the accordion player, came over to Carlos. "With your permission, *patrão*," he said to him, and turned to Laura. "At your service, *senhora*."

But Betta spoke for Laura. "Play the Bleeding Heart," she told Getullio. "Our guest must see how we dance the tango in this part of God's country."

"Does that meet with your approval, *senhora?*" Getullio, who knew his manners, asked Laura.

"I can do the tango," Laura said.

Getullio asked permission to inquire how the *senhora* was enjoying the hospitality of Fabenda Boa Vista. Then he bowed and went to rejoin the orchestra. Now all of them, except for the drummer, they started to play the Bleeding Heart, a mournfully sentimental tune that told of a *vaqueiro* who had stuck a thorn in his *inamorata's* heart because she was unfaithful to him while he was far away from home.

"Shall we dance, Carlos?" Laura said and stood up. "Shall we?" She looked down to Carlos.

"It is not proper that you dance," Betta said to Laura.

"Why not?"

"You are a married woman."

"And a guest of the house," Betta added. "And your man is not present."

"Betta," Laura said, suddenly angrily, "I don't know what you're talking about." Laura felt silly, standing there and being told what to do.

"That is the law," Betta said.

"What law?"

"The law of the land."

"If you ask me—"

"Please," Carlos said. "Sit down, Laura, and I'll explain."

By the time Carlos had explained the law of the land to Laura, the tango was over and they were playing a samba, made livelier by a score of dancing couples.

"A damn silly law," Laura said.

"Maybe," said Carlos. "But the old-timers wouldn't have it otherwise. Should I break the law now they would accuse me of disloyalty to my grandfather, to them, to the ranch. It was a good law in the old days, though, Laura, when men were many and women few, and ..."

Laura followed Carlos' eyes. They were fixed on the dancers. Then Laura saw Betta was standing, gaping incredulously. She reminded Laura of an idiot child. Then Laura grew conscious of the hush that had set in all over the place. Even the music seemed to be softer The dancers moved as if in slow-motion, and every head was turned in Carlos' direction. He sat with his hands clenched on his knees.

Now Laura saw Anteiro walking towards the dancers and heard Carlos snarl, "Come back."

Anteiro hung on his step, faced Carlos.

"Don't interfere," Carlos told him.

"Interfere yourself then, man. You know you must uphold the law."

"Come back."

Anteiro gazed at Carlos unbelievingly. Betta bent over as if to make sure it was Carlos she was looking at. Then she made a sound of incredible contempt. Repeating the sound she turned about and walked toward the house. Anteiro followed her. By now most of the dancers had stopped dancing. They stood, their arms slack about each other, staring at Carlos. Carlos did not move, not even now as Alma and Antonio danced past him, grinning at him challengingly. Not even for tradition's sake was he going to humiliate his true love. Laura realized what it must cost Carlos to behave thus. It was a testament of his love for her.

"Shall we go for a walk, darling," she said quietly.

"No. Not yet, Laura. Let them make sure that I'm what I appear to be." Carlos grinned bitterly. "She beat me to the punch," he said. "Very cunning of her. But that's Alma for you. I should have told them that I was through with her when she made that scene in the dining room. I missed my cue. Now it's too late. Now—"

"I'm your woman, darling."

Carlos stood up. "Don't come with me," he said and walked away.

Laura noticed that the people's eyes followed Carlos as if he were a leper.

Now the moon was high, the house asleep.

Carlos sat up in bed. "Who's there?"

"It's me, darling," Laura whispered in the dark. She stepped out of her nightshirt and slipped into the bed beside Carlos.

"You shouldn't have come here," he said. "Now I'm breaking the law of hospitality, too. Making love to my guest under my own roof."

"But I don't want you to make love to me, darling. I only want to be with you. To be affectionate."

"Passion Fruit," he said and took her into his arms and kissed her.

"That's enough," she said. "Now let's rest. Just hold me."

But already his hand was exploring her body. "Here it is," he said, pinching.

"What, darling?"

"The birthmark." His hand continued on its persuasive mission.

"No," she said. "No." She crossed her legs tight, trapping his hand.

"Passion Fruit."

"Yes?"

"You have a fever."

"No," she said. "I don't. I'm cold. Frigid."

"You're trembling."

"Please don't. Don't, darling," she said, inviting him.

Joyfully tired, Laura then fell asleep in Carlos' arms.

Carlos got out of bed, picked Laura up in his arms and went and stood at the window. The moonlight fell upon Laura's body. Carlos held Laura's body up to the moon as if it were an offering. The moon, who knows all about women, who brings them pain or relief, peace or anxiety—the moon was noncommittal.

Carlos carried Laura back to her room, laid her down on her bed, drew the sheet over her.

Under the sheet, Laura's body looked virginal.

Stepping back into his own room Carlos tripped over Laura's nightshirt lying on the floor. He picked it up and stuffed it under his pillow.

Laura was undressing in the bathing grotto when Alma came in. By showing no surprise at finding Laura there, Alma indicated that she had been waiting, hiding somewhere outside.

With unmistakable purposefulness Alma took off her clothes and stood naked before Laura. Laura finished undressing and stood naked before Alma. The soundless, bloodless contest began. They were almost of a height, and both were long-limbed. Only one was fair, the other dark. One was feminine, the other female. The breasts of one were small and firm, the nipples like ripening berries; the breasts of the other were slightly elongated, the nipples like ripe berries. The navel of one was a soft whorl, the other's a hard knot. The hip-line of one flowed unbroken onto her thigh, the other's swelled superbly. The hair of one was light and soft, the other's black and bushy. The buttocks of one were small and round, the other's small and slightly melon shaped. They both had slim ankles. The feet of one were long and narrow, the other's rather short and broad.

And, as both Laura and Alma had already guessed, they were of approximately the same age. The difference between them was in the sun. The Mato Grosso sun ripens its native fruit more quickly.

"Shall we bathe now?" Laura said.

Alma snatched her clothes off the ground and left the grotto. But Laura read dire thoughts in Alma's glowing eyes.

Judging by the sun it was now about eleven o'clock.

Carlos and Tomaso were in the gun room repairing a *garu-cha,* a weapon that looked like a baby shotgun and fired thumb-sized bullets.

Its owner, Miguel, a cowboy of the olden days, attached such sentimental value to this museum piece that he had resisted Carlos' offer of a new six-shooter.

"Do you think we'll ever fix it, Tomaso?"

"*Si, senhor patrão.*"

Carlos eyed Tomaso. It was painful to be addressed so formally by a man whom he regarded as a special friend. But Tomaso was a loyal son of the ranch and together with the others considered himself dishonored by Carlos' behavior at the dance.

They were working in silence when Anteiro blew into the room like a sirocco.

"Now they are together in the forest," he told Carlos.

"They? Who?"

"God damn you, man. You know who they are." Anteiro rarely cursed. He never took God's name in vain. But Anteiro's proverbial patience had deserted-him now.

Instinctively Carlos looked about him for a handy weapon.

"This is your chance," Anteiro went on. "The chance you would not take last night."

"Why should I take any chance?"

"Alma is your woman."

"*Was.*"

"Still *is*, as far as the ranch knows. You teach him a lesson, as Betta is going to teach Alma one. Let us go."

Carlos did not move.

"Man," Anteiro cried. "What must he do to you before you teach him a lesson? Spit on your grandfather's grave?"

"Say that again and I'll kill you."

"For God's sake, punish the lawbreaker," Anteiro pleaded.

"I can't fight for something I feel nothing about."

"Then fight for us. For the law of the land. Our land."

"Take the land, Anteiro. Take anything you want. But for God's sake stay out of my personal affairs."

"Your grandfather would already have killed you for the cowardly way you behaved last night."

"He would."

"I should have killed you in his place."

Carlos felt sorry for Anteiro, for his fanatical loyalty to the ranch. Now Carlos wished he could put his arms around Anteiro's shoulders and explain to him in simple words how a man's sense of values can suddenly change because at last he has found a woman who can fulfill his expectation of life. But Anteiro would not understand. Anteiro would only grow madder and madder, until finally he would hit Carlos. And then he would never be able to forget it, nor forgive himself for having done it.

"Let's finish this piece of junk," Carlos told Tomaso and picked up the ancient weapon.

"Excuse me, *senhor patrão*," Tomaso said and followed Anteiro out of the gun room.

They were having lunch when Laura remembered and said, "What happened to my nightshirt, darling?"

Carlos started. "Damn it! I put your nightshirt under my pillow and forgot all about it."

"You'd better sneak it back to me before my little chambermaid misses it, and starts asking questions."

"Was your room already made when you came back from your bath?" Carlos asked.

"Yes, darling. Yours?"

"I don't know. I haven't been there yet."

"Hadn't you better see?"

Carlos left the dining room.

"Well?"

"We're lucky," Carlos said as he sat down next to Laura again. "The bed was still unmade. It has never happened before. I threw your nightshirt on your bed."

"That calls for another glass of wine," Laura said. Then, sipping, "I met your ex-woman in the grotto this morning. She challenged me to a beauty contest."

"A beauty contest?"

Laura explained.

"Please stay away from her, Laura. I'm serious. Promise you will."

"I'm not afraid of her, Carlos. I can be a Dr. Jekyll and Mrs. Hyde if I have to. She wanted a contest and I obliged her. She isn't bad at all."

Carlos smiled. "You can afford to be generous," he said. "Have you ever been jealous of another woman?"

"No. Why should I? What's another woman got that I haven't got?"

"Your wonderful sense of humor, for one thing."

"Well, thank you, darling. But I don't think I'm best known for my sense of humor. By the way, what did the critics have to say this morning about last night's performance?"

Carlos grinned ruefully. "Anteiro reminded me that if my grandfather were alive he would have killed me for the performance I gave last night."

"I'm terribly sorry, Carlos."

"It only makes me want you the more."

She blew him a kiss. "How's Rosario?" she asked.

"I saw him this morning. He isn't too bad. But he's an old man and he took a brutal beating. The Negress Mullô's doing her best."

"I'll drop in to see him on my way to my room."

Betta came into the dining room. Ignoring Carlos she handed Laura a black veil. She really tossed the veil at her.

"What's this for?" Laura asked, pretending to ignore Betta's rudeness.

"When you go to chapel you must cover your head."

Well, you're an old sour puss, Laura thought. "Why black?" she asked.

"You are a *married* woman, are you not?"

"Betta," Laura said, to settle the chapel business once and for all, "I'm a Protestant."

"I am a protester too," Betta said. "We all protest in the course of time, except one. That one's guts have gone incurably bad. That one's—"

"Betta," Laura said. "How is it outside?"

"Eh?"

Maybe it started then, at lunch. But there was something in Betta's behavior that antagonized Laura. Although she had sensed at once Betta's sudden, inexplicable change of heart toward her personally, Laura left it out of her consideration. It might have been Betta's attitude against Carlos, or Betta's domineering way that rubbed Laura the wrong way. Especially the latter. It ruffled Laura's temperament.

CHAPTER TWELVE

THE SUN was setting when Betta broke into Alma's house and beat her into unconsciousness. Then she ripped Alma's skirt open in front and spat upon her. "Alma *mala*," she called her. Bad soul. Whore.

Alma went down under the rain of blows almost happily. Her revenge was working out nicely. She had already dishonored Carlos before the whole ranch, and she had not yet given herself to Antonio. She was no fool. She still needed him.

The Negress Mullô kept the news of Antonio's transgression from Uncle Rosario. She knew what kind of a man her patient was and she did not want to upset him. The Negress Mullô warned all visitors to keep their mouths shut, or she would not be responsible for what her patient might do. Sick as he was he might quit the bed, harm his nephew and then quit the ranch, dying on the open road road like a dog.

It was the siesta hour, the safest time of the day to carry on private affairs. Antonio slipped into Alma's house. Alma was so busy sharpening her dagger on a whetstone that she did not hear Antonio come in.

She started when Antonio said, "What are you doing that for?"

"I must have a sharp point to clean the dirt from under my fingernails."

"To hell with your nails," Antonio said. "Let's go to bed."

"I have a belly ache."

"That's what you said yesterday."

"It is the same belly ache."

No one, in or out of the house, could believe that the master of Fazenda Boa Vista would allow Antonio's insult to go unchallenged.

But Carlos continued to live in a world of his own, and even those who loved him best were forced to brand him as a coward. For they all religiously believed in and abided by a self-made code of honor so inflexible as to overrule all other feelings and considerations.

True, they hated Antonio, but still they looked up to him with grudging admiration. The man had guts; Antonio, however, wished he could honestly believe that the rancher, as he called Carlos, was a coward. The hog episode was still fresh in Antonio's mind, and in light of it, Carlos' behavior did not make sense. But then Antonio had a friend, Juan, a good matador, who was mortally afraid of dogs. Maybe the rancher was afraid of men. Thinking of Carlos, Antonio thought of his woman. He had not slept with her yet. Maybe she was playing him for a fool, Antonio thought. She had better not. No one ever made a fool of Antonio and got away with it, he reminded himself, and went about the ranch as if he were Carlos' partner.

Laura thought of Antonio as a bloody nuisance, and kept him at arm's length. Being a man of great pride, Antonio retaliated. He wanted Laura to know, his attitude told her, that he was not in the habit of associating with persons who associated with cowards.

To hell with you, was Laura's attitude toward Antonio.

Fortunately for Antonio, no one could harm him except the "insulted one," or they would have started fighting among themselves for the privilege of being the first to lay hands on him.

Betta was stoutly resisting the temptation to sneak a poisonous snake in Antonio's bed. Anteiro dug his hands deep into his pockets whenever Antonio crossed his path.

Carlos was sorry for his people as he watched their awkward but nevertheless successful efforts to avoid him.

Laura was sad for Carlos' sake, and amazed at his people's behavior toward him. Laura tried to put herself in their place, tried to think with their mentality, because she realized that it was her love for Carlos which urged her to condemn them harshly, and perhaps unfairly.

Laura saw then that they were like hurt and angry children. Children who saw their beloved father being scorned and stoned in the street and doing nothing to defend himself, to prove to his children that he was not a coward.

Their little god had crumbled at their feet, failed them miserably. And like sunflowers which droop when the sun does not come out, they too felt they had no one to look up to now.

This appraisal made Laura realize how deeply Carlos loved her—not to humble his love for her with an outburst of unfelt personal injury, even though it would please and appease his people.

Carlos and Laura were in each other's arms on the mossy floor of the forest.

Laura's will to resist Carlos had completely run down. In her rare sober moments Laura wondered at her love. Was it genuine love? Or was it only lust? She didn't know. She only knew that she could not lessen her passion. Carlos fired it at will. Alone with Carlos, Laura lost all inhibitions. Carlos was the instrument of

pleasure upon which Laura impaled herself with ecstatic abandon. Alone with Carlos, sensations replaced thoughts in her.
She seemed to be inspired only by the sexual demands of her
body. She thought with her eyes, with her hands. Her eyes and
hands had lost all modesty. She could not reason with herself.
The important thing was to live, she kept telling herself.

Laura was greedily making up for her unfulfilled past life.
She was releasing the animal-like energy of a healthy woman
freed from the taboos of her society.

Away from Carlos, and waiting for Carlos, Laura was in a
passion of expectancy. Once with him she was recharged with
fresh rapture. She believed she was dreaming a wonderful dream
that would never end. For a few days at a time she forgot where
she had come from, where she was supposed to be going.

Laura's views and values of long established habits altered.

Laura discovered that bed is really the last place in which to
make love; that love is stifled between sheets; that love loses its
identity in the dark.

Laura discovered that the sun and the moon and the earth
lend strength to love; that they possess that part of the body
which is not being possessed.

Laura experienced the indescribable feeling of awakening
from the ecstasy of love and gazing up at the sun or at the moon
and starlit sky. It was as if she were passing from dream to dream.
It filled her with an ineffable peace that was akin to a silent prayer
of thanksgiving for being alive.

Particularly the earth, Laura felt, was human under her. It
was warmly unyielding. It held her so close to her lover that she
felt as though she were consorting with the earth and with her
lover at once. She loved the odor of the earth. She compared it
to that of black bread fresh from the oven It seasoned love as
perfume never did.

Laura discovered the sensual pleasure of going stark naked in the forest, as, native-like, she now called the jungle. From head to foot her body was now evenly suntanned. Her nakedness was radiant. She had forgotten what lipstick was. The artificial waves in her hair had gone. She had no natural waves, but her hair had a healthier sheen, was rebellious, tomboy-like. She seemed unable to inhale enough air to satisfy her lungs, to feed her upturned breasts. Without the bra her breasts seemed to have gained a richer bloom, like house flowers put out in the sun. Never before had she lived so freely in the open. She felt that life was bursting within her, clamoring for release.

Laura felt like a savage. She had developed the appetites of a savage. She gratified her appetites unashamedly. She yielded to love at the sound of Carlos' voice, at the touch of his hand, of his lips; at the sight of his body which, to her, was like live granite. She looked at his body with bold eyes and touched it with sure hands.

They were madly in love. They played all kinds of crazy games.

Monkeys and parrots saw them pursuing each other naked through the forest. One day he was a caveman who dragged her off to his lair. One day she was an Amazon who overcame him. Now she was a Bororo squaw, and he a white hunter; how she was a mission girl and he a bandit. Once they played a risky game in a tree, crashed down in each other's arms and, half stunned, concluded the episode. They returned to the boat to remember and to reenact their first meeting there. They took each other wherever and whenever the mood possessed them, except in bed—the coldest, most uninspiring place they could think of to be together.

And, like all clandestine lovers, they too thought they were fooling the world.

❧ ❧ ❧

"Senhora."

"Are you speaking to me, Betta?"

"Si, senhora?"

What's come over her? Laura thought. "What is it?"

"When will you ride on again?"

"Whenever Rosario is ready."

"He is an old man. It will take him a long time to regain his traveling strength."

"I'm in no particular hurry, Betta. Why do you ask?"

"We have our own mounts, and guides. At your service, *senhora.*"

"You sound as though you were anxious to get rid of me, Betta."

"God forbid, *senhora.* I know the law of hospitality. You are a guest of the house. It is for you to decide when to go, *senhora.*"

"Say, Betta, what's this *'senhora'* all about all of a sudden?"

"You are a married woman, are you not?"

"Go on."

"A married woman who should be glad to meet her brother soon, and then return to her husband."

"Is there anything else you want to speak to me about, Betta?"

"Should there be anything else we should talk about, *senhora?*"

"You tell me, Betta." *I'll be damned if I'm going to let you browbeat me. You may be Carlos' second mother, and that's fine with me. But to me you're only his housekeeper, and that's fine, too, as long as you mind your own business.* Smiling then, "By the way, I forgot to thank you for the new nightshirt."

"It fits much better, does it not, *senhora?*"

"I didn't mind wearing yours."

"Mine was much too large for you."

"I didn't mind."

"It did slip off too easily, did it not?"

"I didn't notice it." *What is she trying to tell me anyway? Shall I ask her? Don't bother.* "I thought it was perfectly all right."

"Did you?"

Come out with it, Betta. Because I'm not going to let you have the last word if we stay here all day. "I certainly did."

"I have been keeping your riding boots in my room, *senhora*."

"I must thank Almirante."

"And your riding skirt too."

"Riding skirt? I'm used to wearing riding breeches, Betta."

"Is that what you wore?"

"Yes. Rosario thought it was perfectly all right."

"The old guide has dealt with so many foreigners for so long that he has forgotten the customs of the land."

Have it your own way, Betta, as long as we keep peace in the family. It's too wonderful to spoil. "All right, Betta. I'll be glad to wear the riding skirt. What color is it?"

"Gray."

"Gray's fine. Shall I pick it up in your room?"

"I shall send your things to your room, *senhora*."

They decided to go horseback riding to find out how Laura liked her new skirt.

Until now Laura had shown no enthusiasm at all about getting back into the saddle. She told Carlos she had had enough riding to last her for a while. And she reminded him that she still had some more riding ahead of her ... and a cloud passed between them.

The boots were fine. Finer, more comfortable, than the expensive ones she had bought in Cuiaba. Almirante was certainly a pompous rustic, Laura thought, but he was also a fine bootmaker. By the way, she hadn't thanked him yet. Where had he been keeping himself?

The skirt however felt uncomfortable, and would until Laura grew used to it. The waist band was purposely broad, stiffly reinforced and too snug fitting; the skirt was heavy, roomy and ankle length. Within the skirt, Laura's legs felt like bell-clappers.

In Laura's language, it was a perfectly lovely morning. Dry and clear. Not even a small cloud marred the serenity of the sky. There was a shimmering halo of heat around the sun. Only there the sky seemed to be gleefully excited. The horizon wore a treetop-studded belt.

"I've an incoming suspicion, as you say here, that I'll be good and stiff tonight," Laura said.

"Nothing that warm water and salt won't cure," Carlos said. "Betta'll take care of that."

"Not Betta, darling. Betta's gone formal on me. I wouldn't think of exposing my—informality to her. Now she calls me *senhora*."

"I've noticed that."

"And I don't like the way she says it, the way she looks at me when she says it. You don't think she suspects something, do you, Carlos?"

"I wouldn't be a bit surprised if she did. Betta's no fool. The day you arrived she called you daughter. Now she calls you *senhora*. Should be the other way around, shouldn't it?" Then Carlos said, "Why did you lie to me, Passion Fruit?"

"About what?"

"About being married. How simpler everything'd be if you had told the truth."

"I guess you're right. But you frightened me a little bit, and I thought it would be safer to be married. Should I tell Betta now?"

"It's too late now. She wouldn't believe you. Yet she must be told sooner or later. Passion Fruit, when are you going to marry me?"

"I'm your woman, darling."

"Be serious. I want you now as Laura Diaz, mistress of Fazenda Boa Vista."

"Thank you, Carlos. But what about the present mistress of the house? How long has she been holding that exalted position?"

"All her life."

"And do you think she's going to give it up without a fight? Give it up to an intruder—and a foreigner at that?"

"I'm sure you can handle her."

"Perhaps," Laura said modestly. "But give me time to think it over, darling. Where are you taking me now?"

"Nowhere in particular. Just getting you used to your new skirt. There's nowhere in particular to go, nothing in particular to do. You've already seen all there is to be seen. By now you must have a pretty accurate idea of what we did last year, what we'll be doing next year."

Laura tried to read meaning in Carlos' words. Was he telling her what her future life on the ranch would be like?

Laura had thought of that before, but casually, with her eyes only, as it were. That first afternoon in the boat had marked the end of Laura's entries in her mental diary. Since then she had scarcely paid any attention to physical life of the ranch. Sometimes, taken by surprise by Mira, she would look at the child as if she were seeing her for the first time. To Laura the physical life of the ranch was like a calm sea she had admired for the first few days out; then, tiring of it, she had thereafter looked at it with eyes that beheld other sights. Her inner peace was one of the sights. For the first time in her adult life Laura was a happy woman. She felt clean inside, perhaps because of the sun and the moon and the earth—and a man who gratified her sexual urges as fully as those in her wildest dreams. Without realizing it, Laura had simplified life to its most common denominator.

"The house and the people," Carlos was saying. "Work. Horses and cattle. Cattle and horses. A little dancing at night. Then night. And the next morning to begin again. A succession of twin days, months and years. Quite unexciting for a woman from New York, isn't it?"

I love you, Laura thought. I love your honesty. You've just finished asking me to marry you, and now you're telling me how bleak my future'll be if I accept. You're a dear.

"Unless," Carlos was saying, "you want to go out hunting big cats."

"Good heavens, no! I'm not that kind of woman. I'm a home body."

"Passion Fruit?"

"Yes, darling."

"I love you."

Now for the first time Laura noticed that Carlos always spoke that short simple sentence in a peculiar way: aggressively, intensely, passionately. It really sounded more like a command than a declaration of love. And as he spoke the sentence his handsome dark face grew faintly sinister, reminding her of a drawn bow. He takes love seriously, she thought. Maybe too seriously.

Vanity and curiosity prompted Laura's delayed question. "I love you too, darling. I love you even more than you love me."

"Each loves with what he has."

"How much do you love me?"

"My people, my land and my honor. That's all I have and care for."

That was what Laura thought. She remembered that Carlos had said something like that before. It was rather a responsibility to be loved like that, a responsibility a capricious woman could not assume, had better not assume. On the other hand, such a love made a woman feel wanted as she wanted to be wanted, proud and indispensable in a man's life.

All of a sudden Laura wished Carlos were an American. She would understand and appreciate him better, she felt, and try to love him accordingly. As it was, his wonderful, live-granite body distracted her true love for him. The mere thought of his body thrilled her.

By now the sun had traveled half of its allotted distance. The halo of heat around the sun was melting. Men and animals had already taken refuge in the groves dotting the fields. The grass smelled of scorched alfalfa. The horizon was wine tinted and the treetops no longer girdled it. They were stooping under it.

What from the shimmering distance had looked like a solid windbreak began to take shape as Laura and Carlos rode closer to it. It was a long row of low timber buildings fringed with alfalfa. Behind the buildings rose a banana grove.

They were welcomed by three cowboys, old-timers in thought and appearance. They were barefooted and had heavy iron spurs fastened to their callused heels. They carried thin-bladed long knives tucked under colorful sashes. Their faces were like leather and their eyes like shoe buttons tarnished by time. They still wore old-fashioned hats, narrow-brimmed and with the crown up, like a derby. Only one of them was now wearing his knee-length leather work apron. They smelled of milk. Sour milk.

They were wonderful obstetricians and the Tamer had elevated them to the most responsible position on the ranch: the mating and maternity ward of his full-blooded bovine stock.

They spoke in the sonorous language of the jungle herdsmen of long ago, and they welcomed Laura with the politeness of that time. Faultlessly austere.

Of course they had heard of Carlos' cowardice. But for the Tamer's sake they pretended not to believe it and would have killed anyone who disagreed with them.

Carlos asked Luiz, the oldest cowboy, if they could have something to eat.

Luiz looked at the sun and said they were about to sit down to eat the noon meal. He would be honored to share it with the guest of the *casa grande* and with the *patrão*.

Carlos did not like to be called *patrão* by these men. Before them he felt like a recruit before veterans.

Luiz whistled and a stable boy appeared and led Laura's and Carlos' horses away. They followed Luiz and his friends into the banana grove, an oasis of shade in a desert of sunlight. The banana trees smelled sweetly. They sat on cowhide sheets stretched on the ground beneath the trees. From unseen points in the grove they heard the placid lowing of cows, the temperamental snorting of bulls. Under a smoke-licked banana tree there was a fire burning in a pit dug into the earth. The pit was fairly choked with smooth flat stones and the fire snapped and cracked as it struggled through them.

First things came first with these old-timers, and they sat in the lovely shade drinking alcohol, kept in cow guts hanging from a tree, and making polite conversation. The old-timers were sticklers for manners; they would apologize at the slightest provocation and then proceed to tell you what they thought of you. Having drunk three unhurried drinks, Luiz said it was time to eat. The cowboy wearing the apron got up and went to the fire. The other disappeared through the trees, returning quickly with five enormous sirloin steaks wrapped in banana leaves. While he unwrapped them the cowboy with the leather apron took the stones out of the fire with a pair of prongs and arranged them evenly on the ground. Together then the two men broiled the steaks on the stones, turning them over quickly with their long knives. The steaks sizzled and smoked, and the air filled with an odor that made Laura's mouth water. They seasoned the steaks with crushed garlic, pepper and salt and tamarind juice and served them, still sizzling, on leafy platters. They started to eat as they were taught to eat steak: with knife and hand.

Unthinkingly, Carlos asked for a fork for Laura.

The three old-times glowered at Carlos.

Carlos said to Laura quickly out of the corner of his mouth, "When in Rome do as the Romans do."

"I'm an old Roman myself," Laura said.

And the three old-timers glowered at Laura, and again at Carlos, for breaking the silence.

Speech, they declared, disturbs the odor and taste of the meal, not to mention what it does do to the digestion.

So Laura ate her wonderful, mouth-melting steak native fashion, and the three old-timers returned to her the respect they had withdrawn from her. It was a bit messy, the juice trickling down the corners of her mouth. But the steak—it was perfect! And the garlic, the *divine* garlic ... Fortunately, Laura told herself, Carlos had eaten it also."

After the meal they drank coffee in small cups. Then they went back to alcohol, never breaking the silence.

And in silence Luiz and his men each made himself another cigarette for the day. Almost guiltily Carlos offered Laura a paper cigarette and warned her, quickly, out of the corner of his mouth, not to blow the smoke in the old-timers' direction.

From his leather pouch Luiz took out a ten-inch-long maize leaf. He wet it with his tongue, folded it in two lengthwise and ran it between thumb and knife-edge until it was perfectly smooth. Then he cut off the ends and held the leaf between his lips. Next he cut light slices of tobacco from his tobacco rope, rubbed them between his palms until the slices broke up into fine strands, packed the strands into the maize-leaf and rolled it into a cigarette, nine inches long. He lighted it and at once the whole place filled with the strong, sugary odor of burnt molasses.

They smoked in peace. A cigarette dropped out of one man's hand. Another man's chin dropped onto his chest. Luiz himself, the host, was struggling to keep his eyes open. Finally he gathered himself up and kicked his men awake. They said they had been thinking, to save face. The three old-timers bowed to Laura and Carlos and walked away, disappearing through the trees as they went to their quarters to sleep out the siesta hour.

CHAPTER THIRTEEN

"MAY I open my big mouth now?" Laura said.

"Yes, Passion Fruit."

"I've eaten too much. It's killing me." Laura pulled at the waistband of her skirt. "Do you mind?"

"I'll help you," Carlos said and unbuttoned the waistband for her.

Laura let out a sigh of relief. "There'll be hell to pay to button it up again," she said. She stretched out on the cowhide sheet. Her throat was bare, her pointed breasts stood out, the skirt sagged softly between her legs. Carlos leaned on an elbow next to Laura. He bent down and kissed her. They were kissing when they heard a rustling noise. They drew apart. A cow appeared in the trees. It was a beautiful cow, with the sleekest coat and softest eyes.

"And who might you be?" Laura asked the cow.

"Caterina," Carlos said. "She's Zebu's favorite concubine."

"How nice."

Caterina swished her tufted tail at the introduction. Then she withdrew.

Laura closed her eyes. Carlos lay next to her, his hands now clasped under his head. It was fairly cool in the grove. Cool and shady and very peaceful. A cow lowed, a bull snorted, dogs barked in the distance.

Laura sighed deeply. Carlos watched her breasts rise and fall. His eyes ran down her body, journeyed back to her face. It was the face of a perfectly contented beautiful girl. Her lips were slightly parted. Suddenly Laura opened her eyes.

"It isn't polite to be spying on a sleeping woman," she said.

"Go to sleep," he whispered.

Go to sleep. She closed her eyes obediently. The words sounded familiar. They reminded Laura of the place in the jungle they had first stopped to rest the morning after the storm, when Carlos had stood by her hammock, raised her ankle and studied her foot. It was good to be alive, to be loved. She kicked her boots as if they were shoes she wanted to remove.

Laura kept her eyes closed when she felt Carlos pulling her boots off. She helped him by pulling her legs back and in so doing her skirt crept over her knees. Carlos saw the bronzed beauty of her thighs, the fluffy shadow. She heard Carlos unbuckle his belt, the thud of his knife falling on the ground....

"Cruel," was the first thing that Laura said to Carlos when she awoke from her sexual ecstasy. "Damned cruel."

"Did you enjoy it?"

Laura nodded modestly.

He kissed her eyes. She kissed the tip of his nose. And they were two again.

If only their backgrounds could harmonize as their bodies did.

Alone with his thoughts, Carlos was an unhappy man. And he could not share his unhappiness with anyone because he refused to sadden Laura with it and, except for her, there was no one else he would confide in. He could not even unburden himself to Anteiro, who, ever since the argument in the gun room, had been following Carlos about with the mien of a faithful dog unjustly kicked.

Laura admired Carlos' will-power. Carlos was an outcast in his own house, on his own ranch. No one better than Laura knew how warm and impulsive Carlos was. Yet, once challenged, he became a silent man who seemed to fear his own fury.

Laura knew that Carlos could easily have taken the bullwhip down from the dining-room wall and played his grandfather's role, the master of the olden times. But Carlos was an honest man. He knew he had done wrong by his people and he must redeem himself or suffer the consequences.

Thinking of Carlos' honesty, Laura was filled with a creeping uneasiness, a vague sense of guilt, as though she were not quite as sure of her love for Carlos as he was of his love for her.

Laura had moments of soul searching. At times she felt like a tourist having lots of fun with the natives, of whom Carlos was her favorite. At times she felt as though she were Carlos' wife, trying to adjust herself to a new life. Those were the times when she caught herself thinking of America, of New York, of her friends—and longing for them. It was a novel feeling to be longing for something, somebody, hitherto unappreciated. Even disdained.

Distance must indeed make the heart grow fonder, Laura told herself lightly.

Betta's unyielding attitude against Carlos drew Laura closer to him. Laura would have fallen in love with Carlos now merely to antagonize Betta, the high priestess of the house.

Laura no longer gave a hoot whether Betta knew anything about her love affair with Carlos. She hoped Betta did. She believed Betta did—or how else explain Betta's abrupt change of heart, from the affectionate "daughter" to the biting *"senhora."* Laura grinned maliciously at the thought of dethroning Betta.

❧ ❧ ❧

For the first time since the night of the dance, Betta was fairly happy this early evening as she paid her daily visit to Uncle Rosario and saw that the Negress Mullô had removed the bandage from his head.

In her new mood Betta failed to notice the pungent odor of salves and ointments that hung in the room so strongly you could feel it on your tongue.

Uncle Rosario was sitting up in bed looking gauntly sinister; half of his head had been shaven clean and the hair on that side was now a coarse fuzz.

Clad in white and barefooted, calm of mien and relaxed of body, the Negress Mullô was like a greatly magnified native Samaritan as she sat by her patient's bedside.

Betta took a low-burning lamp from a round table in the corner and carried it to the bed, held it close to Uncle Rosario's head as she bent down and looked at the freshly healed wound over his left temple. The healed wound looked like a five-inch-long red worm. Still squirming.

"A rare work of nature," Betta said.

"It has mended properly," said the Negress Mullô.

"Will it leave a scar?"

"Life is marked with scars," said the Negress Mullô.

"And how is the rest of the broken body, Compadre Rosario?"

"Very well, Nhâ Betta."

"Well enough," said the Negress Mullô.

"Well enough to be taken to the races soon?" Betta asked.

"Who knows," said the Negress Mullô.

"We could take Compadre Rosario to the races in a buckboard," Betta said. "It would do him good, the air and the people."

The Negress Mullô said nothing.

"The quicker Compadre Rosario leaves the bed and the shade for his legs and the sun, the sooner he will regain his strength, I think," Betta went on.

The Negress Mullô dug between her deep thighs, produced an earthen tumbler of shrub tea which she had been warming with her vitality, and handed it to Uncle Rosario. "Gather strength," she told him.

"What do you say?" Betta said, returning to her idea.

"This," said the Negress Mullô. "You cannot force the rhythm of time."

Betta looked away. She feared the Negress Mullô would look into her eyes and be able to read her mind.

Exiled from the *casa grande,* and avoided just as much as Carlos was, Alma spent much of her time staring at her sharpened dagger and eating her heart out in brooding indecision. Also fighting off Antonio's increasingly brutal demands that she yield to him.

It came to Alma that Betta's behavior toward her had changed of late. Betta had made the first move, too—greeting Alma, gruffly, to be sure, but still greeting her whenever she met her, and asking her how she was and whether she needed anything.

And while Betta's mouth said one thing her eyes said another. Betta's eyes told Alma, *She is just as bad as you are. But I prefer you to her. You are one of us. But do not do anything foolish, Alma. You have been quiet too long. I know what you are thinking. But do not do it. Do not do it.*

In the dark in her bed Alma saw Betta's eyes talking to her, and she wondered if that was Betta's way of telling her, challenging her, to execute her revenge. The doubt stayed Alma's poised hand. Alma was not going to lend her hand to Betta, whom she had good reasons not to love. If she lent her hand to Betta, Alma felt, she would be carrying out Betta's revenge and not her own. It was of bitter comfort to Alma to know that Betta was suffering just as much as she was.

Laura was ill during the night. An attack of indigestion, she thought. Rather bad, too. Candle in hand Laura went to Uncle Rosario's room and awakened the Negress Mullô, who was sleeping on a mat on the floor.

The Negress Mullô took Laura's temperature by slipping her hand between Laura's thighs. Then she smelled Laura's breath. She disdained to look at Laura's tongue; milk, the Negress Mullô averred, coated the tongue worse than an upset stomach. Finally she completed the examination by placing her ear to Laura's belly and listening for symptomatic rumblings. Then the Negress Mullô went into consultation with herself, from which she emerged saying, "Indigestion? Maybe. Go back to bed now. I will brew a pot of camomile and bring it to you." Which, the Negress Mullô did as she did everything else, with love.

As Laura was sipping the strongly scented beverage, the Negress Mullô said, "When do you respond to the moon?"

After a moment's reckoning Laura said, "I'm not due yet."

"Maybe you are about to respond to the moon before your time."

"It'd be rather unusual. I'm usually on time," Laura said.

"Well," said the Negress Mullô, "the moon is the only one who can force the rhythm of a woman."

The next morning Laura was feeling fine again, except for a bad taste in her mouth.

Carlos and Anteiro rode out on business. For three days Laura missed Carlos hungrily. She wandered through the house like a shadow. She stayed in her room feeling like a prisoner. Laura did not use the three days to take an inventory of her present life. She preferred to waste her energy waiting for Carlos' return.

Carlos and Anteiro were riding to Las Pombas to supervise the selection of the cattle destined for the Planalto and thence to the slaughterhouses in Cuiaba and points south.

Carlos and Anteiro had grown used to working together with a minimum of words. Neither liked it. But they had tacitly agreed that it was better to be silent than to start a conversation that would inevitably degenerate into the same bitter argument.

Anteiro had been sneaking sidelong glances at Carlos for the past mile or so, as if he wished to say something but could not bring himself to speak.

Now he spoke. "Are you going to lead the herds to the Planalto?"

"No," Carlos said.

"You are not going because of the races?"

Carlos looked at Anteiro as if he did not know what the man was talking about.

"The races, man," Anteiro said angrily. "The *main race* you should have been training for."

"Find somebody else to represent the *casa grande* in the main race," Carlos told Anteiro.

"Fear has broken your back for good, man. Everybody thinks so."

"Does it mean that much to you what the others think of me?"

"It means so much that I wish I was dead, man."

"You mean you wish *I* was dead."

"Truly so, man. That would put an end to the make believe."

"The make *what?*"

"You pretending to be a coward."

"You don't believe I'm a coward?"

"No more than you believe you are."

"Does Betta feel as you do about me?"

"Listen, son. Betta told me she might find it in her heart to forgive you if you truly suffered with the sickness of fear. But she also knows that your cowardice is a make believe. She has known it since the day she found her nightshirt under your pillow, and that is why, she told me, she did not make your bed until after you had returned her nightshirt to the guest."

"That was thoughtful of her," Carlos said sarcastically.

"No," said Anteiro. "That was not it. Betta did that because she did not want you to know that she knew and could still go on living under the same roof with you. Son, you should not have broken the law of hospitality. That was even worse than you pretending to be a coward. Because, that was a fact. And, son, was it worth it?"

"Yes. I love her."

"But she is a married woman."

"She's *not* married, Anteiro. She's divorced."

"What does that mean?"

"What?"

"Divorce."

"Never mind."

"Now you are lying to me also. Stop lying, son. Stop pretending. Your pretending is causing much trouble in the house. Me and Betta are fighting all the time now. We do not sleep together any more. All over the ranch old friendships are breaking up. Two men are down with knife wounds. Come, son, *my* son. invite the bullfighter for a ride to the Mountain of Sadness."

"No, Anteiro. I can't do that. I can't try to kill a man who has done me no true harm."

Anteiro shook his head. "I am full of sad confusion," he said. "When I listen to you, Carlos, I understand you. But then there is Betta, and so many others like Betta."

"Does Betta hate our guest, Anteiro?"

"With a hidden intensity."

"Do you?"

"You say you love her. How can I hate her? If I hated her I would be hating you too, no? I hate nobody, except the bull-fighter. I suffer with an urge to take him by the ankles, turn him upside down and tear him apart."

"You know you can't do that."

"I know the law of the land."

"Do you want me to ride in the main race, Anteiro?"

"Yes, son."

"What pony shall I ride?"

"Carlos, you have even forgotten that you have already picked your pony, Tordilho. I have had one of the boys gallop him regularly."

"Is the track the same?"

"No. Not this year. The elders have changed it. It is an incredibly bad track. Become friendly with it before the race."

Laura welcomed Carlos back as a loving wife would welcome her beloved husband returning from the wars. She accompanied Carlos to the river, the same evening he arrived, carrying his fresh linen, soap and towel.

Betta was thunderstruck. She first looked like a deaf-and-dumb exclamation point. Then like a banshee interrogation mark. *They are going too far,* she screamed in her mind. If what she suspected were to happen now, at the river, Betta was going to confront Laura with it and throw her out of the house, even if she had to use force to do it.

Her eyes drilling burning holes into Laura's and Carlos' backs as they walked happily towards the river, Betta bribed two boys to follow the couple and report to her on the situation.

Betta waited for the boys' report as if she had swallowed sulphuric acid. The boys were back about three quarters of an hour later. Betta grabbed them and dragged them into her room. She locked the door and stood the boys against the wall.

"Speak up."

First one boy and then the other boy spoke up, using exactly the same words.

Well, they said, while the *patrão* was washing himself, the green-eyed woman kept walking back and forth some distance from the bathing place, singing a strange song in a strange language, and now and then breaking into a dance.

Betta pounced on that. "What kind of dance?"

Well, the green-eyed woman had her arms out and turned around and around, slowly, as if she were dreaming. "Maybe she is a little crazy, no, Nhâ Betta?"

"No. She is not crazy. Go away now, both of you. And keep your mouths shut, *comprende?*"

Betta did not eat at the dining table that night. She was not quite sure whether her shame was due to her action, or its subsequent failure.

Carlos rode over the race track.

The track was marked with cow skulls mounted on wooden stakes. Two skulls marked the dangerous spots, where man and mount struggled together to overcome permanent oblivion. In the sun now the weather-bleached skulls looked like lyres. The track this year was the worst Carlos remembered.

The contestants rode bareback, barefoot, spurless and whipless. Their talent or gift lay in their hands. And never in the whole history of the ranch was a rider found guilty or even suspected of foul play.

The main race, the Boa Vista, the one Carlos rode to represent the *casa grande,* was a seven mile cross-jungle ride that included wading the river at a point where its bed collapsed and formed a treacherous well.

The main prize, the Boa Vista, was an enormous pair of solid gold spurs. These were coveted not so much for the gold as for the honor of being able to hand them down from generation to generation.

The day of the races dawned clear and mild. A brisk breeze kept the heat from settling.

Throughout the night, from near and far, on foot, on mount, in all kinds of vehicles, and wearing their feast-day clothes, the people had been converging upon the *casa grande* from all points of the ranch.

They arrived, dismounted and bivouacked in the nearby fields where they renewed old friendships. Then, as the sun rose, they assembled before the main entrance of the house. There Carlos welcomed them, Anteiro distributed alcohol to the men, and Betta saw to it that the women's needs were satisfied.

The children, the very small ones, arrived stuffed in twos and threes in each of two baskets strapped like packsaddles to old mules and mares.

The younger boys had been told by their parents that later in life they would be given a chance to ride in the races, maybe even in the main race, and therefore they must behave like men today. Most of the boys wore boots and spurs borrowed from elder brothers, and carried bull whips too long and too heavy for their arms to manage.

One glance at the man with whom he was shaking hands, and Carlos knew that the news of his cowardice had reached the farthest hamlet. They did not exactly look at Carlos with unfriendly eyes, but rather with searching eyes, eyes that sought to find the feature of cowardice in his face, eyes that said, *I see nothing different in his face. Maybe it isn't true. Let's wait and see.* And then they went about gathering the news from the home folk.

CHAPTER FOURTEEN

WEARING her riding outfit, Laura came into the dining room and found Carlos sitting at his usual place. Although it was early morning it was hot in the dining room; the door that led outside was closed and would not be opened until late in the afternoon.

Carlos was alone, sipping black coffee and smoking. He was dressed to ride, a heavy white cotton shirt and pants and a black sash wound tightly around his waist. His insides would take a mighty bouncing by-and-by.

Making sure they were alone, Laura kissed Carlos on the head and sat down next to him.

The service in the dining room was disrupted this morning. Already cooks and kitchen girls and extra hands were busy preparing the evening meal when extra tables would be sec up in the dining room and only God knew how many guests would be eating.

When a girl, Amaya, strayed into the dining room, Laura ordered her breakfast. An egg omelet.

"Good heavens, what is this?" Laura cried when the girl returned with a fried chicken.

As Carlos looked questioningly, at Amaya her rather vacant stare reminded him that she was a little deaf and must have misunderstood.

Carlos explained to Laura who smiled at the girl and said it was all right and thanked her very much.

"Will you help me eat it?" Laura asked Carlos.

He shook his head.

Laura twisted loose one of the chicken's legs and started to eat with her fingers. The chicken's skin was golden brown and crispy, the meat tender. Laura ate with a good appetite.

"What's the matter, darling?" Laura put the drumstick down on her plate. "You're very quiet this morning. You aren't worried about the outcome of the race, are you?"

"No. I'm going to win."

"I'm sure you are, darling."

"Not because I have a good pony and I'm a good rider. They are all good ponies and good riders. The best on the ranch. But because I want to win, and I'm going to win!"

"I understand." Then, with a smile, "I'm broke, darling. May I borrow some money from you to bet on you?"

"If you do," Carlos said, "yours will be the only bet riding on me."

Laura could have kicked herself for trying to joke. She lost interest in the chicken.

Betta came into the dining room, stopped at one end of the table. She stood there like a storm cloud.

I'm not going to speak to her until she speaks to me first, Laura thought to herself.

"You are eating fowl in the morning like a man," Betta said with an unsmiling face. "You are a woman of great hunger."

"It's the wonderful fresh air that does it, Betta. Also your wonderful hospitality that makes me feel at home. At home I always eat meat in the morning."

"With your *husband?*"

"With or without him."

"Eat more of the fowl then."

"No, thank you, Betta. I'm quite satisfied now." *I know what you're thinking and I know that you know and I think you're a damn fool for making it worse. And I'm even a bigger fool than you for letting you upset me.* "May I please have a cup of coffee, Betta?"

"Meat and coffee do not go together, *senhora.* Maybe a glass of the red wine?"

You so and so. "That's a splendid idea, Betta. A glass of wine'll do nicely. Will you bring it to me, please?" *You're a shrewd, domineering woman.* And jealous too. *But don't make me angry, Betta, or I'll make up my mind right now and marry your boy. And where will you be then?* "Thank you, Betta," Laura said taking the glass of wine. *Mud in your eyes, Betta.* Laura drank, looking at Carlos over the rim of her glass. He winked at her.

Anteiro came in to take Laura to the races. It was then that Betta said she would not go to the races. Betta left the dining room without even wishing Carlos the customary *sorte.* Good luck.

Laura stood up. Carlos rose also.

"*Sorte,*" Laura said and put out her hand. Carlos took it. "Bless you, darling," she whispered.

"*Sorte,* son," Anteiro said.

"Thank you, man," said Carlos. They grinned at each other.

Anteiro and Laura left the room. Carlos sat down again. He lighted a fresh cigarette from the one burning in the dish before him.

The last preliminary race was over. The noise at O Brejo, the starting point, was deafening. When Carlos rode to the main line for the Boa Vista race, the riders, thirteen of them, mostly professional bronco busters, each representing a sector of the ranch, avoided Carlos' eyes and drew their ponies so close together that Carlos had to place himself far on the outside.

Next to Carlos on his nervously prancing pony was Rico. Next to Rico was Ricardo. They were two of Carlos' best bronco busters and his friends since boyhood. Now they exchanged no hellos.

And now that all the riders were at the line, the crowd let out a cry of impatience that swelled into a thunderous chorus.

A man with a black poncho wrapped around his neck like a scarf, as if he were cold in the blazing sun, stood up in his stirrups, raised his rifle in the air and cried, "Are the riders ready?"

The crowd quieted down.

The riders stretched themselves upon their mounts as they would upon a woman and almost with the same expectancy, reins twisted around their outthrust hands, their bare feet fairly hugging their mounts' rumps.

The crowd held its breath.

A rifle shot rang out and the ponies were off. The crowd exploded.

Carlos grabbed the lead a few strides after breaking from the line. Half a length behind him in second place were Rico and Ricardo. Here the route was good and Carlos rode well, with Rico and Ricardo close behind him.

Necks pumping, tails stiff and straight out behind them, the ponies came to the river. The riders lifted them into the water and they started to swim across, towards the well, Carlos' pony swimming between Rico's and Ricardo's. It came to Carlos that Rico and Ricardo were squeezing him between them, forcing him to fight for room. But Carlos at once dismissed the suspicion, although the same tactic was repeated when they came to the treacherous well; Carlos' pony neighed nervously for room to fight the swift current and finally gave up and fell a length behind.

Rico and Ricardo broke on top as soon as they reached the other shore. But again Carlos quickly took the lead, although he had to swing wide to get around Rico's pony, now unmistakably hogging the track. Hardly ever slacking their furious pace, they rode three and a half miles—over open rocky ground, where the ponies' steel-shod hoofs seemed to be on fire with myriad sparks; through a pretzel-like course in the thicket, swinging their ponies left and right lest they smash their heads against trees; now lifting their ponies over obstacles and now pulling them up sharply as they came to the spots marked with two cow skulls; now holding their ponies up as the route grew steeper and steeper; then fairly straddling their ponies' necks as the route turned steeply uphill. By now both men and mounts were covered with mire. The men talked to their mounts with voice, heels and hands; the mounts understanding, responded, their bodies coiling, uncoiling and recoiling like springs as they gathered their strength for yet another spurt that never ended.

A few riders had already dropped out, their mounts undertrained for the route.

Now the route swerved sharply to the west, ran through a lime grove, down a sandy embankment, up onto the open road again, back into the thicket, with Carlos still in the lead. Here the track was good again and Rico and Ricardo gained ground, drew abreast of Carlos and rode close together. Carlos looked from one to the other, quickly, and it dawned on him that the two friends had all along been keeping the same pace, doing the same thing. Suddenly now they spurted ahead and, riding knee to knee, barred his way, forcing him to swing wide around them. And no sooner did he have the lead again than they were racing at his sides, crowding him between them, suddenly breaking apart and as suddenly closing in on him again, in an effort to throw his pony out of step and send him crashing to the ground.

Now Carlos was sure that Rico and Ricardo were riding for a purpose, and it was not winning. Again they crowded him behind them. Carlos swung his pony around the outside rider and cut back to the inside. Rico did the same thing and broke on top, with Ricardo now riding so close beside Carlos that the head of Carlos' pony was fairly on the rump of Rico's pony, while Ricardo prevented Carlos from swinging out.

Carlos motioned Ricardo to give him room. Ricardo rode closer to him, if possible. Carlos fought to swing free from the trap. They gave him no ground. Risking his pony's legs and his own neck, Carlos lifted and swung his pony against Ricardo's. The two ponies whined, swayed apart, were brought close together again as the riders held them straight on the bit. The riders fought in silence. Now Carlos jerked at the reins, hard and fast, threw his pony out of step so that Ricardo gained a few strides and thus cleared the way. Then Carlos swung around him, gained on him and passed him.

"Rico," Ricardo called.

Rico looked back over his shoulder and as Carlos came flying past him he reached out and grabbed Carlos' foot and lifted him off his pony's back. Carlos went crashing and rolling into the bush.

Rico and Ricardo came in together at the finish, last.

The crowd showed no interest in Carlos dropping out of the race.

Rico and Ricardo rode up to Anteiro, who was still trying to find an answer to Laura's insistent, "Where's Carlos? What happened to him?" They told Anteiro that Carlos had met with an accident.

"Rotten luck," Laura cried.

"Where is he now?" Anteiro asked.

"We will take you there," they said and looked at each other as if they had sealed their doom.

"You ride back home alone," Anteiro told Laura.

"Of course not!" Laura told him. "I'm coming along."

"Let us ride," Anteiro said.

They found Carlos sitting by the edge of the path removing thorns from his hands. His left shirt sleeve was rent and there was a bleeding scratch the whole length of his arm.

"What happened, Carlos?" Laura said dismounting and running to him. "Are you hurt?" She knelt down beside him.

Anteiro did not dismount. Anteiro sat in the saddle studying the ground.

Carlos looked up at Rico and Ricardo. They met his eyes, not defiantly, Carlos saw, but resignedly; they knew that Carlos could have them kicked off the ranch for having broken one of the ranch's most honored rules, or killed them himself for the personal injury they had done him.

"Find my mount," Carlos said to Anteiro.

Anteiro rode away and soon was lost in the thicket.

Then Carlos stood up. "Speak up, man," he said to Rico. "Why did you throw me?"

"We could not let *you* win the Boa Vista Prize, *patrão*."

Carlos lashed out wildly. Rico went down, blood spurting from a deep gash over his left eye. Laura shuddered as she saw the killer's look in Carlos' eyes. Carlos bent down, grabbed Rico by the chest and pulled him up. "Why not?" he asked.

"We are not afraid of the consequences," Ricardo said.

Carlos let go of Rico and grabbed Ricardo.

And Rico repeated, "We are not afraid of the consequences."

So they thought they were upholding the honor of the ranch by having prevented a coward from winning the Boa Vista prize.

They had placed the honor of the ranch above their lives. Such blind loyalty disarmed Carlos. He let go of Ricardo, told them to go away, to hurry, before he forgot himself again.

They mounted their ponies and rode off. They rode off looking back at Carlos, telling him with their eyes that they were sorry for what they had done, but would do it again.

"Don't tell Anteiro what they did," Carlos warned Laura.

"Of course not, darling."

With Laura between Carlos and Anteiro they rode back home in silence.

Strangely enough, Anteiro never once asked Carlos what had happened to him.

Carlos went to his room, picked up a fresh change of clothes, slipped into his sandals and walked to the river, limping on his left leg.

Carlos felt tired within. The silent struggle to control himself before his people was playing hard with his impulsive, fiery temperament. Carlos was so tired now that he did not even feel the pains and aches in his body. Ruefully he congratulated himself for merely having hit Rico. For a moment it had been touch-and-go. Laura had seen the urge to kill in Carlos' eyes.

But the unvented rage remained with Carlos, seething within him, even now that he was soaking his body in the river.

Laura had been caught in the subway at the rush hour more than once. But compared with what was going on in the dining room this evening, she decided, the crush in the concrete bowels of New York was like a gentle waltz. The crowd in the dining room overflowed far outside.

The walls were lined with extra tables, mostly planks on trestles. There was not one vacant seat. At a table next to the credenza, there was a proud father who had his young son straddling his shoulders, and he kept handing the food up to him. The boy used his father's head as his own private table. Many were eating standing up, many more sitting down on the floor.

Whenever an old-timer came into the dining room a chair or a stool or even an upturned box was squeezed in at the main table for him in deference to his age and long service on the ranch.

The menu ran from baskets filled with hard-boiled Tartaruga Grande eggs, a very fecund turtle, to rabbit stew, served in trough-like receptacles on wheels. There were fried chickens, roasted pigs and calves. Also fish, mostly Dorados. Heaps of fish, baked or broiled as it was brought into the kitchen fresh from the river. There was something like a bucket brigade between the kitchen and the river, only the buckets, which were baskets, were filled with fish. Mounds of vegetables, cooked and raw. Giant round loaves of bread, white and *rosca,* piled in the center of the tables. They tossed the loaves to each other with uncanny aim. It was an enormous joke when somebody inevitably got a black eye or a bloody nose from one of the flying wheat missiles. And there were all kinds of fruit—bananas by the bunches, baskets of tangerines and pineapples, bushels of nuts.

Also in the dining room, there was an unruly mob of strong smells bullying its way through the flavorsome odors of baked, roasted, boiled, broiled, and highly seasoned food. It was a combination of tobacco smoke, the pungent homemade perfume the girls were wearing in the innocent belief that the stronger the perfume the more alluring they would be, the smell of flushed young skin, the tang of sweating mature bodies, the breath of healthy belching, the smell of greased boots and leather. Also the sourish smell of the little ones soiling themselves. That, and the animal-like electricity discharged from the eyes and mouths and gestures of everyone. When the noise abated the smells grew stronger.

Betta was outside supervising the feeding of those who had not been quick enough to find a seat in the dining room.

Bull whip in hand, Anteiro was shadowing Antonio to protect him from harm. Anteiro was not so much worried that some young hothead would take it upon himself to show his loyalty to the ranch. Anteiro feared the vengeance of the old-timers. They were a stubborn, touchy lot.

Valente, the reformed bandit and chief sheriff, was stationed in the dining room. The other three sheriffs were patroling the grounds outside.

Now and then Valente would tap a boisterous drunkard on the shoulder and in brotherly fashion remind him he was a guest of the house. Or he would tap a too-boisterous drunkard on the shoulder and invite him outside for a breath of fresh air, and turn him over to the other sheriffs.

Every child in the dining room was sitting on some older person's lap. Little Mira, wearing an ankle-length white dress with lace and frills, was sitting on Laura's lap. Laura was in her usual place next to Carlos. Laura looked at Carlos and she was sorry for him. She felt as though Carlos was in some kind of a pillory.

Carlos sat at the table tonight because it was his duty, as all the present guests were from distant parts of the ranch and had been given preference over the home folk.

Bursts of women's happy screams, of men's laughter, of children's squealing, kept the dining room in a turmoil. But at moody moments the dining room would also be very quiet, as if the guests remembered the same thing and shared the same thought at the same time. They would then sit in mute reproach, casting accusing glances at Carlos, who pretended not to notice.

In spite of the good spirits prevailing in the dining room, Carlos knew that his presence at the table was putting a damper on the guests' true festive mood and he was waiting for a favorable chance to sneak away unnoticed.

Now commotion broke out in that region of the table occupied by two toothless old men with flowing white hair and beards. One of the old-timers was brandishing his long knife at three young men who were obviously drunk and eager to show off.

In his anger the old-timer imagined himself to be a young man of twenty again, and he was challenging the three young men to step outside. He would fight the three of them at once, he said in thundering tones. In the same tones he defined them as disrespectful puppies. He declared that he spat in the milk that had nourished them, and went through the motion.

The three young men wanted to know if the old-timer had a son or sons. The old-timer, as if stung by a snake, shouted he did not need a son or sons to fight his fights.

The three young men laughed and laughed at the old-timer, who by now was about ready to commit a bloody feat. He was holding his knife flat against his forearm, the point touching his elbow, which meant he was going to toss it either from the side or underhand.

Valente, who had been squinting at the three young men from a distance, now came over to them and tapped them hard on the shoulder and thumbed them outside. After a tense moment's hesitation, the three young men got up and walked out of the dining room. The old-timer wanted to follow them outside and settle the question. But Valente spoke to the old-timer in soothing tones and the old-timer allowed himself to be appeased.

Carlos never knew what the commotion was about. He took advantage of it, though. He patted Laura's knee under the table, got up and sneaked away.

On his way to his room Carlos passed by the chapel.

The chapel was still open and crowded with pious women from distant parts of the ranch. They took this day to do their praying in a proper place of worship. Many of them had come to the races only to pray in the chapel. The happy experience lasted them the whole year.

Prudencia, the dressmaker, was in charge of the chapel. She saw to it that virgins and married women were properly veiled, and that they did not use the chapel as a place to exchange gossip or indulge in any other irreligious activities.

Laura left the table and the dining room soon after Carlos. Holding little Mira by the hand, Laura mingled with the crowds.

There was music, dancing, contests of strength, storytelling. Each feature was crowded with participants and spectators. An old Negro woman was telling fortunes. She was surrounded by earnest virgins. The boys were having their own special contest: knife throwing. They removed their shoes, spread the toes of one foot on the ground and tossed the knife between the toes. Except for two boys, who looked like proud bantams, all of the other boys had bleeding wounds on their right feet. Laura asked them if they were crazy. No, they told her, surprised. They were just training, that was all.

As always, the best patronized attraction was the cockfights. The betting was heavy and the crowd delirious as the mad-eyed, steel-spurred birds fought one another to death. The sight revolted Laura. She asked one of the men what they did with the dead cocks. They buried them, naturally. How? Laura wanted to know. In a coffin, naturally. Were they given a religious service too? *Answer that one,* Laura thought. Naturally. By whom? Their owners. *You win.*

Dragging the sleepy-eyed, heavy-legged child by the hand, Laura went from place to place until she turned the child over to a woman of the house.

Then she took a short walk down the road and finally retired to her room.

Even before she had lighted the lamp Laura felt someone was in her room. Then she saw Carlos sleeping in her bed. He had all his clothes on except for his sandals. He looked tired. He was frowning in his sleep. Maybe the fall from the pony had hurt him more than he liked to admit.

Laura had seen Carlos drinking rather heavily at the table, and now she wondered whether he had mistaken her room for his, or just come to her room to wait for her, something which he had never done before.

Laura had been up since early morning. It had been a long hectic day and she fell asleep almost at once, in spite of the noises reaching into her room from within and without the house.

Laura awoke suddenly, crying out in pain and fear. Carlos was beating her up. In his sleep Carlos was fighting Rico and Ricardo. He was thrashing about wildly and had miraculously missed hitting Laura's face.

Laura shook Carlos violently by the shoulder, pulled his hair in an effort to awaken him. She failed. She took his flushed face in her hands and kissed him, softly called him by name. And Carlos quieted down and slept peacefully in Laura's arms.

Two days after the races, four old men mounted their horses at the four points of the ranch and rode toward the cemetery.

They sat in old-fashioned saddles with bell-shaped wooden stirrups which they gripped with the big toe and the next. They wore white kerchiefs wrapped around their heads, tied at the back, and narrow-brimmed black hats over the kerchiefs. Their ponchos were waist length, the sides rolled and tied over their shoulders with leather strings. Each carried a ball-tipped lasso wound around his waist, and a two-barreled pistol.

Grim of mien and hard of body they rode through the day and into the evening, coming within sight of the cemetery as the sun was setting on the bluish-purple horizon.

The cemetery lay on a hilltop east of Dois Pointos and in the sun's spent glow the hill rose golden and green on the plain. It looked like an upstanding ripe pineapple with its crest of stiff leaves.

Night caught up with the four old men as they were beginning to climb the hill from four different sides.

Their rendezvous was at the Tamer's grave.

The first to arrive was Vovo Olivera. Vovo Mello followed him. Then came Vovo Juaru. And finally Vovo Augusto.

As they arrived they exchanged solemn greetings and sat down by the Tamer's grave. They sat and smoked long maize-leaf cigarettes.

"*Bom,*" said Vovo Mello. "Let us share our thoughts."

"The man Antonio who has broken the law of the land is still alive," said Vovo Juaru. "I have told my grandson Rico to provoke him and shoot him down. But I know he will not do it—not out of fear, but in obedience to the law of the land."

"I have told my grandson Ricardo to be ready to provoke the man and knife him through," said Vovo Olivera. "But I too know that he will not do it, for the same reason. And that is why we are meeting tonight, to agree to break the law of the land and kill the man ourselves."

"He must die," said Vovo Augusto.

"True," said Vovo Mello. "But not so painlessly as all that."

Moved by the same wish, the four old men turned and looked at the Mountain of Sadness.

In the moonlight the distant mountain looked like a huge artichoke. They looked at the mountain longingly, but then they bowed their heads, oppressed by the same thought: they were too old to fight in such a place.

"With your permission," said Vovo Mello. "I must think."

The others set themselves to wait.

These old men knew how to wait. They had spent half of their long lives waiting or watching. For long ago, when the Tamer had been but a young man, he had used them as a picket fence for his herds. Those were the days when a yard of barbed wire was worth a dozen men. And these veterans had spent half of their lives alone in the open, each watching one spot. They had been the foot soldiers of the ranch. They would not have deserted their posts even in the face of a cattle stampede. And they suffered with the sickness of pride. Their sense of honor had ben instilled into them by the Tamer himself. They were the elders and considered themselves the keepers of the ranch's honor. Now they met to decide the worst way to vindicate the insult Carlos had received at Antonio's hands and allowed to go unpunished, thereby disgracing them all.

"I have an opinion," said Vovo Mello raising his head. "She must die too."

"She is a woman," said Vovo Juaru.

"That is why she must die first," said Vovo Mello. "Experience has taught me that no man can make love to another man's woman unless she wants him to. For it is the woman who holds the bait. The man is but a fish. Therefore, the hand that holds the bait and throws it to the fish has got to be cut off first. She dies first."

"No," said Vovo Augusto. "They die together, and it must be a painful death, an example to all the daughters of the ranch not to break the law of the land."

"Yes. An exemplary death," Vovo Olivera said.

"I have the death for them," said Vovo Mello.

"Speak."

"We shall lasso them together, lash them to a plank and float them in the river so that the piranhas can eat them alive, at leisure, bit by bit."

"That is the proper death," said Vovo Olivera.

"When?" asked Vovo Juaru.

"Tomorrow at this time."

"Where?"

"At her place."

"Will he be there?"

"We shall wait until he comes."

One after the other the four old men drew their knees under their short ponchos, dropped their heads over their knees, and were silent.

They looked like tombstones.

CHAPTER FIFTEEN

IT WAS NOW the evening of the next day.

Although every seat at the table was taken, the dining room was like an oasis of solitude compared with the carnival it had been the night of the races.

Betta noticed how well Laura was eating and drinking. Betta was sure that Laura and Carlos were touching knees under the table. Betta knew that Laura and Carlos had been together under the same roof again because Carlos' bed had not been slept in the night of the races. Betta's face was ashen.

Anteiro, sitting in his usual place next to Betta, to whom he hardly spoke, reached for another hunk of roasted meat and was tearing at it with his teeth when a kitchen girl came hurrying to him and began to whisper in his ear.

Anteiro looked at Carlos as he listened to the girl. Then he dropped the mangled hunk of meat on his plate and left the dining room through the door that led out to the courtyard.

He heard a whistle that sounded like the tearing of canvas. He followed the whistle and found Ricardo in the shadow of the eucalyptus trees.

"What is it that is so important?" Anteiro asked Ricardo.

"They are going to kill him tonight."

"Who?"

"The man called Antonio."

"How do you know that?"

"My grandfather told me to provoke the man and knife him through," Ricardo explained. "I told Rico about it. And Rico told me that his grandfather had told him to do the same thing, only with the gun. And then yesterday my grandfather mounted his horse and rode off. I became suspicious and followed him at a distance. Rico did the same thing, following his grandfather. And then we saw Vovo Mello and Vovo Augusto join them and decided to watch them. With the rising moon tonight they mounted their horses and rode off again. We followed them. They dismounted a mile from Alma's house. Then Rico and I decided they were going to ambush the man and kill him themselves. I left Rico watching them and I rode here to warn you."

"Why warn me?"

"Because you know the law of the land as well as any of us. No one can touch that man unless the master does that himself."

"True," Anteiro said. "So why did you not send for the master instead of sending for me?"

Ricardo looked at Anteiro, said nothing.

But Anteiro understood. He laid his huge hand on Ricardo's shoulder. "No, son. You are wrong," he said and shook Ricardo by the shoulder. "The master will not allow anyone else to do the killing for him. I will now send the master to you. And you will tell him what you told me. But do not tell him that I know, *comprende?*"

Riding Ricardo's horse, Carlos went past four knee-haltered horses grazing in the thicket about a mile from Alma's house.

When Carlos came in sight of Alma's house and saw the light burning in her bedroom, he dismounted and went on on foot. He was walking down the lane, hugging the edge, when something hit him in the back. He turned and saw Rico hiding behind a tree. Rico was surprised to see Carlos. He had mistaken him for Ricardo.

"Where are they?" Carlos asked.

"You know, *patrão?*"

"Where are they?"

"I lost them. For fear of being seen I was following them at too great a distance. They suddenly disappeared, like ants into the earth."

"I must find them before they do something foolish."

"Yes, *patrão.* The ranch would then believe that you had your own men doing the killing for you."

"I see that you understand, Rico. So I don't have to tell you to keep your mouth shut."

"I understand, *patrão.*"

"Where can they be, those old foxes?"

"They are hidden in the neighborhood, *patrão.* Somewhere in the neighborhood."

Carlos looked down the lane. Then he turned to Rico. "You'd better go before your grandfather finds out you're involved in this."

"He would kill me." And Rico disappeared.

Hugging the edge of the lane, Carlos walked down towards Alma's house. When he came abreast of Alma's house he stopped, then slowly started to cross the lane. Chills were running down his spine. He hoped the old men would not shoot. He thought of Laura. Maybe he would never see her again. What does a man think when he stands before a firing squad? Does he still hope? So did Carlos, as he walked on, as he put one foot before the other, his mouth feeling as if it were full of cotton.

As Carlos reached the middle of the lane he heard a swiftly approaching swishing sound, and then he was whipped across his torso and across his ankles. He saw the balls of the higher lasso revolving against each other around his chest, pinning his arms down to his sides, while the other lasso was drawing his ankles tightly together. For a moment he stood, swaying, and then he dropped. At once the four old men piled on top of him, and one of them, Vovo Mello, while trying to gag him, recognized him.

"*Patrão.*"

"*Patrão,*" echoed the others.

"Be quick," Carlos told them. "Unlasso me before Alma comes out and tells the whole ranch that I hired four old men to do the killing for me."

They unlassoed Carlos quickly.

"Come away," Carlos told them.

The four old men followed Carlos down the lane, into the thicket. Carlos stopped and faced them. He rubbed his arms as he spoke. "Four old men," he said looking from one to the other, "who are too old to remember that no one can fight my fights have taken it upon themselves to dishonor the ranch throughout this country."

"*Patrão—*" began Vovo Juaru.

"Shut up."

"No, *patrão.* I will not shut up. It is you who have dishonored the ranch," said Vovo Juaru.

"I can dishonor what's mine," Carlos told him.

"What is yours is ours by the law of loyalty," said Vovo Mello.

"True," Carlos said. "Except for my personal affairs."

"The only personal affairs on this ranch is when man and woman take one another," said Vovo Augusto. "We share and share alike, in happiness and sorrow. In honor and dishonor, *comprende, patrão?*"

"I do. And now it's my turn to share your dishonor. Four old men doing the killing for me."

"There is no more dishonor to be shared," said Vovo Olivera. "You have dishonored us completely, even as a drunk cannot become drunker when he is already drunk."

Carlos knew he could not successfully argue this point with the four old men. They religiously believed every word they said. It was part of their lives. It was the ranch speaking. And Carlos tried to bluff them.

"True," he said. "I have dishonored you. And I'll make amends for it."

"Are you going to fight him then, *patrão?*" the four old men asked together.

"No," Carlos said. "I'll be in the saddle at sunrise, on my way to Cuiaba—to sell the ranch."

Vovo Mello was the first to recover. "You are going to sell us?"

"You are not my slaves," Carlos told him. "Those days are over. It's my ranch and I can sell it. And then it's up to you to stay here with the new rancher, or go away."

"You are robbing the earth from under us," Vovo Olivera said. "This is the only earth we know, feel for, and want to be buried in."

"In that case," said Carlos, "you can stay here with the new rancher, and be buried in this earth that you love so well."

"What would the Tamer say?" Vovo Juaru said.

"I don't know," Carlos told him. "Nor do you. But one thing I'm sure he'd say: 'You cannot walk out of the smoke into the flame.' And you can't protect the honor of the ranch by adding more dishonor to it—as you were about to do."

"Fight him, *patrão.*"

"I suffer with the sickness of fear," Carlos said simply.

The four old men were silent.

Then Vovo Olivera spoke. "Do not ride at sunrise, *patrão,*"

"Why not?"

"We shall share your sickness with you."

"Peacefully?"

"In silence and in shame. But without violence," said Vovo Augusto.

"All right," Carlos said. "Let's go. Come and spend the night at the *casa grande.*"

The four old men looked at each other.

Vovo Juaru spoke for the others. "Much obliged, *patrão.* But we already have a place to sleep."

"Where?"

"At the cemetery. By the Tamer's grave."

The Negress Mullô had an elephant's memory.

"*Senhora,*" she called to Laura one noontime as Laura passed by Uncle Rosario's room on her way to the dining room.

Laura stepped into the room.

Uncle Rosario was sitting in a rocking chair by the window. His neck looked much scrawnier than it really was because he was wearing a dark shirt much too large for him. And his face had a peculiar, naked look because his long mustache had been trimmed short. He had a partly healed fever blister on his upper lip. He seemed cheerful in his own solemn way.

"Congratulations," Laura said with feeling. "How are you, Rosario?"

"Very well," Rosario said.

"Well enough," said the Negress Mullô.

"At your service, *senhora,*" Uncle Rosario said, meaning, I'm ready to ride again.

"Not yet," said the Negress Mullô. "You still need to eat much red meat to thicken your blood. I will also put you on a steer-blood diet. Three glasses a day."

"I will be well in a week," Uncle Rosario said to Laura.

"This old man is a fool," said the Negress Mullô kindly. "This old man wants to force the rhythm of time."

Then she said to Laura, "Let us go outside. I want to make speech with you."

Laura said good-bye to Uncle Rosario. The Negress Mullô followed Laura outside and closed the door after her.

"What is it?" Laura asked.

"Breathe in my face," said the Negress Mullô.

"What the devil for?"

"Breathe." The Negress Mullô fairly stuck her nose into Laura's mouth. "Breathe." The Negress Mullô sniffed and sniffed at Laura's breath. "Your breath is healthy," she said.

"Thank you."

"You are late," she continued. "You have not yet responded to the moon as you said you would by this time."

Laura went cold from head to foot. In her lotus-land interlude she had lost all notion of time, and left the regularly recurrent time-marking event outside her consciousness.

I'm caught! was the first fearful thought that crossed Laura's mind. The word "abortion" followed instinctively.

"Yes, I'm late, Negress Mullô. But I've been late before. Lots of times," Laura said, forgetting that she had told the Negress Mullô she was usually on time.

"Woman to woman," said the Negress Mullô, "what say about man?"

"What am I supposed to say about man?"

"Do you enjoy man?"

"I'm a woman."

"Much woman, although you are small and frail," said the Negress Mullô who was thrice Laura's size from hip to hip. "Have you been sleeping with man?"

"Don't be absurd! And don't ask impertinent questions!"

The Negress Mullô smiled blandly. "A woman is like a cart wheel," she said. "It has got to be greased regularly or it will creak and squeak. Man greases woman. There is nothing impertinent for woman to sleep with man. What say?"

"I told you. Now let's drop the subject."

The Negress Mullô smiled blandly. She seemed to have seated her patience in a comfortable place and was ready to wait indefinitely.

I'm afraid, Laura was telling herself, seeing herself pregnant here, among these people, who all of a sudden lost their warm, exotic charm. Everything suddenly appeared cold to Laura, and everybody looked like a bad picture of himself.

"Negress Mullô, you're a midwife …"

The Negress Mullô waited.

"What should I do to bring it on?"

"Let us see, dear child," said the Negress Mullô, who was a wise woman. "Commence drinking the milk. Also swallow a raw egg every morning. Then eat the lean meat."

"What for?"

"They are good for a forming baby."

"You fool!" Laura walked away, back to her room.

Laura sat down on the edge of her bed, clasped her hands on her lap, and tried to think.

The rude awakening and revulsion were as violent as Laura's rapturous mood had been a short while ago. Had someone fired a shot close to her ear, she would not have reacted differently. She didn't want to be pregnant. But she was pregnant. She was pregnant without her consent. Her nature rebelled. She felt that Carlos had forced the pregnancy on her. She couldn't help hating him. Laura's reaction was no different from that of any other woman caught in the same predicament. Instinctively she blamed the man.

Between Laura and her emotional fancies, which she now mistook for honest thoughts, stood Carlos, also looking like a bad picture of himself.

I've been under his spell, Laura told herself, as though she were no longer the strong-willed, wide-eyed woman of the world, but an innocent milkmaid. This was an understandable reaction however, for the smarter the woman is, the harder she tries to excuse her *faux pas*. So it was with Laura now. And yet, even though she was working herself into her present mood, doubt was already pecking at the back of her mind. Already Laura knew, or at least sensed, that this was not her honest, final reaction. But like any woman in the throes of hysteria, Laura wallowed now in her present synthetic mood.

If I tell him I'm pregnant, he won't let me out of his sight any more. (Carlos himself could not have expressed it better.) *I'll be his prisoner until I have the child. It's his child and he'll want it whether I marry him or not. If I marry him I'll share the child with him, here. If I don't marry him I can go back home, without the child.*

I must go to William. Good heavens, I'd forgotten him. Will I tell him? No, of course not. Not now. I'll just visit with him, come back here and go back home. I must bring my child up among civilized people. Now Laura was starting to rationalize her flight, which was utterly incompatible with her nature. She had never run away from anything or anybody before, and down deep inside she knew she was rationalizing even now. But in her present mood she had to make these simple, friendly people appear like savages.

If I stay here, he'll bring up my child as his grandfather brought him up. He hates civilization. I won't stay here. I can't stay here. Nothing to do all day. Nothing at all. He told me so himself, the day he asked me to marry him. No theaters, no movies, no radio, no books, no newspapers, no one to talk to intelligently. I'd go crazy. I must get away. Then Laura thought, as if she were already back in America, *I'll write him. It's all right if he joins me. I'll marry him in America, if he stays in America. Now I want to be by myself, to get used to the idea of being pregnant. What about Rosario? Never mind the old man. He'll be all right by the time I come back.*

They were on the boat. Carlos had been swimming. Now he pulled his white pants on and seated himself cross-legged on the floor of the boat before Laura, who was sitting under the canvas roof.

Laura had not gone into the water. She couldn't. She was unwell, she had told Carlos.

"Darling," she said now with a smile. "Be a good boy and do me a favor."

"I'll do you the favor."

"Lend me one of your men and a horse. I want to go to see my brother."

"No sooner said than done, Passion Fruit. I'll take you there myself. It's a four-day ride, if we ride steadily."

"Thank you, darling. Very sweet of you." Then, reluctantly, as if she were denying herself the pleasure of Carlos' company, she said, "No, darling. You'd better not come with me. I haven't seen Willian in five years. I want to visit with him alone."

"I'd like to meet my future brother-in-law," Carlos said. "But I understand. I'll give you Anteiro."

"I wouldn't think of taking Anteiro away from you," Laura said. "He's much too valuable to you on the ranch. Just give me a man who knows the way."

"You're too precious to me to be entrusted to one man. I'll give you two. Two good men."

"Do I know them?"

"Yes. Rico and Ricardo, remember? The ones who stopped me from winning the race. They placed, or misplaced, the honor of the ranch above their lives. They'll die to protect you, a guest of the house."

"Thank you, darling."

"When will you go?"

"Tomorrow."

"So soon?"

"The sooner I go the quicker I'll be back."

So Laura rode off at sunrise with Rico and Ricardo and a pack mule.

Laura rode off to meet a crushing disappointment. William Burgess had taken his sabbatical leave and gone to surprise his sister. He had left for America about a month or so ago. But for the storm, brother and sister might well have met on the road.

Now five days had passed.

Laura was riding ranchward with Rico and Ricardo, and the pack mule.

Carlos had missed Laura. Twice he had got into the saddle and ridden off to join her. Miles later he had turned back, not to displease her.

Betta was happy. Now that the foreign woman had gone to visit her brother she would go away as soon as she returned. Betta would see to it that she did.

Uncle Rosario was up and about, feeling remarkably fit. Laura's riding off with two other guides had been a severe blow to Uncle Rosario's pride, and the best medicine for his health. Fearing that Laura would finish the trip with the other guides, Uncle Rosario had quit the rocking chair and started to eat red meat and drink steer blood until he was ready to burst.

The Negress Mullô had dismissed her patient. "Ride with God," she told him.

"God bless you," Uncle Rosario told her.

The Negress Mullô had packed her belongings in her vast basket, slipped her arm under the handle and gone to bring happiness and comfort to someone else waiting for her tender ministrations and healing vitality.

There had been a terrible argument between Uncle Rosario and Antonio. What the Negress Mullô had been able to avoid, by keeping the news of Antonio's transgression from leaking into her patient's room, happened on the first day Uncle Rosario was able to sit outside in the sun.

Except for a few blows which the irate old guide had dealt his nephew, who had not even bothered to protect himself, Antonio had really got the better of the argument.

Antonio had blamed his uncle, "Rosario *the* guide," as he called him, for not telling him beforehand about the laws of this part of the country. He was only a good bullfighter, a man of the city. How the hell was he to know the imbecility of these people?

Alma was still being ominously quiet, like a storm cloud forming or hovering in the sky. She was no longer feeding her revenge with her jealousy; she now was reasoning it out, or trying to. She was subjecting her untrained mind to cruel punishment. With some degree of consternation, she had discovered that she could conceive a thought and follow it half-way through, whereas before she followed her impulses only. She felt it to be a great responsibility, to be able to think. It destroyed her true nature, and stayed her hand. She had finally slept with Antonio, once. And while he satisfied himself, she had been staring at the ceiling, thinking. It was a horrible revelation. She had never imagined that a thing like that could ever happen to her, that she could be with a man and be thinking of extraneous matters. Maybe she was aging before her time. Maybe Carlos' treachery had killed her womanhood. A woman without womanhood might as well be dead. She thought of the river; she looked at her sharp dagger. Maybe she could kill two birds with one stone—take Laura along with her. They would be buried side by side and Carlos would come to visit them, and want to kill himself also. Or would he? She should never have learned to think. The more she thought, the less she knew what to do. Once upon a time (so long, long ago, it seemed to her now) she would have done it without thinking.

CHAPTER SIXTEEN

THE sixth day of Laura's absence dawned.

Lying in bed, Carlos reckoned that Laura had met her brother two days ago. As it would take Carlos four days to join her, she would have been with her brother six days by the time he got there.

Carlos decided that six days were enough for brother and sister to hold private reunion. He jumped out of bed, dressed, inspected his rifle and revolver, tested the edge and point of his knife, packed his saddlebags, ate breakfast, had his skin-flask filled, mounted his mule and rode off. Meanwhile, Laura was riding homewards with Rico and Ricardo and the pack mule.

Laura was now two days away from the ranch. Around sunset tomorrow she would ride through the outer gates, arriving in time for the evening meal.

Rico and Ricardo had shared and still were sharing Laura's bitter disappointment as a personal one. But Laura was in no mood for sympathy. The two men's clumsy efforts to console her only irritated her more. She wished they would stop feeling sorry for her. Finally she bade them mind their own infernal business. The two men, who were tough and brave, winced with mortification, which Laura could not fail to notice in spite of her despondency. She felt she ought to apologize. Instead she swelled with anger at the thought that these two men, so well-meaning and simple, were like all the rest she would have to live with if she married Carlos.

Ye gods, Laura cried inside. *Why did I have to be so careless, so downright stupid?* Why didn't I demand that Carlos take precautions? *Go ahead,* she told herself spitefully, *lock the stable after the horses are stolen.* She was pregnant. Laura could not divorce her future from her present predicament. *If he didn't take precautions while we were lovers, he certainly won't do it when we're married. He'll have me with child every year. Oh, no, he won't! He isn't even going to give me a child this time. I'm going to get rid of it the day after I'm back in New York.* Laura thumbed through her memory. She had a friend who knew a certain doctor.

Will you go through with it?

Why not?

Why should you? You loved its father.

It wasn't love, really. It was an infatuation. A damned tourist's infatuation.

Was it, really?

Maybe there was some love mixed up with it. I owed it to him. He saved my life twice. He lost face with his people because of me. He's been very kind. Laura couldn't help adding, *He's a man.* And for a moment her memory took Laura away from her present mood and led her back over the path strewn with their lovemaking.

Laura cried out in anger at the recollection of her wonderful experience—that had ended in such a pedestrian fashion. Pregnant!

Are you going to tell him?

I don't know. I don't know what to do. If I tell him, I'm finished.

By now Laura was over her original reaction. She was entering a new emotional stage. She felt she was weakening, putting up token resistance against something she would ultimately do.

A shadow fell across the open road. Laura looked about her, as if awakening. Then she looked for the sun. The sun had dropped behind the treetops. It was evening, the day's heavy make-up was beginning to fade. Laura had been in the saddle about seven hours today. But she wasn't tired, hungry or thirsty. She wanted to ride on and on, to avoid sitting still with her honest self.

At the next turn in the road, Laura's mule pricked her ears and broke into a fast trot. She had sensed the *pouso*, resting camp.

The *pouso* was by a stream, half a mile into the thicket. This *pouso* was a bad but unavoidable one—a pavilion covered with a broken-down straw-thatched roof beneath which a pit for a fire had been dug into the earth.

Laura and her party had spent the night at this *pouso* on their way to her brother. Then, as now, Rico and Ricardo unloaded the pack mule, quickly set up Laura's tent, safely outside the *pouso*, and brought her things in.

Laura stepped into the tent. She removed her hat, dropped her revolver belt on the sleeping mat on the ground. She removed her spurs. She took the oval mirror from her pack and hung it on the center pole. She looked at herself in the mirror. She wasn't interested. She took a towel and the thinning bar of soap and left the tent. She walked into the bush.

Meanwhile, night was fast approaching.

Her face and hands clean, her hair combed back from her forehead, smoking a paper cigarette and sipping gin from a tin cup, Laura sat on the ground before the fire, waiting to be fed. Three iron pots hung from an iron rod over the fire—beans, rice and coffee.

Laura stuffed beans and rice into her mouth mechanically. She did not notice how meaty the beans were, how well done the rice was. She did not even notice the man-sized portion Rico had served her. She could have eaten a camel without realizing it, she was so nervous. By tomorrow she must have her decision made and she must stick to it, one way or the other.

Laura laced her black coffee with gin, a great deal of it. She lighted a cigarette and settled down to wait for sleep, if sleep would ever come.

The dishes done, the traveling gear in, the mules attended to, Rico and Ricardo sat on the ground by the fire opposite Laura. Each rolled himself a maize-leaf cigarette. Laura told them to help themselves to the gin. Politely they reminded Laura that they were pinga drinkers, that their supply had run out, that they did not mind it as they would be home tomorrow, and that they would drink sugared water now.

"Sugar is very good for the eyesight, no, *senhora?*"

"Since when?"

"Since sugar was discovered, *senhora.*"

"Oh yes. I'd forgotten about that." Live and learn.

So simple and calm and credulous they were. So devoted. So respectful. They were his men. They would be her men if she married him. Spend a lifetime among simple, calm, credulous people, so devoted and respectful. How wonderful! And how damned boring after a while. She would be a very rich woman if she married him. She knew that. But where would she spend her money? Maybe in Cuiaba once a year, for a few days. Cut it out, Laura warned herself. You're talking yourself into marrying him.

Rico kindled the fire. Night had fallen. A serene night, that would make happy people happier.

Laura poured herself another drink of gin. Then, on second thought, she shook her skin-flask. It was almost empty. She told herself to take it easy with her present drink. She took a long swallow, wiped her mouth with the back of her hand. She wished she could play poker with Rico and Ricardo. Might as well start being one of the gang. She looked at them and was shocked at the expressions on their faces. They reminded her of the two lions on the steps of the Public Library in New York. Like the lions they were absolutely still and contented. She did not know that night had bedded their simple souls.

It was growing cooler. A milky mist began to rise. As it rose higher and higher, it left the leaves of the bushes and trees sparkling in the moonlight. Small drops of moisture began to fall from the edge of the broken-down roof. The heavier the mist grew, the stronger the smell of wet vegetation. Urubus hooted. A tree branch shook violently: birds disputing a sleeping berth. Now and then a sound, like a heavy body crashing through a fence, reached into the *pouso* faintly. Sometimes not so faintly. Then the "two lions" pricked their ears, and Rico fed the fire.

"Look, *senhora*."

She did. A caravan of thumb-sized black ants was carting away the food that had been spilled on the ground.

"There is a reason why God commanded the snakes to crawl," Rico said and paused.

"Why?" Laura asked, knowing that Rico would not go on until she asked.

"To be stepped upon."

"How nice."

"But I cannot understand why God commanded the ants to crawl, too. They are very intelligent."

"It's a tragedy, Rico. A damn rotten tragedy."

"True, *senhora*."

The curtain of silence descended between Laura and her guides again.

Now Rico leaned forward, cocked his head to one side. He looked at Ricardo. Ricardo nodded. They stood up, picked up their rifles and went to stand behind Laura.

Laura looked up. "What is it?"

"Do not be disturbed," Rico said.

And now Laura too began to hear a faint thumping sound that grew clearer as it drew nearer. It was the laborious plodding of a mount finding its way carefully in the pitch-dark forest.

Then Laura heard Rico exclaim, "The *patrão*." And she saw Carlos riding out of the darkness into the dim light cast by the fire.

Carlos pulled up, dismounted and walked into the *pouso*. They made a group of very puzzled people. The presence of his men restrained Carlos from taking Laura into his arms. He stood before her, looking at her questioningly.

The explanation over, Carlos said he was very sorry and with Laura sat down on the ground before the fire. Carlos asked Ricardo to bring him his skin-flask of alcohol. In his happiness to be with Laura again, Carlos soon forgot how sorry he was supposed to be.

Here was a man who had been in the saddle the whole day—he had taken a wrong turn while daydreaming, which explained his late arrival. A man who should be out of sorts, tired and hungry, and who was instead smiling sheepishly at her because he was too conscious of his desire for her. A desire which he obviously intended to gratify later on, as soon as his men were asleep.

All was confusion within Laura. Confusion and doubt. Laura marveled at, and at the same time was repelled by, Carlos' savage energy. She knew that if she should sleep with Carlos tonight he would stampede all over her body. She remembered what Carlos had told her the first night by the river bank. *I need your body to tell you how much I love you.* And then she remembered the kind of passionate love he had made to her the next day on the boat.

And it came to Laura now that the moment Carlos stopped making love to her he started loving her more ardently than ever. In one way or another he loved her around the clock.

This kind of love was rare to come by, Laura told herself. To reject this kind of love was to deny happiness; to accept this kind of love was to sacrifice all else. And what would happen when the flame of this love started to burn lower and lower, as it must in time? Would she become an embittered exile, tortured by the gnawing memory of a folly committed in a moment of weakness?

Laura looked at Carlos. He was sitting on the ground facing her, enjoying his drink of alcohol as if it were the elixir of life, adoring her, devouring her with his eyes, waiting for his men to fall asleep. She looked at him. He was a handsome man. The most handsome man she ever met, in his dark, faintly sinister sort of way. Warm and loyal and generous. A man.

But do I love him? If I do love him, why don't I throw my arms around his neck now and tell him that I'm going to be a mother? That would be love, wouldn't it? Why don't I do it? What's stopping me?

"Give me a drink, Carlos."

"I'm drinking pinga, Passion Fruit."

"That's all right."

Carlos poured out a drink and handed it to Laura. "Like a true native," he said.

"Yes," Laura said, "like a true native."

Laura drank, staring into the darkness surrounding her.

Why don't I nestle close to him and tell him that I'm pregnant? It would make him very happy. He would take me into his arms, kiss me, make ardent love to me.

Laura could not help thinking of her pregnancy now as another disillusionment in her life. She felt she had been deceived—not by Carlos any more; she was over that. Now she felt that she had been deceived by her own merciless destiny. Her destiny had got her pregnant to punish her for having at long last found love … if it were love.

Wasn't it?

Don't let's start that again!

Whatever it was she had enjoyed it greedily, and she was grateful to Carlos for having revealed her to herself. If this pregnancy hadn't happened she might have gone on living her lotus-land interlude until—

Until when?

And suddenly Laura knew.

Until she might have genuinely fallen in love with Carlos. Yes, that was it. Instead she had been roughly awakened in the middle of the interlude, and robbed of the time which she needed to find out what her true feeling was for Carlos.

Whatever it was, she was pregnant, and she couldn't and wouldn't forget that Carlos was the father of the child she was bearing. She wished she could think otherwise, could disregard the father's rights and feelings altogether. Sneak away, have an abortion. But her conscience said no. No, no matter what. And because Laura was not going to be dictated to, even by her own conscience, her conscience and her rebellious nature came to grips and fought themselves to an impasse.

But Laura now knew for certain that she did not love Carlos with a true love, with the love he deserved. But she was carrying his child. What was that about being caught between Scylla and Charybdis?

To hell with Scylla and Charybdis.

"Give me another drink, Carlos."

Carlos half-filled Laura's tin cup again.

"Thank you, Carlos."

Maybe, Laura thought, I'll learn to love him later, in America.

And she began. "How's Rosario?"

"As good as new."

"And Betta?"

"The same old Betta."

"And little Mira?"

"She misses you very much."

Laura started to pull her net in. "Dear child," she said. "So affectionate." She must send Mira a gift from America. In America they had such beautiful things for children. Asking forgiveness for saying so herself, Laura said that children in America were the best brought up children in the world. She meant materially cared for. But she was not in the mood for stopping, thinking, choosing the correct words. Carlos was hanging upon her every word, she thought. She didn't want to break the spell. So Laura went on telling Carlos all about America. She was indeed a splendid ambassador of good will. Relatively speaking, Laura pointed out to Carlos, America and Brazil were only a stone's throw from each other. Carlos never batted an eyelash. He kept adoring her, devouring her with his eyes. "You ought to visit America, darling. You'll like America very much. Darling, would you like to live in America?"

"Passion Fruit," Carlos said as if he had lost his voice.

"You could live in America eight, nine months of the year," Laura went on. "Spend the rest here, looking after the ranch. That would be nice, wouldn't it, darling? You'd make me very happy. You do want to make me happy, don't you?"

"I'll make you happy. My people and my land are at your feet, Passion Fruit. You'll be the queen of Boa Vista, with a little prince or princess every year. I love you."

"*Carlos,* you haven't heard a word I said."

"What did you say, Passion Fruit?"

"Nothing. Nothing at all."

"We'll be married in Cuiaba," Carlos said, taking her hand. "No, we'll be married right here on the ranch"—Laura took her hand away from Carlos—"and declare the day an official holiday, to be celebrated every year, as the little princes and little princesses grow in number. I love you." Then he said, "Go to your tent now, Passion Fruit. But don't go to sleep. Wait for me."

"Don't come near me," Laura snapped. "I'm unwell."

"Unwell? But you were unwell when you left the ranch. You wouldn't go swimming because of that," Carlos reminded her.

"I've got a splitting headache, that's what I meant," Laura said and got up and went into her tent.

She undressed and lay down on her sleeping mat, staring into the darkness, watching with an inner eye as her conscience and rebellious nature broke the impasse and started fighting again. They fought nearly all night.

The jungle awoke before the sun had fully risen. Monkeys were jabbering hysterically, birds were singing, and the jungle sounded like a music box playing one hundred different pieces at once.

Laura woke up. She lay still on her sleeping mat, staring at the ceiling of the tent, listening to the sounds and noises outside. She thought over her decision, and felt a creeping loneliness overcoming her. But she knew she would have to abide by her decision, because it was the honest one. She could never live in peace with herself if she lied to him. It was his child, too. She must tell him—and leave her future in the hands of the gods.

Laura bade farewell to America, which she now longed for poignantly; to her friends, whom she now missed and loved, and even to the life she had known and once thought she hated.

Would that she could go back now, erase the past, and start a new life altogether—a simple, active, productive life.

The storm and the jungle and Carlos had taught her a great deal about herself. If she could only start living all over again with her new self! Too late. She was pregnant. Her first duty was to her forming baby, and then to Carlos, to whom she would be kind and considerate even though she did not love him with a true love.

A mule snorted outside. Laura heard Rico's voice. Then running steps. She wondered where Carlos was. Now that she had made up her mind she was almost eager to see him, to tell him, to watch his reaction. She began to smell the strong aroma of coffee brewing in the *pouso*. She tasted the coffee in her mind. The strong coffee she would have to drink from now on. Stop feeling sorry for yourself, she upbraided herself. Get up.

Laura stirred under the cotton blanket. She suddenly lay still. Something she had hopelessly dismissed from her mind was happening to her—unless nature were playing the cruelest sort of joke. She sat up with a start, looked down. And there it was, on the sleeping mat—the lovely, wonderful, worry-destroying red stain. Laura could have cried for joy. She felt like hugging herself. Then she sobered up, remembering her anxiety. She felt as though she had been granted the new lease on life that she had so fervently wished for a few moments ago, and solemnly she promised herself to use it wisely. She listened to her conscience. Good girl, it said to her, referring to her honest decision and to her new plans for the future.

It was toward noon, riding steadily on the open road, that Laura turned to Carlos, riding beside her, and told him, kindly but firmly, that she was not going to marry him. Laura told Carlos she was going back to Cuiaba as soon as he would be kind enough to provide her and her guides with the gear and mounts necessary for the return trip. Laura mentioned money she had left at the hotel for safe keeping. Was that necessary? she asked herself, feeling like a bloody fool.

Quietly Carlos asked Laura why she had changed her mind, what had made her change her mind.

"Carlos," Laura said, kindly but firmly, "you took a great deal for granted. I haven't changed my mind at all. I've simply made my decision. I'm sorry, darling, if I gave you the wrong impression." Laura was truly sorry, perhaps because she could afford it now.

"Don't call me darling," Carlos told Laura quietly. And then he was silent. A silent man who seemed to fear his own fury.

CHAPTER SEVENTEEN

U NCLE ROSARIO was a happy man. Perhaps the happiest man at the dining table tonight. At sunrise tomorrow he would be in the saddle again, homebound.

Uncle Rosario looked at his client, sitting as usual next to her host.

She is a woman of great determination, Uncle Rosario thought. A woman who gets things done quickly.

For no sooner had Laura and Carlos ridden through the outer gates a few hours ago, than Laura, with Carlos' silent assent—he had merely nodded—had taken Uncle Rosario to Anteiro and told him to tell Anteiro what he needed for the return journey. Then she had told Anteiro please to have everything ready as soon as possible. Maybe by tomorrow?

"Now, if you want to," Anteiro said, and further explained that the mules and the saddles and the weapons and the pack mule were all there.

Then Laura had gone to her room, removed her riding clothes, freshened up, slipped into her dress and sandals and, for some feminine reason of her own, she had gone to break the news to Betta personally.

"You have already done the damage," Betta told her. "You will go away tomorrow. But we will remain here, spending the rest of our lives repairing what you have helped ruin. The honor of Boa Vista."

You'd have liked to kill me, wouldn't you? And you won't for-give me, if that's the word I want, Laura thought. *We part enemies. We are all enemies now.* Then she said, "May I say something that may help your mood, Betta?"

"What is it?"

"I'm not married."

"I don't believe you."

That's what I thought.

And now at the table Laura felt that it would be damn rotten of her to carry on a conversation with Carlos for appearance's sake. She respected his mood. And they were silent. Later, Laura noticed that Carlos was not drinking. She wondered why. Carlos did not trust himself to drink in his present mood.

By a strange coincidence, Laura's last meal at the *casa grande* was almost exactly like her first one. Again the table was laden with shoulders and legs of mutton, sirloins of beef and breasts of veal, mounds of vegetables and fruit, and two kinds of bread. And as on that far, far distant evening, the same unrestrained joy of living also prevailed in the dining room tonight. Only it sounded like an echo to Laura now.

"My nephew will miss a good meal," Uncle Rosario said to Anteiro, who pretended not to hear him.

The venerable Porfirio was there, like a landmark, his hands dancing in his lap. They were all there, the familiar faces Laura had grown to know so well.

Maria, the forelady at the spinning house, leaned towards Betta and said, pointing at Almirante, "That skunk has been exciting my girls the whole day."

"Give him the back of your hand," Betta said.

"That skunk is not strong enough to stand a woman's slap."

"Agreed," Betta said. "Try your foot on him."

Tomaso, the gunsmith, and Felicia, the apprentice dress-maker, were sitting next to each other. They were whispering excitedly, prodding each other insistently, as if one wanted the other to do or say something.

Little Mira, looking like a painted Dresden doll, was sitting between the Old One, the beekeeper, and Aurelio, the man in charge of the distillery.

Almirante was waiting for the opportunity to make an impression. Meanwhile he was telling his neighbors that he was getting mighty bored with the present company, needed a change of air, and would therefore personally escort Laura to Cuiaba.

Now Tomaso stood up in his place. *"Patrão,"* he called to Carlos. "With your permission."

The noise subsided. Everyone looked at Tomaso, fidgeting and ill at ease. Felicia lowered her head. She was blushing so violently that even her scalp where the part in her hair showed was pink.

"What is it, Tomaso?" Carlos asked.

"An announcement."

"Yes?"

"I and Felicia have resolved to be married."

"That's fine."

"And we want your consent."

"My consent?"

"Si, patrão."

"You don't need my consent, Tomaso. Go right ahead, get married and be happy. That's what marriage is for, isn't it?"

"The blessing of the house, *patrão,*" Tomaso said.

Carlos frowned. He stood up. "Tomaso," he began. "Tomaso—"

"The *master* of Boa Vista seems to have forgotten the blessing of the house," Betta said vindictively from the other end of the table. "Son of the house," Betta began, standing up in her place, "may the house bless you and Felicia. May you and Felicia live in this house as your forefathers lived in it before you. God bless you."

"Yes," Carlos said, still standing. "And let me know if you need or want anything."

"But he only wanted the blessing of the house," Betta said vindictively.

Carlos sat down, wondering what satisfaction he would derive from slapping Betta on the face. Hard. Very hard.

"*Viva patrão!*" little Mira shouted and threw her arms up and clapped her hands.

Betta called Felicia to her, and as she kissed and blessed her she told her she would take her friend, Inocencia, back into the house.

Anteiro embraced Tomaso. Glass in hand, everyone at once was congratulating and wishing happiness to Felicia and Tomaso.

Carlos looked at Laura. She looked away.

When some semblance of order was restored, Laura promised Felicia and Tomaso a gift from America.

Meanwhile Almirante was trying to make a speech. They shouted and laughed at him. But Almirante was not to be discouraged easily.

"Ladies and gentlemen. Listen, please. A word. One little word of friendship and felicity to our dear friends. In this sublime hour, when love is in the saddle, racing—"

"Almirante."

"Pronto, Nhâ Betta."

"That is enough."

"I must finish my speech. Where was I?"

"Nowhere. Sit down."

"*Viva Almirante,*" little Mira cried, throwing her arms up and clapping her hands.

"Little one," Almirante said to Mira solemnly. "You are the only one with some intelligence. Thank you, my dear child." As Almirante was sitting down a piece of meat struck him in the face.

"Who did that?" Almirante cried raging mad. "I challenge the capon to stand up." He unsheathed his knife. "Who did that?"

"I did it," said Pepe, the pottery-maker, who fancied himself a ventriloquist.

"Who are you? Where are you?"

"Look into your pockets."

Almirante was so mad that he actually started to look into his pockets.

Even Laura had to laugh. The comedy was indescribable — when a scream pierced the festive tumult and lingered echoingly in the startled silence that followed.

Little Mira was wriggling in Antonio's hands like a fish on a hook. Antonio had lifted the child out of her chair and was holding her at arm's length before him, telling her to be still, to be a good little girl and go and eat in the kitchen.

Under different circumstances it might have been funny the way the child cried, "Let me go, let me go, you ugly man," and kicked and thrashed about.

Laughing, Antonio put the child down on the floor, to grab her again at once as she tried to scramble back into her chair.

"Give the child her seat," Anteiro said, getting up.

There was a challenge in Anteiro's voice and Antonio accepted it. He sat down in the child's chair. "Friend," he said to Anteiro. "In all well-managed houses children eat in the kitchen, especially when there is no room for them at the table."

Anteiro moved down the side of the table toward Antonio, who followed his approaching figure with the deadly calm eyes of a matador sighting a bull for the kill.

"Anteiro," Carlos called. "Go back to your place. Don't interfere."

Anteiro stopped, hardly able to believe his ears. Not again, he thought, as did all the others as they turned to Carlos.

"Get off that chair," Carlos told Antonio.

"I am your guest," Antonio told Carlos. "Would you deprive me of the pleasure of sitting at your table for the last time?"

Carlos got up and walked down to Antonio. He tapped him on the shoulder. Antonio stood up.

"Take your seat, child," Carlos said to Mira.

Antonio made as if to bar Mira's way.

Carlos hit Antonio across the mouth with the back of his hand—a vicious, backhanded blow that sent Antonio reeling backwards. He tripped and fell, leaped to his feet again and was about to rush Carlos when Uncle Rosario threw his arms about him from behind, holding him back. Antonio struggled to free himself from his uncle's grasp. Antonio's eyes were bloodshot, his mouth and nose bleeding (the blood dripped on Uncle Rosario's wrists), and he snarled, "Let me free, uncle. For God's sake, let me free."

"Wait, nephew," Uncle Rosario said, and his arms tightened around Antonio's chest.

"You will pay for this with your blood," Antonio said to Carlos.

"Tomorrow," Carlos said.

"Now, coward. *Now.*"

"Tomorrow," Carlos repeated. "Ride off with the dawn and meet me at sunrise—at the Mountain of Sadness."

At the mention of the mountain, a cold draft blew into the dining room, chilling it. Uncle Rosario let go of Antonio and stood looking at Carlos with reverential fear. Although free now, Antonio did nothing. He sensed that something like a terrible curse had been spoken. He saw it in his uncle's eyes, and in the superstitiously awed faces of the men and women seated around the table.

To Antonio the Mountain of Sadness was only a name, another place where he would knife this man dead. And at once Antonio regained his self-confidence.

"The Mountain of Sadness," he said. "Any place suits me."

Uncle Rosario shook his head. "Go outside and wait for me, nephew."

"Child," Carlos said to Mira. "Take your seat."

Antonio left the dining room.

Uncle Rosario turned to Anteiro. They eyed each other, these two old friends and veterans of the jungle, and spoke with strained politeness.

"I have neither leather nor tools," Uncle Rosario said.

"We have. At your service," Anteiro said.

"Where is the leather house?" Uncle Rosario asked.

"I will show you."

"Do me the favor."

"At your service."

They went back to their seats, picked up their hats from the floor beneath their chairs and walked out of the dining room together.

Carlos went back to his seat. Laura did not look at him. She knew what kind of look Carlos had in his eyes.

The men and women looked at Carlos. There was pride in their eyes now. Pride, love and fear. Betta sat in her place with her head down, her hands flat on the table, her bosom heaving like that of an asthmatic.

They tried, but failed to recapture the spirit of the party. Even Almirante sat quiet and frightened in his place.

Laura did not know what to do, what to say. She kept stealing glances at Carlos, clearly realizing now what was going on inside him.

Abruptly Carlos got up and left the dining room.

Getullio and his musicians were playing a merry tune and the people were dancing happily in the glare of the flaring torches before the main entrance, as yet unaware of what had happened in the dining room.

Carlos was standing in the shadow, listening to the music and watching the dancers. And now he saw the children first and then the other and finally Betta and Laura appear at the dance. Laura and Betta sat down in wicker chairs. Then Carlos sent word to Getullio to keep playing, no matter what Betta's orders might be. And to make sure that Betta would not dismiss Getullio for the night he sent word to Betta not to interfere with him.

Beta asked the boy who brought her Carlos' message where Carlos was. The boy pointed. Betta turned in that direction. Carlos had disappeared.

Meanwhile, Antonio was squatting on his heels in the leather house, listening to Uncle Rosario's instructions and advice.

"You understand clearly, nephew?"

"Yes, uncle. And do not worry over me. I am a bullfighter. A matador. No cow has yet given birth to the bull that can destroy me. How could a man who is a coward destroy me then?"

"You speak with confidence, nephew."

"I have confidence."

"Think of Carlos Diaz as a brave man."

"It would grieve me immensely if he should not turn up tomorrow."

"He will. For honor and for spite."

"And I will kill him for the pleasure of killing a man who has scorned me by pretending to be a coward."

Uncle Rosario said nothing.

Antonio got up.

"Where are you going, nephew?"

"A woman is waiting for me."

"Sit down."

"My interest in the fight is exhausted, uncle."

"Stay."

"Why?"

"To become friendly with the weapon you will use tomorrow."

Antonio sat down on a pile of uncured hides. "The stink is insufferable," he said. "The imbecility of these people."

Uncle Rosario reached for the lamp burning before him and got up. Holding the lamp at arm's length over his head, he looked for and found the whip he wanted hanging from a broken wooden peg on the wall facing the door.

Uncle Rosario took it down and examined it. The whip had a seven-inch-long metal handle, a wrist chain and a serpentine lash. It was not quite a bull whip. Uncle Rosario tossed the whip on the ground, next to a cowhide tool box he had been sitting on. Then he walked up to a corner where there was a mound of brine-cured leather that was used for roofing and was as stiff as steel. With a sharp, curved knife Uncle Rosario cut two strips of this leather, eighteen inches long and three inches wide, and went back to the tool box. He sat down on the ground. He cut off the lash from the whip, an inch or so from the handle. Then he opened the tool box, found two different sized awls and a roll of waxed thread, and set to work.

As Antonio watched his uncle's progress his lips unconsciously drew tighter together, and a novel expression came into his eyes that would have surprised him had he been able to see it.

For Uncle Rosario had sewn the two strips together into a double thonged piece that was as long and wide and hard as a machete blade, and now he was beginning to whittle the sides to a razor's edge.

Then Uncle Rosario would round one end of the thong and attach the other to the metal handle.

Meanwhile, Anteiro was having trouble awakening Pardo in the saddle house.

As usual Pardo was drunk. Now Anteiro lost his patience and kicked him. Pardo turned over. As usual Pardo was sleeping booted and spurred. The wheels of his spurs were as large as saucers, thus revealing his profession: bronco buster, before he was kicked in the spine and crippled permanently. Born on the ranch, a splendid horseman, crippled in the service of the ranch, he had been retired by Carlos, who put him in charge of the saddle house and the corrals surrounding it.

Pardo lorded it over a dozen boys, all of them bronco buster apprentices. The boys respected Pardo for what he had been, and loved him for the wonderful stories he told them.

Again Anteiro lost his patience. He grabbed Pardo by the shoulders and shook him so brutally that it seemed as if Pardo's head would come loose at any moment.

Finally Pardo woke up.

"What is it?" Pardo looked at Anteiro reproachfully, his bleary eyes glinting greasily in their round sockets.

"Get up."

"Do not make a joke, companion," Pardo said.

Anteiro looked at Pardo's withered legs, with the beautiful boots and enormous spurs. "I forgot, companion," Anteiro said.

"But I can sit up," Pardo said. And did. "What news?" he asked.

"Have four horses at the main entrance before dawn."

"Saddles?"

"Campeiro."

"All right. Before dawn. At the main entrance. Four horses. Campeiro saddles. Good night, Anteiro."

"You are not going to get drunk again, are you, Pardo?"

"Immediately."

"You will not forget, will you?"

"I will forget it immediately after I have relieved myself of my responsibility," Pardo said, sticking two fingers in his mouth and letting out a piercing whistle.

"Good night, Pardo," Anteiro said. "Put out the candle before you get drunk again. You do not want to burn yourself to death, do you?"

"I do not mind if I do."

As Anteiro walked out of the saddle house, a boy came running in.

The musicians finished playing for the night.

In groups or in couples the ranch hands went their ways.

Betta got up from her chair and walked away.

"Good night, Betta," Laura called.

Betta did not answer.

"Betta," Laura called angrily.

Betta stopped and faced Laura.

Laura got up and walked up to Betta. "All evening I've heard people whispering about the Mountain of Sadness. What is it?"

"It is a mountain. It has no significance to you."

"Maybe not. Still I'd like to know."

Betta eyed Laura. Then she faced east. She pointed. "There," she said, and her forefingers stabbed the darkness.

In the distance in the moonlight the mountain now looked forlorn and forbidding.

"There they will try to destroy each other," Betta said. "They will try to destroy each other with unmentionable pain and cruelty. For at the Mountain of Sadness you do not fight with knife or gun. That is the law. You fight with the whip."

"The whip?"

"The whip. And it is not the whip that kills. It is the drop."

"The drop?"

"The drop. And if it is the drop that kills it cannot be said that you were killed by a man. No bullet holes, no knife cuts to prove differently. So it was an accident. And if it was an accident there is no call for revenge on the part of kin or clan, *comprende?*"

Laura bowed her head.

"Listen," Betta went on hatefully. "You fight on the brink of a precipice on the mountain top. You fight with the whip. And you try to whip the other off the brink. He slips and falls. He dies because he lost his footing, *comprende?*"

Laura walked away.

"Sleep well," Betta called softly.

The hours of darkness were passing.

Betta was alone in the dining room. She was sitting at the center of the table, a colored candle burning before her.

The heavy shadows in the dining room seemed to be converging upon the candlelight, like a dark shade.

Betta had her hands clasped on the table and her lips were moving in silent prayer. Her face was in mourning.

Betta started when Laura whispered her name. She turned and saw Laura standing beside her.

Laura had a blue shawl over her nightshirt. She was barefooted.

"I knew that you would come," Betta said. "I knew that you would need to make speech with me."

Laura sat down in a chair next to Betta. The heavy chair screeched loudly as Laura pulled it out and the dark stillness seemed to crack and snap like heated sandalwood.

"What is it that you want to tell me?" Betta said.

"About tomorrow."

"It is already tomorrow."

"Must he fight?"

"Yes."

"Can't you stop him?"

"No."

"Have you tried to stop him?"

"No."

"Won't you try?"

"No."

"Why not?"

"He cannot play the coward twice for you. It would break my heart to see him dead. But I would rather have him die as a man than live as a coward. You—you are a bad woman."

"Don't be angry with me, Betta."

"Go to bed."

"Will you see him before he goes?"

"Yes. I will see him soon now. Day is breaking."

"Will you tell him that I—"

"I will not tell him anything that has to do with you. Go away."

CHAPTER EIGHTEEN

THE LAST HOUR of darkness was passing.

Carlos was sleeping in his room.

Anteiro was in his hammock, awake.

Wrapped in her blue shawl, Laura was sitting in a chair by the window in her room.

Uncle Rosario was listening to Antonio's breathing as he slept in the bed next to his.

Little Mira was having a bad dream in her white hammock, and she cried and struggled while the spotted puppy that slept with her whimpered restlessly.

Betta was still in the dining room. The colored candle before her was dying out.

Uncle Rosario sat up in bed. He sat lost in thought for awhile. Then he got up and started dressing in the dark. When he was finished he lighted the candle.

The flickering light of the candle caught and squinted on the wrist chain and metal handle of the whip lying on the other end of the table. For a time Uncle Rosario stood looking at the whip as if it were a human being to whom he was trying to convey something. Then he walked over to Antonio's bed.

"Wake up, nephew," he said and shook Antonio by the arm. "Wake up."

Antonio got out of bed and pulled his shirt and pants on. Then his boots.

"Remove the spurs, nephew."

Antonio removed the spurs and held them in his hands. Uncle Rosario took the spurs from Antonio and laid them on the table next to the whip.

"Let us ride, nephew," Uncle Rosario said and picked up the whip.

The wrist chain rattled against the metal handle of the whip.

"One moment, uncle," Antonio said. "This is a fight for life, you said, even as in the ring against the bull. I am a bullfighter. I must pray." Antonio knelt down before the candle, crossed himself, joined his hands and in a quiet voice recited the matadors' prayer. Uncle Rosario nodded his head over him, as if punctuating the prayer, his eyes stonily sad. Then Antonio finished, crossed himself three times, kissed his fingers and stood up.

"We ride, uncle."

Betta shuffled into Carlos' room. Carlos' room, facing the west, was still deep in shadows. As Betta approached Carlos' bed she tripped over Carlos' boots standing in the middle of the room.

Carlos mumbled in his sleep and turned over on one side. For a time Betta stood looking down at Carlos. Then she reached down and shook him by the hair.

"It is time, son," she said. "Day is breaking. The others have gone."

Carlos got out of bed and stood in his shorts before Betta.

She looked at his fine body with infinite tenderness and sadness. She watched him dress in silence.

Carlos dressed slowly. He took a particular long time setting the creases in his boots. Then he got up from the floor and looked for his hat. He found it beneath the chair beside the window. He picked it up and put it on. He tightened the chinstrap. Then loosened it a bit. He looked at Betta, looked away, looked back, undecided. Then he went up to her and threw his arms about her. Poor woman, he thought. Poor woman. Aloud he said, as he used to when he was a child, "Your blessing, Betta."

"Forgive me, son, for having hated you," she said.

"Your blessing, Betta."

Betta shook her head. "I am not qualified to give you my blessing on this grave occasion," she said. "Kneel, son. Pray. Let us pray."

"I never prayed when I was happy," Carlos said. "I will not pray now because I am in fear."

"Kneel, son. Pray."

"No."

"For the sake of your mother, pray."

"I never knew my mother."

"You may meet her."

Carlos said nothing.

"Pray, son. Pray for my sake."

"Give me your blessing, Betta."

"I feel no power, son. I have no power on this occasion."

"You have, Betta, as far as I'm concerned. For you I can touch. You I can see. Your blessing, Betta."

"Kneel before me then, son."

Carlos looked at Betta. There were tears in her eyes. It was the first time he had seen her weep. It was perhaps the first time in her life she had ever wept. And she did not know how to weep. Her face was distorted in a clownish grimace.

Carlos removed his hat and knelt at Betta's feet. She prayed over him, her head thrown back, oily tears rolling down her devoted face. He studied her bare feet, solidly planted on the floor, wider than they were long, the stumpy toes, the hard, gnarled, ivory-like nails.

Anteiro came into the room. The whip was dangling from his wrist. He stopped a few steps from the threshold and waited.

"Take the spurs off your boots," he said to Carlos when Betta had finished.

Carlos put his hat on. He sat down on the floor and removed his spurs, left them there.

"We ride," Anteiro said.

Betta turned away.

Carlos and Anteiro left the room.

They walked through the sleeping house, out into the open.

The moon was weary eyed. The stars were waning. Dawn smelled of day. The tall grass was stirring with the shifting hour. The mist was rising in puffs, like smoke signals. Silence was spying on the plain and the jungle.

They mounted their horses and rode off at a canter, Anteiro's spurs jingling in time to his horse's lope.

The ranch hands' quarters were dark and quiet. Watch dogs were sleeping with one eye open.

A light suddenly blinked on the left side of the house. Someone was praying in the chapel.

They rode through fields that were crowded with cattle that had been assembled for the past several days and were now ready to be moved on to the southern pastures before the rainy season.

They rode past four heifers standing alone. The heifers were cream colored, smooth coated and fat. Each heifer had a black ribbon tied to its right horn.

These heifers were called Bleeding Virgins or Sacrificial Virgins. As a herd came to a river infested with piranhas, a Virgin would be wounded and sent bleeding into the water to draw off the piranhas, while the herd crossed the river safely. It took about half an hour for the piranhas to eat the heifer through to its carcas, churning the water into a bloody boil. It had to be done to protect the herd. But even veteran cowboys did not enjoy the scene, and some of them did not eat beef for some days afterwards.

Carlos and Anteiro rode past cowboys sleeping in the saddle, rifles hanging from their necks and lying horizontally across their chests. At their approach the cowboys raised their heads and then their right hands in silent greeting.

"Ride with God," some of the old-timers said.

"With God we ride," Anteiro responded.

They left the fields and rode into the jungle, onto a wide path that led to the foot of the mountain.

Now the path narrowed into a mule track and the horses slowed their gait.

"Up, up," Anteiro said and spurred his mount.

Carlos kicked his.

The track looked like a crooked, crusted wound deeply imbedded in a hairy surface, mossy and dank smelling here, rugged and craggy as they climbed higher, holding on now to their horses' manes.

Birds were awakening in the trees.

The horses' hoofs stabbed and scooped the earth in sullen rhythm. The riders rocked in their saddles.

The sun rose and the mountain top was dyed an oxblood hue. The light flowed down the mountain sides, sweeping the shadows before it, undressing the mountain, revealing its tortuous body.

Anteiro pointed to the track ahead. It was littered with fresh horse dung. Birds were pecking at the dung. The birds scattered as Carlos and Anteiro drew near, gathering again on their feast as soon as they had passed.

They came to a tree whose cankerous trunk bent and reached all the way across to the other edge of the track.

Uncle Rosario was sitting at the foot of the tree.

Carlos and Anteiro pulled up before Uncle Rosario. They looked at each other.

Anteiro slipped the whip from his wrist and handed it to Carlos.

It was an arm-length oxtail whip, double thonged, brine-cured, stiff as steel. Carlos slipped his right hand through the wrist chain. Then he looked at Anteiro.

Anteiro's eyes were like the twitching lips of a suffering deaf-mute listening to his own feelings and trying to express them out loud. Carlos remembered seeing that expression in Anteiro's eyes when he had first left the ranch to go to Europe. He still loved Anteiro with a child's love, and now found some measure of con-solation in knowing that if something should happen to him, all his earthly riches would go to Anteiro and Betta. A small reward, indeed, for what they had given him of themselves.

With his eyes Carlos tried to tell Anteiro not to worry too much. Anteiro looked away. Carlos kicked his horse. The horse's hoofs drew sparks from the stones as the horse leaped forward.

Anteiro sat in the saddle looking after Carlos until he disap-peared around a turn ahead. Then he dismounted and sat down on the other side of the track, opposite Uncle Rosario.

Birds were singing in the trees.

Antonio turned around when he heard Carlos' horse approach-ing the mountain top. He gripped his whip hard, and waited.

Carlos dismounted and slapped his horse away.

The horse went to join Antonio's, idling by one of the few shaggy clumps on the arid mountain top.

Carlos walked to meet Antonio. They faced each other not far from the brink of the precipice.

The chasm below was humming a windy song.

Antonio's eyes flashed as he quickly and agilely stepped to one side and put the whole weight of his body behind the lightning whip blow that caught Carlos across the side of the neck, opening the flesh. Blood spurted, as Carlos moved backwards under Antonio's rain of blows that he parried with his whip-thong or received on the back of his hand, which was beginning to open up like a bloody rose.

Carlos tried to circle around Antonio. But he always met Antonio's hissing whip, now slashing at his left shoulder, now cutting his right hand again, and he found himself being driven closer and closer to the brink of the precipice.

Meanwhile they sat and waited, Anteiro and Uncle Rosario, the narrow track between them. Whenever their eyes met, each knew what the other was thinking, hoping for, wanting to happen more than anything else in his life.

Their souls came to grips as cruelly as the other two were slashing at each other on the mountain top.

They uttered no sound, made no gesture and not a quiver changed the dull expression of their set faces.

They sat and waited.

They started as the air was suddenly rent by the shrill cries of a bird. The bird alighted on the track between them. A small bird with a yellow breast and purple crest. Its feathers bristling, it skipped about fearfully until another bird of the same size, but of different coloring, swooped down upon it and began pecking at its head, drawing blood from it. They fought cruelly, shedding feathers, chirping viciously, until the first bird took flight with the other in pursuit.

Uncle Rosario looked at the sun. The sun had moved one foot in the sky. Uncle Rosario ran his hand over his face, looked at the palm of his hand, wiped it on his leg. He caught Anteiro watching him. With his eyes Uncle Rosario told Anteiro to give up all hope.

Anteiro told Uncle Rosario the same thing in the same language.

They suddenly stiffened and together looked up the track where it turned to the left, where Antonio first and then Carlos had disappeared. They heard the noise of rolling stones, the halting plodding of a horse carefully picking his way through the stones.

They stood up, faced the turn and waited, forgetful of each other.

A small avalanche of stones rolled down the track. They heard the horse stumbling, struggling to regain his footing, then stop, then plod on and soon afterwards they saw Carlos appear at the turn.

Carlos was slumped in the saddle. His head was rolling nervelessly, his legs were flapping against the horse's flanks and the reins were swinging loosely beneath the horse's neck.

Uncle Rosario reached down for his gun. Anteiro held Uncle Rosario's hand against the gun with his left hand and looked at him, said quietly, sadly, "It was an accident, as you know. And that is the law."

Uncle Rosario bowed his head.

Anteiro went to meet Carlos, trying all the while to peer under the brim of Carlos' hat, which had fallen low over his eyes and revealed only his lips and chin.

Carlos did not see Anteiro and would have ridden past him if Anteiro had not reached out for the reins and halted the horse. Anteiro looked up at Carlos and sucked his breath in.

Carlos' black pupils were stagnant in pools of blood. His nostrils and the corners of his mouth were clogged with blood. The side of his neck was slashed and bleeding. The shirt on the left shoulder was soaked with blood. The back of his right hand was crisscrossed with bleeding gashes.

Anteiro slapped Carlos' leg hard. Carlos raised his head slowly, sighed tiredly and then collapsed upon himself again. Anteiro pulled the whip off Carlos' right wrist. The whip handle was pasty with blood. The thong was sodden with blood, looked like a slab of liver.

As Anteiro led the horse down the track by the bit, Uncle Rosario came riding slowly up the track.

They passed each other in silence.

As they gained the main road Anteiro mounted his horse and rode close to Carlos, knee to knee, keeping an eye on him, now and then pulling or pushing Carlos' body back into the saddle.

A great cloud of red dust was spreading out in the distance in the east where the herds were on the go.

Carlos roused from his exhaustion, looked about. "This is the way to the house."

"Naturally," Anteiro said.

"Not in this condition."

"Where do you want to go then?"

"To the river."

Anteiro led Carlos' horse into a cool, fresh-smelling lane that ended at the river. Here Anteiro dismounted and then pulled Carlos down from the saddle. He undressed Carlos and laid him on the ground. Then Anteiro undressed himself, lifted Carlos up in his arms and walked into the river.

The water revived Carlos, and he told Anteiro to put him down. Carlos walked back to the bank unaided and sat down. The sun dried him, and the wounds, particularly on his neck and left shoulder, smarted badly. He told Anteiro to ride home and bring him some clothes and the medicine to treat the wounds.

Anteiro told Carlos to lie in the shade, and he helped him up on his feet and then down at the foot of a tree. Then he mounted his horse and galloped off.

The hot breeze caressed Carlos' naked body. Though in pain he felt relaxed and glad to be alive. He thought of Laura. No, he did not hate her. He felt at peace within. Sleep surprised him.

The sun rode higher in the sky, paused overhead, rode on.

Carlos was awakened by someone pulling his hair gently and he saw Betta kneeling at his side, her sweat-lacquered face beaming radiantly close to his.

Carlos grew embarrassed as he realized he was naked and said to Betta, "Where's your modesty?"

"Modesty, you say?" Betta boomed and burst out into one of her famous peals of laughter, due in this case to hysterical happiness. "I have seen you born," she shouted. "I have washed your dirty little body for years on end. I know your body like the palm of my hand, and now you ask me where is my modesty. What is there about your body that can surprise me now that it did not then?" She took Carlos' head in her arms and rocked him.

When Betta had calmed down, Carlos pulled on a pair of white pants and sat up.

From a leather pouch Betta took out some bandages and the pomada, an Indian healing salve that stops the severest bleeding almost immediately. She applied it with her fingers to the wounds and the wounds turned gray and then white as their edges slowly closed up like clams. Then she bandaged them.

Carlos' bloodshot eyes were beginning to clear.

Carlos rode home, between Betta and Anteiro very slowly as Betta was riding sideway on a bast-matted, fat old mare that seemed to have forgotten how to walk.

It was past the siesta hour when they came in sight of the house.

As they rode up the well-kept road that led to the house they saw Laura sitting outside the main entrance. Uncle Rosario was standing beside her.

Betta slipped down from her mare. Carlos climbed out of the saddle, holding on to the saddlehead until he had both feet on the ground. Anteiro remained mounted and led the animals away.

Laura came to meet Carlos. Impulsively she put out her hand, and then at once took it back as she realized that Uncle Rosario was present and watching her.

They walked up to the main entrance and sat down in wicker chairs.

Carlos noticed that Uncle Rosario's right shirt sleeve and his pants were torn in several places and he was covered with dust from head to foot. He wondered what had happened to him.

Uncle Rosario came over to Carlos. "I have been waiting for you, Carlos Diaz."

Carlos hoped Uncle Rosario would not make a scene.

"I am leaving your house," Uncle Rosario went on. "I am going to stay at the western *pouso* until my client is ready to ride off."

Carlos turned to Laura. "When?"

"At sunrise tomorrow."

Carlos nodded.

"One favor I am forced to ask you, Carlos Diaz," Uncle Rosario said.

Carlos waited.

"All morning and throughout the afternoon I have tried to reach the bottom of the precipice. But strength failed me and I could not get near to him. I could not even see him. One favor, Carlos Diaz."

"Bury him for me. I was fond of him."

"Rest assured of that, Rosario. Your nephew shall be buried in our cemetery. With a cross with his name on it. And you can come and visit him whenever you wish."

Uncle Rosario bowed his head, overcome with grief. Then his head lifted and he spoke again.

"Carlos Diaz, evening is here. Night will soon follow. The vultures and the beasts of the night will then go on the prowl and he—he lies there defenseless."

"He shall be protected, Rosario. Please, send Anteiro to me.

"Much obliged, Carlos Diaz. I wish I could shake hands with you. But my heart says no."

Uncle Rosario turned to Laura. "We ride at dawn, *senhora*." He touched his hat and walked away.

Carlos and Laura sat in silence.

Anteiro appeared from within the house carrying a tray with glasses and a bottle of brandy. He poured out three drinks.

As Anteiro handed Carlos a drink, Carlos said, "Send two men out to watch over him throughout the night. And have them bring him down tomorrow and bury him in our cemetery."

"He is not one of ours, Carlos."

"You don't mean that," Carlos said quietly. "Not you, Anteiro."

"I spoke in anger," Anteiro said.

"Send the men out," Carlos told him.

"I will send Joaquin and Ignacio. They are not afraid of ghosts." Anteiro swallowed his drink, put the glass on the tray and was leaving on his errand when Carlos called him back.

"Rosario's pretty well broken up."

"And Rico and Ricardo always wanted to go to Cuiaba."

"Always. That lying Almirante once told them that the women in Cuiaba are built differently from our women and they have been excited ever since."

"Have Rico and Ricardo replace Rosario's nephew."

"Somebody has to go to bring back the gear and the mounts. I will send them. Let them find out for themselves how differently the women in Cuiaba are built from ours," Anteiro said and went on his errand.

Little Mira came running from the eastern side of the house, stood breathless and excited before Carlos.

"Come," she said and took him by the hand. "Nhâ Betta is waiting for you. She wants you to eat."

"Tell her I'm not hungry."

"No no," little Mira said. "Nhâ Betta told me not to believe that. She said you would say that."

"Betta's a mind reader," Laura said.

Little Mira turned to Laura. "I know," she chirped. "You are riding away tomorrow. Tomorrow is the *hora dos adeus*."

Laura drew the child to her. "Yes," she said. "Tomorrow is the hour of farewell."

The child nestled in Laura's arms, looked up at her with pleading eyes. "Do not ride, beautiful dear one. Why must you ride then?"

Carlos got up, excused himself, walked into the house.

Dawn was breaking.

Booted and spurred, her broadbrimmed hat hanging from her arm by the chinstrap, and holding her revolver belt in her hand, Laura took a last look at her room. She told herself not to think, not to remember. She put out the lamp, walked out of the room, went through half of the house, into the dining room. Anteiro and Betta were having coffee. They exchanged good mornings.

"Sit there," Betta said, pointing to the center of the table. Laura did not try to read a meaning in Betta's gesture. She laid her hat and revolver belt on a chair and sat down next to it.

A lamp was burning in each corner of the room, casting its tremulous light about its immediate surroundings. A tall candle was burning in the center of the table, before Laura.

Betta left the dining room and returned with Laura's breakfast, a platter of ham and eggs.

Laura was eating when Carlos came in. His face was ashy and drawn, his eyes feverish. He exchanged greeting with Laura and sat down at his usual place, at the head of the table. They looked at each other across the distance that separated them. Each pair of eyes said nothing to the other, in an effort to spare each other's feelings.

Betta brought Carlos his coffee. He lighted a cigarette.

The house slept.

Rico and Ricardo came into the dining room, rifles slung over their shoulders, knives tucked under their belts. "All is in readiness," Rico said to Carlos. "Any instructions, *patrão?*"

Carlos shook his head.

"We ride," Rico said. "We have to meet the old guide at the western *pouso*. "And together they walked out of the dining room, their bronco buster spurs clanging after them.

Laura stood up, picked up her revolver belt and fastened it on. Then she put on her hat. Anteiro squatted on his heels before Laura and examined her spurs. He tightened the left spur one hole. He slapped the leggings of her boots. "That is as it should be," he said and stood up, not knowing what else to do or say.

And Anteiro's attitude awakened in Laura the memory of the storm, the wind and the rain, the agony of fear in the mud. She spoke to Carlos when she said, "Thank you Anteiro. Thanks for everything," and put out her hand.

Anteiro shook it. "Ride well, woman. Ride with God," he said.

"Good-bye, Betta."

Betta said nothing. Laura went up to her. "Don't be angry with me," she said.

"Ride well, *senhora*. Ride with God," Betta said then.

Laura turned to Carlos. She held out her hand to him. He got up and walked over to her and shook her hand. "Ride well," he said. "Ride with God."

They all walked out of the dining room, though the quiet house, through the main entrance, outside.

Rico and Ricardo were in the saddle, a loaded pack mule idling nearby. A boy was holding Laura's mule by the halter. A poncho was thrown across the saddlehead. The stirrups were hooded.

The horizon was growing a pink as the sun pushed through from below. They stood in silence, watching the birth of the new day.

As she stood there Laura had a feeling of being spied upon. She turned her head in time to see two glowing eyes fixed upon her from behind the western corner of the house. Within a few seconds Laura's memory bridged the gap between the first time she had seen the same eyes spying on her and now.

Laura got into the saddle. Anteiro held the stirrup for her. Then he went back to join Carlos and Betta standing at the main entrance.

"Ride, men," Anteiro called to Rico and Ricardo.

They whipped the pack mule and started off.

"Good-bye," Laura called.

Carlos and Anteiro raised their right hands.

Laura remained looking at the small group at the main entrance a moment longer. Then she set spur to her mule, hard. The mule leaped forward and galloped away.

They went back into the house.

Carlos closed the door behind him.